W9-DFF-921

The Stain
on the Snow

Georges Simenon (1903–1989) was born in Liège, Belgium. At sixteen he began work as a journalist on the *Gazette de Liège* but moved to Paris in 1922 and became a prolific author of popular fiction, writing hundreds of novels and innumerable short stories under many pseudonyms. In 1931 he published the first books featuring Maigret, his most famous and enduring creation, and he continued to write Maigret stories alongside his psychological novels for more than forty years, until he retired from fiction writing in the 1970s.

crimemasterworks

Georges Simenon

The Stain
on the Snow

translated by John Petrie

ORION

La Niege Était Sale first published 1948
This translation first published by
Routledge and Kegan Paul 1953

This edition published in Great Britain in 2003 by Orion Books
an imprint of The Orion Publishing Group
Orion House, 5 Upper St Martin's Lane, London WC2H 9EA

A CIP catalogue record for this book
is available from the British Library

ISBN 0 75285 378 3

Typeset by SetSystems Ltd,
Saffron Walden, Essex

Printed and bound in Great Britain by
Clays Ltd, St Ives plc

Contents

Part One
Timo's Patrons

B ut for quite a chance incident, what Frank Friedmaier did that night would have been no more than relatively important. Of course, Frank had not foreseen that his neighbour Gerhard Holst would be passing along the street. However, Holst had passed, and what with that, and his recognizing Frank, everything was changed. But that too, with all that was to follow, Frank accepted.

So it was that the entire series of events underneath the tannery wall that night was very different in its present and future effects from, say, the loss of one's virginity.

Yes, that had been Frank's first thought; and he found the comparison both amusing and disturbing. His friend Fred Kromer – admittedly Kromer was twenty-two – had already killed a man the week before, just as he was leaving Timo's. (Frank too had been at Timo's a few minutes before he found himself hugging the tannery wall.)

Did Kromer's dead man really count? Kromer had been making his way to the door, buttoning up his overcoat and looking important, as usual, with a fat cigar between his fat lips. He was glossy. Kromer always was glossy. He had a coarse skin that looked as though it was oozing with grease, like a certain type of orange.

Someone had likened him to a young bull that could never find satisfaction. Certainly you were reminded of something essentially sexual at the sight of his broad, glossy face, his damp eyes and his inflated lips.

A scraggy little man, rather pale and sickly – the sort you saw so many of, especially at night – had stupidly got in Kromer's way. No one would have thought, to look at him, that he had enough money to go drinking at Timo's. He had clutched Kromer's fur collar and begun to hurl abuse at him.

What shady deal had Kromer cheated him over?

But Kromer had passed on his way, dignified as ever, drawing on his cigar. The little undernourished creature – there was a woman with him and perhaps he had wanted to show off to her – had followed Kromer out on to the pavement and started to shout.

In Timo's street nobody was ever much surprised at hearing an uproar. The patrols went that way as seldom as possible, though if some of these gentlemen had happened to pass in their car, they would have had no option but to come and investigate.

'Go to bed, little man!' Kromer had said to the gnome, whose head, too big for his body, was crowned with a mop of startling red.

'Not before you've heard what I have to say, my friend . . .'

If you had to stop and listen to everything people had to say to you, you'd soon be up against it.

'Go to bed!'

Perhaps the redhead had had too much to drink? Actually, he looked more like a drug addict. Maybe Kromer was his source of supply, and the stuff had been adulterated? Anyway, what the hell?

In the middle of the alley, a river of black between its white banks of snow, Kromer had taken the cigar out of his mouth with his left hand, and with his right struck out, once. And then there were two arms and two legs sticking up in the air, literally like a marionette. After that, the black shape lay embedded in the heap of snow at the edge of the pavement. The oddest feature of the incident was that just by the head there was a piece of orange peel – something that could not have been found any-where in the town except outside Timo's.

Timo himself had come out. No waistcoat, no cap – just as

he served behind the bar. He had felt the marionette, and then pushed out his lower lip half an inch.

'He's had his,' he had grunted. 'He'll be stiff inside an hour.'

Had Kromer really killed the redhead with one blow of his fist? That was his story. The fellow couldn't contradict him. Timo never wasted his time, and on his advice the body had been dragged the couple of hundred yards to the old dock basin, and thrown in just where the sewers debouched and prevented the water from freezing.

Kramer could, then, claim to have killed his man, even if Timo had had a good deal to do with it, even if the marionette, which they had once had to lift over a low brick wall, had not been really quite dead.

The proof that Kromer didn't count this as a serious achievement was the way he continued to relate the case of the strangled girl. Only, that had not taken place in the town, or anywhere else the others knew. There were no proofs. At that rate, anyone could boast of anything he liked.

'She had enormous breasts, practically no nose, and pale eyes . . .' Kromer would say.

That part of the story he never changed. But each time he told it he added various details.

'It was in a barn . . .'

Well and good. But Kromer had never been a soldier, and he loathed the country. What was he doing in a barn?

'We had made love in the straw. I was in a temper because bits of the damn stuff had been tickling me all the time. . . .'

While telling the story, Kromer would suck wetly at his cigar and look straight in front of him, with an aloof, rather bashful air. There was one other detail he never altered. Something the woman had said.

'I hope you're going to give me a baby.'

He always said it was her saying that which had really touched him off. The idea of having a child by this stupid slut, whom he had to work on like a lump of dough, struck him as grotesque and unacceptable.

'Abso-lutely un-accept-able,' he said.

And then, he said, she grew more and more tender and clinging.

Without even closing his eyes, he said, he could see a monstrous head, fair and pallid, and quite featureless. That was what a child by him and that woman would have been like.

All this fuss because Kromer had brown hair and was as hard as teak?

'It turned me up,' he concluded, letting fall the ash of his cigar.

A clever chap. He knew just the right gestures. He even had nervous twitches to make him more interesting.

'I made certain of it by strangling the mother. That was the first time. Oh well, it's dead easy. Nothing to make a fuss about.'

Kromer wasn't the only one. Who, at Timo's, had not killed at least one man? In the war or otherwise? Or by denunciation to the authorities, which was easiest of all. You didn't even have to sign your name.

Timo made no boasts about it, but he must have killed dozens. Otherwise the occupiers would never have let his place stay open all night without coming to see what was going on. True, the shutters were always closed; true, you had to go down the alley and get yourself recognized through the door. Even so, they weren't so simple as not to know.

When, long since, Frank had lost his virginity, in the technical sense, the thing had been entirely unimportant. There were others who made a whole incident out of it, which they went on recounting with embellishments for years afterwards, like Kromer and his story of the girl he had throttled in the barn.

When Frank did kill his first man, at nineteen years old, his initiation into murder was hardly more exciting than the earlier initiation into sex had been. And, like the earlier one, it was quite unpremeditated. It was an event without context. It was as though a moment came when it was both essential and natural to take a decision – a decision which in reality had already been taken long before.

No one had pushed against Frank. No one had laughed at

him. Anyway only fools allowed themselves to be influenced by what their friends did.

For weeks, perhaps months, past, probably because of a vague inner sense of inferiority, he had been saying to himself:

'I *must* try it . . .'

Not in a brawl. That was not his style. For the thing to count, his type of mind found it essential that it should be done in cold blood.

The opportunity presented itself almost at once. Was it because he was on the lookout that it seemed like an opportunity?

They were at Timo's, at their table near the bar. Kromer was there, with the inevitable overcoat, which he kept on even in overheated places. With his cigar, of course. And his glossy skin. And his bulging eyes which really did have something bovine about them. From the way he never bothered to arrange the large notes in a pocket-book, but stuffed them into his pockets in crumpled balls, Kromer evidently felt himself to be of a different order of creature from the rest of the world.

Sitting with Kromer was a chap Frank didn't know, a stranger from a different environment, who said straight away, by way of introducing himself:

'Call me Berg.'

He must have been at least forty. He was frigid, secretive. He was somebody. You could tell that from Kromer's manner towards him: it was almost humble.

Kromer told the story of the strangled girl, coolly and dispassionately, as much as to say it was really nothing, just a joke, a bit of passing fun.

'Look, Frank,' he said, 'look at the knife my *friend* here has just given me.'

And the knife, like a jewel whose brilliance is enhanced by being taken out of a luxurious case, became all the more fascinating for being fetched from the warm depths of the overcoat and exhibited on the chequered tablecloth.

'Feel the edge.'

'My word!'

'Can you read the maker's name?'

It was a Swedish knife with a safety catch, so lively, so cleanlined, as to suggest that the blade must be endowed with an intelligence of its own, must be able to probe its own path between the fibres of the flesh.

Frank never knew why he said, slightly ashamed at the involuntarily childish tone of his voice:

'Lend it me.'

'What for?'

'Nothing.'

'Toys like that weren't made for doing nothing.'

Berg smiled, rather patronizingly, as if he were listening to the boastings of a couple of street urchins.

'Lend it me.'

Certainly not to do nothing with it. But he didn't yet know what. That was the moment when he saw the sergeant at the corner table, under the lamp with the mauve silk shade. The sergeant was already crimson in the face – he looked purple in that light. He chose that moment to take off his belt and dump it on the table among the glasses.

Everyone knew the sergeant. He was almost a mascot, a sort of family pet people get used to seeing in his place. He was the only one of the occupiers to come regularly to Timo's without concealment, without taking precautions, without telling them all to be discreet.

No doubt he had a name. Here he was simply called the Eunuch. He was huge, so fat that his flesh bulged his uniform into rolls, making sausage-like pads at the waist and under the arms. He made one think of a matron undressing, her soft flesh ribbed by her corset. He had more sausages of fat at the back of his neck and under his chin; and on his skull fluttered a few silky, colourless wisps of hair. He always sat in the same corner, always with two women. Provided they were thin and dark, it didn't matter who they were. It was said that he preferred them hairy.

Some of Timo's patrons would look startled, when they came in and saw his uniform – that of the occupation police. Timo scarcely took the trouble to lower his voice. He just said: 'Don't worry. He's not dangerous.'

Did the Eunuch hear? Or understand? He would order spirits by the carafe. With one woman on his knee, and the other beside him on the seat, he would tell stories, speaking very low in their ears, and laughing. He drank, he told his stories, he laughed and made them drink, while all the time his hands were beneath their skirts.

Probably he had a family somewhere in his own country. Nouchi, who had played with his wallet, swore it was stuffed with photographs of children of all ages. He called the women by names different from their own. That amused him. He paid for them to eat. He loved watching them eat, expensive dishes to be found only at Timo's and at certain establishments even more difficult to get into, reserved, in fact, for the high-ranking officers.

He would almost force them to eat. He would eat with them. He would fumble them in full public view. He would look at his fingers, and laugh. Then, quite regularly, the moment would come when he would unbuckle his belt and dump it on the table.

Fastened to the belt was a holster containing an automatic.

All this was in itself supremely unimportant. The sergeant, the Eunuch, was just a lecherous fatty, whom people spoke of only to make fun. Even Lotte, Frank's mother.

She knew him too. Everyone in the neighbourhood knew him, for twice a day he used to cross the tram route and go down as far as the Old Bridge, in order to get into town, where his office would be.

He didn't live in barracks. He was billeted on Frau Mohr, an architect's widow, two blocks above the tram route.

He was one of the locals. He appeared at his set time, always pink and smartly turned out, despite his evenings at Timo's. He had a smile of his own. Some people thought it crafty, but it could be no more than a baby's smile.

Whenever he met little girls, he turned back, preened himself in front of them, sometimes gave them sweets which he fished out of his pockets.

'I bet we'll be seeing him come upstairs one of these days,' Lotte had said.

Her profession was prohibited by law. True, she had a perfect right to run a manicure salon in the old dock basin neighbourhood, even if, to all appearances, nobody would ever think of climbing up three floors, in a block crammed with tenants, to have his nails attended to.

It was, in fact, common knowledge, not only in the street, but throughout the town, that there were bedrooms at the back.

And the Eunuch, who belonged to the occupation police, must also know it.

'He'll come. You see.'

Simply by spotting a man through the third floor window, Lotte could tell whether or not he would eventually come up. She could even reckon in advance how long he would take to make up his mind, and she was seldom wrong.

The Eunuch had, in fact, come up once. It was a Sunday morning – he was in his office all week – and he had been quite stupid and ill at ease. It so happened that Frank was not there, much to his disgust, for there was a fanlight by which he could see into the bedroom if he climbed on to the kitchen table.

He had been told about it afterwards. There was no one there that day but Steffi, a great carthorse of a girl with a leaden skin, just capable of lying on her back with her eyes gazing at the ceiling.

The sergeant had been disappointed, no doubt because there was nothing you could do with Steffi except go the whole hog. She wasn't even smart enough to listen properly to the stories she was told.

'You're nothing but a receptacle, my girl,' Lotte would often say to her.

The Eunuch had probably expected quite a different form of entertainment. Perhaps he really was impotent. Anyway, he never had a woman with him when he left Timo's.

Or perhaps he got his satisfaction spontaneously, unseen, while he was fumbling the women? It was possible. With men, anything is possible, as Frank knew, having graduated in the subject with his feet on the kitchen table and his eyes at the fanlight.

Was it not natural that it should occur to him, since he had to kill someone some day, to try his hand on the Eunuch?

For one thing, he simply had to use the knife which had just been slipped into his hands. It really was a beautiful weapon. You could feel the urge just to try it, in spite of yourself – to see how it would behave when it entered flesh, to find out whether it would slip between the bones.

There was a trick he had been told of. Once the blade penetrated the ribs, you should turn your hand ever so gently, as though turning a key in a lock.

The belt lay on the table, with the smooth, heavy pistol in its holster. What couldn't one do with a revolver! And what a man you were bound to become!

Then there was this forty-year-old, this Berg. He was a friend of Kromer's, and hence somebody very reliable, a man in the top class, without any doubt. People must have been talking to him about Frank as they would about a kid.

'Lend it me just for an hour, and I'll christen it. Nuts if I don't come back with a gun.'

All this at that particular moment was entirely commonplace. Frank knew the spot to lie in wait. There was in Grünestrasse, along which fate would inevitably lead the Eunuch on his way up from the dock basin to the tram route, an old, blind building. It was still called the tannery, though no leather had been worked there for fifteen years. It had in fact been idle for as long as Frank had known it, though local gossip had it that, when working on army orders, it had employed as many as six hundred hands.

There was nothing but great bare walls in black brick, with tall windows like a church; the windows didn't start till twenty feet above ground, and every pane was broken.

A dark entry, barely a yard wide, separated the tannery from the rest of the street.

The nearest lighted gas-jet – plenty of them in the town were twisted and broken – was a long way off, at the tram stop.

So it was all very simple, not even enough to make you feel anything. There he was in the entry, hugging the tannery wall with his back. Around him was silence, broken only by the piercing whistles of the trains on the other side of the river. Not a light in the windows. People were asleep.

Between the two walls he could see a fraction of the street – the street as he had always known it during the winter months. On the pavements, the snow was heaped up in two dirty grey banks, one close beside the houses and the other along the kerb. Between them ran a narrow blackish path, which was kept more or less clear with sand or brine or ashes. Before each door the path was crossed by another leading to the roadway, where the depths of the wheel ruts varied according to the district.

So simple.

Kill the Eunuch . . .

Uniformed men were killed every week, and it was the resistance organizations that got into trouble – hostages, councillors, prominent citizens, who were shot or carried off God knows where. Anyway, they were never heard of again.

For Frank it was simply a question of killing his first man and giving the Swedish knife its baptism of blood – the sergeant's blood.

That was all there was to it.

His only worry was having to stand up to his knees in caked snow – no one had thought of sweeping the entry – and feeling the fingers of his right hand gradually stiffen. But he had decided to leave his glove off.

He felt no stir of emotion when he heard footsteps. Anyway, he could tell it was not his sergeant. His heavy boots would have made much more of a crunch in the snow.

Frank was curious, no more. It was not a woman, the strides were too long for that. It was long after curfew. People of his own kind, Kromer, for instance, or Timo's patrons, might not worry about it, but the law-abiding locals were not in the habit of walking abroad at night.

The man neared the entry and already, before he could see him, Frank knew who it was – guessed rather, and his guess brought him a certain satisfaction.

A small yellow light played uncertainly on the snow. It came from an electric torch which the man was swinging as he walked.

The long, almost silent, stride, soft and yet surprisingly swift, automatically brought to Frank's mind the silhouette of his neighbour Gerhard Holst.

The encounter came about quite naturally. Holst lived in the same block as Lotte, on the same floor. The door of his flat was exactly opposite theirs. He was a tram driver, and his working hours changed every week. Sometimes he would leave very early in the morning, before daybreak. At others he would descend the stairs towards mid-afternoon. Always with the inevitable tin box under his arm.

He was very tall. He walked silently, for he wore boots he had made himself out of felt and rags. It was only natural for a man who spent hours on end on the platform of a tram to try to keep his feet warm. Yet Frank, for no real reason, always felt a kind of unease whenever he saw those shapeless boots, grey like blotting paper – they even seemed to have the texture of blotting paper.

Holst was the same grey throughout, as if he were made of the same material. He seemed never to look at anybody, never to be interested in anything, unless it was the tin dinner box under his arm.

Nevertheless, Frank would turn away his head to avoid Holst's glance, or else deliberately look straight into his eyes with an aggressive stare.

Holst was about to pass the entry. What then? There was every chance he would walk straight past, directing the bright circle of his torch ahead of him, over snow and black path alike. Frank had no reason at all for making a noise. Hugging close to the wall, he was practically invisible.

So why did he have to cough just at the moment when Holst was arriving at the mouth of the entry? He hadn't got a cold. He hadn't even got a dry throat. He had scarcely smoked all evening.

The fact of the matter was, he coughed to attract attention. And it wasn't even out of bravado! What interest could he have in showing off before a poor man who drove trams?

True, Holst was not a genuine tram driver. It was obvious

that he came from elsewhere, that he and his daughter had led a different kind of life. The streets were full of such people, not to mention the queues outside the bakers' shops. You never stopped to look at them. *They* were the ones who were ashamed at feeling not quite like other people; they were the ones who went humbly.

All the same, Frank did cough, and did it deliberately.

Was it because of Sissy, Holst's daughter? That made no difference at all. He wasn't in love with Sissy. She was a little thing of sixteen, and made no sort of impression on him. On the contrary, it was Frank who made an impression on her.

Wasn't it she who would half open her door when she heard him climbing the stairs and whistling? Wasn't it she who would run to the window when he went out, and didn't he see the curtain stir?

If he wanted her, he could have her whenever he liked. A little patience, maybe, and some nice manners, which was not difficult.

The astonishing thing was that Sissy undoubtedly knew who he was and what his mother's trade was. The whole block despised them. Few people greeted them.

Holst never acknowledged them either, but then he never acknowledged anyone. It wasn't just out of pride. Rather out of humility, or because other people just didn't interest him, because he lived with his daughter in a narrow little circle, and never felt the need to go outside it. There were people like that. There wasn't even any mystery about him.

Was it perhaps plain devilment that made Frank cough? The thing was too easy, too dull.

Holst wasn't frightened. His stride did not falter. He didn't believe he was the man who was being watched for from the entry. That too was odd. When you came to think of it, it wasn't for nothing that a man flattened himself against a wall in the middle of the night, with the temperature below zero.

As he came opposite the mouth of the entry, Holst altered the direction of his torch just a fraction, just for a second, just long enough to light up Frank's face.

Frank did not bother to turn up his overcoat collar, to turn away his head even. He remained there quite unconcealed, with that settled and absorbed air he always wore, even when he was thinking of trifles.

Holst saw him, and recognized him. He had only a hundred yards to go before he reached the block. Then he would take the key out of his pocket. As a night worker, he was the only tenant to have a key to the main door.

Tomorrow he would learn – either from the newspapers, or in the queue in front of some shop – that the sergeant had been killed at the corner of the entry.

Then, he would know everything.

What would he decide to do? The occupiers would offer a reward. They always did when it was one of their men – even more so when it was an NCO. Holst and his daughter were poor. They probably didn't taste meat above once a fortnight, and then usually scraps stewed with swedes. You could tell what the people in each flat had to eat from the smell creeping out under the door.

What would Holst do?

No doubt he wasn't exactly delighted at Lotte's trade being carried on just opposite his flat, where Sissy had to spend her days.

Wouldn't this be an opportunity for Holst to rid himself of them?

Yet Frank had coughed, and did not dream for a moment of abandoning his purpose. Quite the opposite. For some seconds, he even prayed after a fashion that the sergeant might turn the corner before Holst had had the time to get indoors.

Holst would hear him, would see him. Perhaps he would wait for a moment, key in hand, and so be a witness when the thing happened.

But it didn't turn out like that. A pity. Frank was all keyed up to the idea. It seemed to him that there was already a secret link between himself and the man who was now climbing the stairs in the darkness of the block.

Certainly, it wasn't on Holst's account that he was going to kill the Eunuch. The deed had been predetermined before Holst had appeared.

Only then – at the time of deciding on it – his act was without point. It was almost a practical joke, a piece of devilry. What was it he still called it? Losing his virginity.

Now, it was something quite different that he desired and accepted, well knowing why.

Now, there was Holst, there was Sissy, and himself. The sergeant was fading into the background, and Kromer and his pal, Berg, completely lost their importance.

Holst and himself.

And it really seemed as if he had deliberately picked out Holst – as if he had always known that Holst would arrive at a given point, at a given time, because Frank would not have done what he was going to do for any person other than the tram driver.

Half an hour later he was knocking, in the arranged manner, on Timo's little door at the bottom of the lane. Timo opened the door himself. There was practically nobody left there now, and one of the tarts who had been drinking with the Eunuch was being sick in the kitchen sink.

'Kromer gone?'

'Yes . . . he asked me to tell you – he had a date up in town . . .'

The knife, wiped clean, lay in Frank's pocket. Timo paid no attention to him and went on rinsing glasses.

'Having a drink?'

Frank had to say yes. But he would have preferred to prove to himself that he wasn't in the least shaken, that he had no need of liquor. All the same, he had had to strike twice, so thick had been the layer of fat on the sergeant's back. The revolver was bulging his other pocket.

Should he show it to Timo? There would be no risk. Timo would keep his mouth shut. But that also was too easy. It was just what everybody would have done.

'Good night.'

'Sleeping at your mother's?'

He had got into the way of sleeping almost anywhere, sometimes in the shack behind Timo's, where tarts lodged, sometimes at Kromer's, where there was a nice bedroom with a couch, sometimes at other friends' places, just as it turned out. But there was always a camp-bed for him in Lotte's kitchen.

'I shall go home . . .'

It was dangerous on account of the body still lying across the pavement. It was even more dangerous to go the long way round by the main street – and back across the bridge – because that way you might run into a patrol.

The dark heap was still lying on the pavement, half on the black path and half on the mound of snow, and Frank had to step over it. That was the only moment when he felt frightened. Not merely of hearing steps behind him, but of seeing the Eunuch raise himself.

He rang the bell, and had to wait some time for the janitor to open the main door by pressing a button at his bed head. He climbed the first flight pretty fast, then slowed down and finally, as he passed Holst's door, under which a slit of light showed, he began to whistle, to show who it was.

His mother was in a deep sleep. He did not go into her room. He lit the lamp in the kitchen and undressed there. Then he got into bed. The place reeked of soup and leeks, and the smell was so strong he couldn't get to sleep.

In the end he got up, half opened the door at the back, and shrugged his shoulders.

Bertha was in the bed that night. Her big stale body was warm. He gave her a push in the back and she grunted, stretching out an arm which he had to bend back to make room for himself.

A little later, he nearly had her because he couldn't get to sleep. Then he thought of Sissy, who must certainly be a virgin.

Would her father tell her what Frank had done that night?

2

When Bertha got up, Frank half woke, opening his eyes just enough to see the huge frost flowers on the window.

Still barefoot, the fat girl went to turn the light on in the kitchen, leaving the door slightly open, so that the bedroom was lit by reflected light. Then he heard her putting on her stockings and underclothes, pulling her frock over her head, and finally going out and shutting the door. The next noise would be the rattle of the poker on the fire bars.

His mother knew how to bring them to heel. She always took care to keep at least one girl in the flat for the night. Not for the customers' sake, for at eight o'clock every night the downstairs door was shut, and nobody could come up after that. But Lotte needed company. Even more she needed waiting on.

'I went hungry often enough when I was young and stupid,' she would say. 'Now I can take it easy. I've earned it. Turn and turn about, I say.'

It was always the simplest, poorest girl she chose to keep back. She would find some excuse – the girl lived too far away, there was a nice fire, or there was a good dinner ready.

Whichever girl it was, they all had to wear the same mauve flannelette dressing-gown. It was so long that most of the time it trailed on the ground. The girls were always between sixteen and eighteen. Older than that Lotte wouldn't take them. And, with rare exceptions, she never kept them longer than a month.

The customers liked change. It was no good telling the girls that in advance. They thought they had found a good home, especially the country ones – and it was nearly always those who slept in.

Lotte was probably following Frank's example and lying half asleep. He was conscious of the time, of where he was, of the noises of the flat and in the street outside. So he lay, automatically waiting for the clang and clatter of the first tram. Its approach could be heard from a long way off in the frozen emptiness of the streets, and he almost felt he could see its big headlight.

Then, suddenly, there was the clatter of the two coal buckets. The early morning was always the toughest part for the girl on duty. One had even left because of it, for all she was as strong as a horse. The job was to take the two black iron buckets, go down the three flights of stairs, then down the cellar stairs, fill the buckets and then bring them all the way up again.

Everyone in the block got up early. It was like a house of ghosts, for, with all the restrictions and power cuts, people now used only the weakest electric bulbs. Besides, they had no heating. They were lucky if they got a trickle of gas to heat their acorn coffee.

Every time a girl left the flat with the coal buckets, Frank would listen. No doubt Lotte, lying in her bed, did the same.

Each tenant had his little cellar, secured with a padlock. But which of them had any coal or wood?

When the girl climbed the stairs with her buckets, flushed in the face and with her arms pulled half out of their sockets, doors were usually half opened as she went by. Ugly looks were aimed at her and her buckets. Women exchanged loud-voiced comments. Once a tenant on the second floor – he had been shot since, but not for that – had overturned the buckets, spitting out as he did so:

'Whore!'

All of them, from top to bottom of the barrack-like block, went muffled up in overcoats, with two or three waistcoats. Most of them wore gloves as well. And there were children who had to go to school.

Bertha had gone down. She was not afraid. Perhaps because she was so strong and placid, she was one of the few who had stuck it for more than six weeks.

But she was no good in bed. She set up such an odd roaring noise that a man was quite put off.

'What a cow!' thought Frank.

Just as he thought of Kromer as a young bull.

The two of them ought to have been put to stud together. Bertha was lighting the fires in the stoves, including the one in the bedroom, leaving the kitchen door ajar again. There were four fires in the flat, more than in all the rest of the block put together – four fires just for them alone. It wouldn't be surprising if one day people came to steal a little warmth by pressing themselves against their outer wall in the corridor.

Did Sissy Holst have a fire?

He knew how it went. He knew all about the little blue flame coming out of the gas-ring, and that only between seven and eight in the morning.

People used to warm their fingers on the kettle. There were some who put their feet, or their belly, on the gas-ring. And covered, at that, with cast-offs, with everything they could find to heap on their backs, anything on top of anything, all anyhow.

Sissy?

Why had he thought of Sissy?

The block opposite was a poorer type of place than theirs, being older and already half in decay. The people had stuck brown paper over the windows to keep out some of the cold, leaving only little holes in the paper to let in light and enable them to see out.

Could they see the Eunuch? Had the body been discovered?

There would be no fuss when it was. That sort of thing never caused a fuss. A lot of people had already gone off to work, and the women were now going out to get places in the queues.

Apart from the possibility of a patrol – which was unlikely, since patrols scarcely ever went along Grünestrasse, leading as it did to nowhere in particular – the early risers must have been the first to see the dark heap in the snow – and then hurry on to the tram stop.

Now that it was light, the others must be able to make out the colour of the uniform. That would only make them all the more anxious to get away as far and as fast as they could.

The discovery would be reported by one of the janitors. They had a kind of official position. They couldn't pretend they'd seen nothing. A telephone was provided for them in the lobby of the building.

From the kitchen came the smell of kindling wood breaking into a blaze. Then the sound of avalanches of ashes being cleared from the other stoves, and finally the music of the coffee grinder.

Poor fat stupid Bertha! A moment ago she had been standing barefoot on the rug, rubbing herself all over to get rid of the wrinkles which the sheets had engraved on her skin. She had put nothing on underneath her skirt. She was all greasy. Probably she was talking to herself. Two months earlier, at that time of day, she would have been feeding the hens, and doubtless talking to them in a language only they could understand.

Then there was the inevitable tram, stopping abruptly at the corner of the street, where it braked by discharging sand on the rails. Frank was used to it, and yet he waited, in suspense as it were, for it to start off again with its metallic clatter.

Which of the janitors had been frightened enough to telephone the authorities? All janitors were afraid. It was an occupational disease with them. One of them was there now, waving his hands in front of two or three cars full of occupiers.

At one time they would have cordoned off the neighbourhood and searched the houses one by one. But that was already a thing of the past. Hostages too. It seemed as if men had grown philosophic on both sides of the barrier. But was there still a barrier?

They would act as though there were.

A fat pervert was dead. How could that affect them? They must have known him for what he was really worth. The disappearance of the revolver would worry them more, because the man who had taken it might be thinking of using it against them.

They too were afraid, quite definitely afraid. Everyone was afraid. Two cars, three cars, drove by, then drove back. Another was going from house to house.

That was just for appearance. Nothing would come of it.

Unless, of course, Holst took it into his head to talk. But Holst wouldn't talk. Frank had confided in him.

Yes, that was it! Now he had the clue. It wasn't perhaps the precise phrase, but it served as a hint at what he had been thinking, in a muddled sort of way, the night before. He had confided in Holst.

Holst must be asleep. No. He would be up by this time. Soon he would be going downstairs, for when he was not on duty, it was he who did the queueing.

At Lotte's there were certain commodities they would queue for, some articles which even they found worth while to put themselves out for – to the extent, that is, of sending one of the girls to do it. But for the rest – no!

All the doors in the flat were open. The heat from the kitchen stove seeped through into every room until the temperature was just right. Then the smell of coffee, real coffee, began to spread through the flat.

Over on the other side of the kitchen was the manicure salon. It had an entry from the landing, just to the left of the staircase. A stove was always kept going there.

And each stove, each fire, had its own peculiar smell, its own private life, its own fashion of breathing, its own more or less ill-assorted repertoire of noises. The one in the salon smelt of linoleum, recalling the traditional parlour with its highly polished furniture, its upright piano, and embroidery and pieces of crochet work on the occasional tables and the arms of the easy chairs.

'The worst,' Lotte always maintained, 'are the bourgeois. And they love to take their dirty little pleasures in an atmosphere that reminds them of their own homes.'

That was why the two manicure tables were so tiny, almost

invisible, you might say. And that was also why Lotte taught her little drabs to play the piano with one finger.

'Like *their* daughters, d'you see?'

The bedroom, the big bedroom as it was called, where Lotte was lying at this moment, was crammed with rugs, hangings, and little bits of needlework.

It was Lotte again who said:

'If only I could shove in the portraits of their fathers, mothers, wives, and children, I should be a millionaire.'

Had they taken the Eunuch away at last? Probably. The cars had stopped their coming and going.

Gerhard Holst, his long nose blue with cold, with his string bag in his hand, must be standing, upright, motionless, and dignified, in some queue in the neighbourhood. Some people accepted that sort of thing; others did not. Frank had never accepted it. Not for anything in the world would he stand in a queue.

'Others can do it, dear . . .' his mother had said to him once, but she found him full of pride.

Could you imagine Kromer in a queue? Or Timo? Or so-and-so?

Had Lotte got coal? Would not the first thing she did, as soon as she was up, be to talk food?

'At my place, we eat,' had been her answer once to a girl who had never sold herself before and was asking what her earnings would be.

And it was true. They ate. Or rather, they stuffed. They stuffed from morning till night. There was always something to eat on the kitchen table, and a whole family could have been fed on the left-overs.

It had become a sort of game to hunt out the dishes that were hardest to come by, those containing the most fat or unobtainable ingredients. It was a form of sport.

'Bacon? Run along to Kopotzki's. Tell him I sent you. Say I'll send him some sugar.'

Suppose one threw in some mushrooms?

'Take the tram as far as Blang's. Tell him . . .'

Every meal was a wager. A wager and a challenge, for the smell from their kitchen penetrated the entire block, seeping through keyholes and under doors. For a while the doors would be left open. Meantime, the Holsts made do on a bone boiled with swedes.

What compulsion was it that kept bringing him back to the Holsts? He got up. He had been in bed long enough. He went into the kitchen rubbing the mists of sleep out of his eyes. It was eleven o'clock. A girl he didn't know had arrived – a new one. She looked prim and correct. She had not yet taken her hat off, and was wearing a white blouse like a young lady.

'Don't be frightened of helping yourself to sugar,' Lotte said to her. Lotte was sitting in her dressing-gown, with her elbows on the table, drinking her breakfast coffee in little gulps.

That was how it always went. They had to be broken in. At first, they didn't dare. They looked at the sugar lumps as though they were jewels. The same with the milk, with everything. Then, after a while, they had to be put out because they were looting the cupboards. Though it was true they would have been put out anyway.

They were on their best behaviour. They kept their knees together when they sat down. Most of them wore a little tailor-made, like Sissy, with a dark skirt and a light-coloured blouse.

'If only they'd stay like that.'

That was what the gentlemen liked. Not this early morning display of bosom, for instance. Still, who knew about that? There they were, all together in a family circle, unwashed, with shiny noses, drinking coffee, eating whatever they liked, smoking cigarettes, and hanging about.

'Would you press my trousers, mother?' Frank asked.

The power point was in the drawing-room, so Lotte set up a board there between two armchairs.

The Eunuch?

No doubt some of the neighbours were frightened because of him – all those who had seen the body that morning. They would not be easy in their minds for the rest of that day.

The only thing that worried Frank was the revolver. About

nine o'clock he had got up for a moment, with the idea of taking it out of his overcoat pocket and hiding it somewhere.

But where? And from whom?

Bertha was too weak and soft to give anything away except out of sheer stupidity.

The other one, the little girl in the tailor-made whose name he didn't yet know, would keep quiet because she was new, because she was in their flat, because she was hungry.

As for his mother, he never gave her a thought. He was master of the house. She might sometimes try to rebel, but it was no good. She knew that the last word was not with her and that she would always do what Frank wanted in the end.

He was not tall. If anything, he was on the small side. He had once tried – but long since given up – wearing high heels, women's heels almost, to make himself taller. He was not fat either, but well covered and square shouldered.

He had a pale complexion, like Lotte's, her fair hair and her grey-blue eyes.

He was only nineteen, yet the girls were afraid of him. Why? There were moments when he might have been taken for a child. He could probably show tenderness if he wanted to. He didn't take the trouble.

What was most astonishing at his age was his coolness. When he was quite tiny, barely able to toddle, with his big head covered in ringlets, people used to say that he looked like a little man.

He didn't throw himself about. He didn't talk with his hands. He was rarely seen running, rarely angry. It was even more seldom that he raised his voice.

One of the girls, whose bed he often went to, had taken his head in her arms and asked why he was always so sad.

She had refused to believe him when he broke free, and replied in a flat, hard voice:

'I am not sad. I have never been sad in my life.'

That was true perhaps. He was not sad, but he never felt the need for laughter or fun. He always remained calm and unmoved and that, no doubt, was what led people astray.

So even now, even while he was thinking about Holst, he was

quite unmoved. He felt not the slightest anxiety. He was hardly even curious.

Here in the flat, there was sugar to put in your coffee, and real cream, and butter and jam or honey to spread on your bread. And the bread was almost white. Nowhere else in the neighbourhood would you have found anything like it, except at Timo's.

What had they got to eat, there in the flat opposite? What was Gerhard Holst eating? What was his daughter Sissy eating?

'You've had practically no breakfast, Frank dear,' said Lotte. She had tucked in heartily, as usual.

She had been so terribly hungry herself long ago, when other people were eating. Now she was always afraid that he wouldn't eat enough, and so tried to cram him like a Strasburg goose.

He lacked the courage to get dressed. Anyway he had nothing to do out of doors at that time of day. He just idled. He watched Lotte carefully pressing his trousers and scratching off food spots with her lacquered nails. Then he followed the new girl round with his eyes. He watched her setting out the manicure instruments she didn't know how to use on the little table.

The nape of her neck was still thin. The skin was very fine, reminding him of a chicken's. There were little stray hairs on it, which every now and then she tried to push up with a mechanical movement of her hand.

Sissy often did the same, when she was going up or down stairs.

The new girl called him Herr Frank, as Lotte had told her to do. Out of politeness he asked her her name.

'Minna.'

Her skirt was well cut, the material scarcely worn, and she looked clean. Had she ever been to bed with a man? Probably, otherwise she wouldn't have come to Lotte's. But she couldn't have done it for money, whoever he was.

Soon, when a customer came, Frank would climb on the kitchen table. He was quite certain that once they had got together she would turn towards the wall, and fiddle with her shoulder straps for a long time before she stripped to the skin.

Sissy was just on the other side of the landing. When you

stepped off the wide staircase, there was one door on the right, and one on the left, before you reached the corridor from which other doors opened. Some tenants occupied a whole flat, others a single room only, and there were three more floors above their heads. There were always people going up and down stairs. The women carried string bags and parcels, and as time went on they found the climb harder and harder. One of them – she was only thirty or so – had fainted away on the stairs only a few days before.

He had never been into Holst's flat. He knew some of the interiors, because occasionally some of the tenants left their door open. Women did their washing in the corridor, although that was forbidden by the proprietor.

By day the whole place was pervaded by a harsh, almost icy light. The windows were tall and wide, and the white paint of the stair well and corridors, and the white of the snow outside, were reflected glaringly throughout the block.

'Did you ever learn the piano?' Lotte asked the new girl.

'I play just a little, madam.'

'Well, then, kindly play us a piece.'

By the time evening came, Lotte would be calling her 'darling', but she always treated them more formally to begin with.

Lotte was a reddish blonde, without a single white hair. Her face had stayed young. If only she hadn't eaten so much and allowed the fat to pile up, she would have been very good-looking. As it was, she laughed at her figure, and you would have thought she took a delight in putting on weight. Her wrap was always left half open – deliberately, it seemed – so as to reveal her deep, soft breasts which quivered at every movement.

'Your trousers are done. Going out?'

'I don't know yet.'

He would have been perfectly ready to sleep all day. That was not possible, because the bedrooms had to be done and some-times a customer was to be heard at the door as early as midday. None of Frank's acquaintances really began to live until the end of the day. So he would just hang about, sometimes for hours on end, idling the time away.

Often he would stay in the kitchen in his dressing-gown, without brushing his hair or washing, with his feet on the oven door, or even in the oven itself, reading the first book that came to hand. Or, if he felt like it, he would climb on the kitchen table when he heard voices in the bedroom next door.

Today, without really being aware of what he was doing, he prowled round the new girl as she played the piano, and not badly either. But in reality it was not she he was interested in. His thoughts were continually reverting to Holst, to Sissy, and that irritated him. He didn't like an idea pestering him like a fly when a storm is brewing.

'The bell, Frank.'

The piano had almost drowned the noise of ringing. Lotte tidied away the ironing board and the iron, made sure everything was neat and said to Minna:

'Go on playing, please.'

Then she opened the front door and, recognizing the caller, murmured without enthusiasm:

'Oh, it's you, Herr Hamling. Come in. Minna, you may leave us.'

And, holding her wrap with one hand, she pushed forward a chair for the visitor.

'Please sit down. Perhaps you'd better take off your galoshes.'

'I shan't be stopping long.'

Minna had joined Frank in the kitchen. In the next room Bertha was making the bed. The new girl was nervous, worried.

'Is it a customer?' she asked.

'It's the chief inspector of police.'

That upset her all the more, while Frank remained calm and slightly contemptuous.

'Don't be frightened. He's a friend of my mother's.'

Which was almost true. He had known Lotte before, when she was just a girl. Had there been something between them? Maybe. Anyway, Hamling was now a man in his fifties, with strong broad shoulders and not an ounce of spare flesh. He was almost certainly not married. If he was, he never spoke of his wife, and wore no wedding ring.

The whole neighbourhood went in fear of him, except Lotte.

'You can come in, Frank.'

'Good morning, Herr Inspektor.'

'Good morning, young man.'

'You might get Herr Hamling a drink, Frank. And I wouldn't mind one myself.'

The chief inspector's visits always followed the same pattern. As he came in he really looked as if he were a good friend and neighbour who had just dropped in to pass the time of day. He would sit down in the proffered chair, accept the drink he was asked to take. He would smoke his cigar, unbutton his heavy black overcoat, and give a little sigh of content, like a man delighted to warm himself and relax for a moment in a cosy and congenial atmosphere.

You always felt he was going to say something definite, or put a question. At first, Lotte was convinced that he was trying to find out what went on under her roof.

For all that they had once been acquainted, they had lost sight of each other for years, and he was after all the chief inspector of police.

'It's good stuff,' he said, putting his glass down on a little table.

'The best we can manage to find these days.'

Then there was silence, and silence never bothered Kurt Hamling in the least. Perhaps he did it on purpose, because he knew it threw others off their balance – especially Lotte, who stopped talking only when her mouth was full.

He gazed calmly at the open piano – so innocent it looked – at the two little tables with their manicure kits. He had spotted Minna when she left the room to go into the kitchen. He must have realized that she was new. He had heard the piano while he was on the landing.

What did he think? Nobody had the faintest idea. They had argued about it time and again.

He was uncannily well informed about Lotte's affairs. One day – though it was the only time he had ever done so – he had come in the afternoon, at a time when there was a customer in the bedroom. From the salon they could hear noises that nobody could make any mistake about.

Pleading that she had to keep an eye on her cooking, Lotte had gone through the kitchen to tell the man he was not to leave until she gave him the word.

On that occasion, exceptionally, Hamling had stayed a good two hours, without any excuse, maintaining throughout his appearance of paying a purely social call.

Perhaps he knew Minna? Perhaps she had relatives who had warned the police?

Lotte was all smiles. Frank, on the other hand, stared at him grimly, without trying to conceal how little he liked Hamling's company. Hamling was hard-featured, with a hard body. He was a man of stone, which rendered only the more striking the contrast with his little eyes asparkle with irony.

'Our friends have had some work in your street this morning.'

Frank did not tremble. His mother could scarcely keep from looking at him, as if she knew her son was somehow involved.

'A fat sergeant was killed near the tannery, not a hundred yards from here. He spent the night in the snow. He was coming away from Timo's.

All this was said as if with no purpose. He picked up his glass, warmed it in the hollow of his hand and very slowly wetted his lips.

'I heard nothing,' said Lotte.

'There was no shot to hear. He was knifed. They've already made an arrest.'

Why did Frank immediately think:

'Holst!'

It was absurd. All the more because the tram driver was not in the least involved.

'I expect you know him, Frank. He's a lad of your age who lives in this block with his mother. On the first floor, right at the far end of the corridor on the left. He's a violinist.'

'I have sometimes met a young man carrying a violin case.'

'I forget his name. He states he never left his flat last night, and his mother tells the same story, of course. He also says that he has never set foot inside Timo's place. However, it's not our business. Our friends are busy with the investigation. All I've heard is that he is supposed to have used his violin as a blind, and that the black case he always carried under his arm was more often than not full of papers. It seems he belonged to a terrorist group.'

Why should Frank stir uneasily? He lit a fresh cigarette.

'He looked like a TB case to me,' he said.

Which was true. On the stairs he had more than once met a tall, emaciated youth, always dressed in black; his overcoat was too thin and he had a violin case under his arm. He was always pallid, with patches of red under his eyes and a mouth too red to be healthy. Often he had to stop on the stairs to cough himself out of breath.

Hamling had said 'terrorist', just as the occupiers did. Other people used the word 'patriot'. Still, that needn't signify. When it came to officials, of all people, it was very difficult to guess what they were thinking.

Did Hamling despise them, his mother and himself? Not because of the girls; he wasn't interested in that sort of thing. But because of all the other things – the coal, their intimacy with lots of people, because of the officers who so often came to the flat?

Supposing Hamling wanted to do Lotte a bad turn, what then? Lotte would go to see various important persons she knew in the military police, or perhaps Frank would have a word with Kromer, whose arm was very long.

When all was said and done, 'our friends' would summon the chief inspector of police to appear before them, and would order him to lay off.

That was why Lotte was not really frightened. Did Hamling realize?

There he was, sitting in her flat, warming himself at her fire and accepting her drinks.

And Holst?

With some tenants you knew precisely what they were thinking. Most of them loathed and despised Frank and his mother.

Certain lips would curl back in a snarl of anger when they went by.

With some of them it was simply that Lotte had coal and plenty to eat. Perhaps they would do the same as she did if they had the chance. With others – especially middle-aged women and fathers of families – it was because of her profession.

But with others again, the case was quite different. And they were just the ones who made least parade of their feelings. These did not even look at them, but pretended, out of a sort of shame, not to know that they so much as existed.

Was that the way of it with Holst? Did he, like the young man with the fiddle, belong to an underground network?

It was not very likely. Frank had thought so for a moment, because of Holst's calm, his apparent serenity. And also because Holst was not a genuine tram driver, because you could perceive the intellectual type in him. Perhaps he was a professor, who had been dismissed for his views? Or had he resigned of his own accord to avoid having to do violence to his principles?

Outside working hours he never left the flat, except to go queueing. No one came to see them. Did he yet know of the fiddler's arrest? He was bound to hear of it, eventually. The janitor always had the latest, and he told all the tenants, except Lotte and her son.

Meanwhile Hamling stayed put, without saying another word, day-dreaming, drawing on his cigar and puffing out little clouds of smoke.

Even if he knew or suspected something, how could that affect Frank? He wouldn't dare say anything.

The man who really mattered was Gerhard Holst, who must by now have come back from his shopping and shut himself up in the flat opposite, with Sissy.

What had he got? A handful of vegetables, some swedes, perhaps a tiny morsel of rancid bacon, the kind that was issued from time to time?

They saw no one, spoke to no one. What in the world could they talk to each other about, those two?

And Sissy would look out for Frank, would lift a corner of the curtain to watch him disappearing up the street, would half open her door when she heard his whistling on the stairs.

Hamling sighed, and got up.

'Another little drink?'

'No, thank you. I must be off.'

There was a glorious smell coming from the kitchen. He sniffed it mechanically as he left, and the smell crept after him into the corridor, and perhaps made its way under the Holsts' door.

'He's an old bastard,' said Frank calmly.

3

It wasn't the sort of place Frank liked: he'd only gone in there to avoid hanging about in the street. There were two steps down, then a floor paved with flags, like a church. There were old beams in the ceiling and panelled walls: the bar was flamboyantly carved and the tables were massive.

The landlord was Herr Kamp. Frank knew him by name and by sight, and no doubt Herr Kamp knew him. He was a little bald man, quiet and polite, always shuffling around in his slippers. He had probably been fat once, but his belly was getting slack, and his trousers had become too big for him. Of course, there was nothing to drink but vile beer. It was always the way in this sort of house, where they kept to regulations, or at any rate pretended to when strangers were about. You could tell you weren't wanted. You could always count on finding half a dozen regulars there, old men from the neighbourhood. They would sit smoking their long china or meerschaum pipes and go dumb when you came in. Then they would keep quiet all the time you stayed, pulling on their pipes and watching you.

Frank was wearing shoes with thick soles of real leather. His overcoat was warm, and the price of his fur gloves would have kept any one of these old men for a month, family and all.

He kept a look-out through the little window for Holst to arrive. Holst was why he had come out: he wanted to get a look at his face. The driver had come home at midnight the night before, and today was Monday, so he'd be leaving home about two-thirty to get to his depot by three.

What had they been talking about before he came in? Anyway, what did it matter? One of them was a cobbler with a tiny shop a little further up the street, but he was doing practically nothing now, materials were so short He was probably squinting at Frank's shoes and pricing them, righteously indignant because the young fellow hadn't bothered to protect them with galoshes.

The fact was, there were places where you could go, and places it was better to keep out of. At Timo's, he was in place. Here he was not. What would they say about him when he'd gone?

Holst too must have been fat once, but he was thin now. Men like that formed a kind of race apart: you could pick them out the moment you saw them. Hamling, now, was huge, but you could sense that he was hard as well. Holst even bigger, with shoulders that had probably been wide once, but now his lines had gone soft. And it wasn't only his clothes that were worn out and sagging. His skin had become too big for him, and probably hung in wrinkles. Even the skin of his face was crumpled.

Ever since the start of the troubles – he'd been barely fifteen then – Frank had felt a contempt for misery and for those who abandoned themselves to it. It was rather a sort of repugnance or disgust. Even for the girls who came to his mother's, thin and too white, who threw themselves on the food the moment they saw it. Sometimes they would cry openly as they heaped their plates, and then find they couldn't eat.

The street where the tram ran was black and white, and the snow was dirtier there than anywhere else. The rails, black and shining, underlined the perspective as far as you could see, curving together where the two tracks joined. The sky was low and too clear, with that luminosity which is more depressing than real grey. That whiteness, livid and translucent, contained something threatening, precise, eternal. Colours became harsh and jarring, the brown or dirty yellow of the houses, the deep red of the tram, which looked as if it were afloat and wanted to mount the pavement. And there, opposite Kamp's, trailed the lumpish queue at the door of the tripe shop, the women in shawls, the thin-legged little girls clacking their wooden soles on the pavement to warm themselves.

'How much?'

He paid. The price was a mockery. It was almost irritating to have to unbutton one's overcoat for so little. The prices really were ridiculously low in these cafés. Though it was true you got no more than your money's worth.

Holst was on the kerb, all grey, with his long shapeless overcoat, his balaclava, and his famous boots tied up to his calves with twine. In other times, in other countries, people would have stopped to look at him, got up like that. He probably had newspapers under his clothes for warmth, and he held his precious tin box clutched under his arm. What sort of food could he take to work?

Frank went over and joined him, as if he too were waiting for the tram. He walked up and down: he came opposite Holst for the tenth time, and looked him full in the face, puffing out little spurts of cigarette smoke. What if he threw away his butt? Would Sissy's father pick it up? Perhaps not in front of Frank, for fear of what he might think, though up in town plenty of people did it who were neither beggars nor workmen.

He had never seen Holst smoking. Had he smoked in the old days?

Frank was cross. He felt he must look like an ill-tempered little dog trying in vain to attract attention. He took a turn round the long grey silhouette, but the still figure didn't seem to notice he was there.

All the same, Holst had seen him in the entry that night. He had heard the news of the sergeant's death. He knew too, he must know – for the janitor drew every tenant, one at a time, into his lodge – that the violinist from the first floor had been arrested.

Well! Why didn't he move? It wouldn't have taken much to make Frank speak to him out of sheer bravado. Perhaps he would have done in the end, using the first words to come into his head, if the dark red tram had not arrived with its usual clatter.

Frank decided not to get on it. He had nothing to do in town at that time of day. All he had wanted to do was to see Holst, and that he had done at his leisure. Holst took his place on the forward platform: then he turned and leaned out as the tram started, not to look at Frank, but to stare up at his flat, his window, where you could sense, rather than see, the whiteness of a face between the curtains.

That was how father and daughter said good-bye to each other. After the tram had gone, she stayed at the window, because Frank was in the street. Quite suddenly, Frank took a decision. Taking care to keep his head down, he went back into the building, climbed the three flights of stairs without hurry, and, with a tightness in his chest, knocked at the door opposite Lotte's.

He had nothing planned, no idea what he was going to say. He had simply decided to put his foot in the door to prevent its being shut – but it wasn't shut. Sissy looked at him in surprise: he felt almost as surprised himself. He smiled. It was not often that he managed a smile. He tended rather to cultivate a frown, looking grimly in front of him, even when he was quite alone, or else to wear such an impassive air that people were frozen by it.

'And yet,' Lotte would sometimes say, 'when you do smile, you can ask for anything you like. You've kept the smile you had when you were two.'

It wasn't deliberate, that smile. He smiled because he was embarrassed. He couldn't see Sissy properly. She was between him and the light. But on the table he could see little saucers, brushes, pots of paint.

'Painting?'

'I decorate china. I have to help my father.'

He had seen saucers like that, cups, ashtrays, candlesticks, in shops up in town. Artistic, they were supposed to be. They were mostly bought by the occupiers, as souvenirs. They had flowers painted on them, or a girl in peasant costume, or the spire of the cathedral.

Why did she stare at him like that? It would be easier if she didn't look at him. She devoured him with her eyes, so naïvely that he felt shy. It reminded him of the girl that morning, Minna, the new one, who was probably busy now. She too had studied him all the time with a sort of stupefied respect.

'Do you work hard?'

'It's a long day.'

'Do you never go out?'

'Sometimes.'

'Do you ever go to the cinema?'

Why did she blush? He took immediate advantage of it.

'I'd like to go to the cinema with you some time.'

But she wasn't all that interesting to him, he realized. He looked round him and sniffed, just as Hamling did when he came to see them. From the door you went straight into the kitchen, where there was a folding bed pushed back against the wall. That was probably where her father slept – with his feet sticking out over the end. Through an open door he could see Sissy's bedroom – she gave that away by her confusion when he looked in that direction.

There was a fanlight, as in their own flat, but it had been covered with cardboard because it gave on to next door.

They were still standing. She hadn't dared ask him to sit down. To keep things going, he held out his cigarette-case.

'No, thank you. I never smoke.'

'Don't you like it?'

There was a pipe lying on the table, and a tin box with butts in it. Did she suppose he didn't understand?

'Try one. They're very mild.'

'I know.'

She had recognized the foreign brand. Those cigarettes represented more than banknotes. Everybody knew just how much each one of them was worth.

She jumped. Someone had knocked at the door. The same thought passed through his mind as through hers. Could Holst have come back for some reason, perhaps because he had seen the young man at the tram stop?

'Excuse me, Fräulein Holst . . .'

It was an old man Frank had seen before about the corridors, a neighbour, the one in fact from the flat beyond the fanlight. He scarcely disguised his feelings, looking at Frank like a mess the cat had sicked up. But he was very gentle and fatherly to Sissy.

'I just came to ask if you happened to have a match?'

'Of course, Herr Wimmer.'

But he didn't go. He stuck there, with his hands on top of the stove, where there was still a small fire. He said flatly:

'We'll be having snow before long.'

'I expect so.'

'Of course, there are some people who don't mind the cold.'

That was one for Frank, but Sissy moved across to him with a covert glance.

Herr Wimmer was sixty-five or thereabouts, and his face was covered with white bristles.

'Yes, we'll certainly have snow before the week's out,' he repeated, waiting for Frank to go.

Frank risked a bold move.

'Excuse me, Herr Wimmer . . .'

Up to a minute ago he had not known his name, and the old man looked at him in shocked surprise.

'Fräulein Holst and I were just going out.'

Herr Wimmer stared at the girl. He was certain she'd deny it.

'Yes,' she said, taking down her coat from its hook. 'We've got an errand to run.'

That was one of their best moments. They almost burst out laughing, both of them. They were no more than a couple of children playing let's-pretend, and Herr Wimmer, to complete the picture – for all his lack of a tie, and the brass collar stud on his Adam's apple – looked like a schoolteacher as they beat their retreat.

Sissy damped down the stove. She turned back to pick up her gloves. The old man didn't budge. You would have thought he was going to let himself be shut in the flat by way of protest. He watched them go downstairs, and he couldn't have helped sensing the spring of youth in their steps.

'I wonder whether he'll tell my father.'

'He won't tell.'

'I know my father doesn't like him, but . . .'

'People never tell.'

He said it firmly. It was true. He knew it from experience. Had Holst denounced him? He wanted to talk about it to Sissy, to show her the revolver which was always there in his pocket. He was risking his life with that weapon on him, and she didn't even suspect. Once in the street, she asked:

'What are we going to do?'

What an extraordinary moment that had been, so utterly unexpected – when he had answered the old gentleman, and she had taken down her coat: when they had walked past the old boy, as miserable as a dose of salts, and had begun to go downstairs just like a couple beginning to dance.

For a brief instant she might quite naturally have taken him by the arm. But here they were, in the street, and it was over already. Did Sissy realize? They didn't know which way to go. Lucky he'd mentioned the cinema. He said, with exaggerated solemnity:

'There's a good film on at the Lido.'

It was the other side of the bridges. He didn't want to take her by tram. Not because of her father, but because he wouldn't know how to behave. They had to walk past the old dock basin. As they crossed the bridges, the north wind prevented them from talking, but she didn't dare take him by the arm, though she kept close to him instinctively.

'We never go to the cinema.'

'Why?'

He was sorry he had asked that. Couldn't afford it, of course. The thought of money coming up like that suddenly embarrassed him. He would have liked to take her to tea at a cakeshop, for instance. There were still a few where you could order anything you liked, once you were known. He even knew two where there was dancing, and Sissy would probably have been glad to dance.

Likely enough, she'd never danced. She was too young. Before the troubles she had been just a little girl. She had never drunk liqueurs or cocktails.

It was he who was embarrassed. He pushed her into the foyer of the Lido. The lights were on already, making a false daylight.

'Two boxes.'

The phrase grated on his nerves. Because he had often been there. His friends did the same. When they made a pick-up they took a box at the Lido, as everyone knew. The boxes were very dark, with such high partitions you could do practically anything you liked in them. He'd several times found girls for Lotte that way.

'Working, darling?'

'The works shut last week.'

'Like to earn some money?'

Sissy followed him just like the others, excited at entering the warm cinema and being shown to a box by an usherette in her little red cap with the gold-lettered word 'Lido' on it.

Just like the others! That was enough to put him back in his black mood again. In the dark she turned towards him to smile, because she was happy to be there, because she was grateful to him: and she said nothing, she hardly even flinched when he stretched his arm along the back of her seat.

Soon that arm would be round her shoulders. She had thin shoulders. She was waiting for him to kiss her. He knew she was waiting, and he did it rather reluctantly. Her mouth was half open, and it was wet and slightly sour. She gripped his hand in hers and squeezed it hard, then clung to it like a captured prize.

They were all the same! She took it all in. She hushed him when he whispered in her ear. They had come in half-way through the film, and she was trying to follow it. Sometimes her fingers went stiff with excitement.

'Sissy . . .'

'Yes . . .'

'Look . . .'

'What?'

'In my hand . . .'

It was the revolver, gleaming dully in the half-light. She shuddered, looked round.

'Be careful.'

It had produced some effect, but she hadn't really been surprised.

'Is it loaded?'

'I expect so.'

'Have you used it?'

He hesitated. He spoke the truth.

'Not yet.'

At once he took his chance to lay his hand on her knee and push back her skirt the least little bit.

She let him do that to her too, just like the others. He was seized by a dumb rage, against her, against herself, against Holst. Yes, Holst too, though he couldn't have said why.

'Frank . . .'

It was she who had spoken his name. So she knew it. She repeated it deliberately, even while trying to push his hand away.

Now he was done with emotion. Or rather he was angry. Huge images danced on the screen, monstrous heads came and went, black, white, voices, music. What he wanted to know, what he *would* know, whatever she did, was whether she was a virgin. He still had that left to hang on to.

That meant he had to kiss her, and every time he did it she yielded, softened. He gained ground on her naked thigh, where a feeble hand pushed back at his as it explored the rough track of a suspender.

He must know. Because if she wasn't even a virgin, Holst was the one who would lose everything, who would look utterly absurd. Frank too. What had come over him to get himself mixed up with these two?

Her skin must be white, like Minna's. Chicken's skin, as Lotte would say. Chicken's thighs. Was Minna in the bedroom at that very moment, naked before a man she didn't know?

It was warm. He pushed on. She lacked the strength to stiffen herself all the time, and when she lost ground her fingers gently squeezed Frank's as if by way of entreaty.

She put her mouth close to his ear to stammer:

'Frank . . .'

And by the way she said it she acknowledged defeat. He

would have said it would have taken him eight days at the very least, but he was there already. Now it was only a matter of inches. The flesh was smoother, warmer, quite moist.

She was a virgin, and he stopped short. Not out of pity. He wasn't moved.

Just like the others!

He knew now that it wasn't her he was interested in, but Holst, and how incongruous it was to be thinking of Holst when he had his hand where it was.

'You shouldn't have done that.'

He said politely:

'I beg your pardon.'

And suddenly he became well behaved again, while in the dark Sissy's face must be registering disappointment. It would have been worse if she could have seen him. When he was on his best behaviour he became quite terrifying, so calm, so cold, so aloof that you didn't know how to get at him. Even Lotte was frightened of him then.

'Go on, make a fuss!' she would say to him in exasperation. 'Scream, kick, do something, anything!'

All the worse for Sissy. He was no longer interested in her. Several times lately, when thinking of her, he had called up the image of those couples who walked along the street hip to hip – the long-drawn-out kisses in dark corners. He had genuinely thought he would find a thrill in that. One detail in particular had always fascinated him – the misty breath issuing from the two creatures as they closed for a kiss under a gas lamp.

To mingle breaths!

'Shall we go and have something to eat?'

All she had to do was to follow. Besides, she would be only too happy to eat some cakes.

'We'll go to Taste's.'

'But they say it's full of officers.'

'What about it?'

She had to learn that he wasn't just any young fellow, a sort of cousin, the kind you sent little notes to. He didn't even let her see the end of the film. He dragged her out. And when they passed lighted shop windows he could see she was looking at him furtively, curiously and, already, with respect.

'It's expensive,' she ventured again.

'Well?'

'I'm not dressed to go there.'

That too he was used to – the coats too short and too scanty, with a collar added from mother's or grandmother's fur. She would meet her sort at Taste's. He could have told her that was how they always came – the first time.

'Frank . . .'

It was one of those rare doors still framed in neon lights, of a very soft blue. There was a thick carpet in the dim corridor, but here lack of light did not mean poverty. On the contrary, it was to make people feel rich, and the liveried commissionaire was as well dressed as a general.

'Go in . . .'

They went up to the first floor. A brass strip glistened between each step, and electric brackets tried to look like candles. Between mysterious hangings a young woman held out her hand to take Sissy's coat.

And meekly, Sissy questioned:

'Should I?

Just like the others. Frank was at home. He smiled at the cloakroom girl, handed over his coat, paused in front of a mirror to run a comb through his hair.

In her black knitted frock Sissy looked like an orphan. He parted the hangings to reveal a hot and scented room throbbing with soft music, where the women's complexions vied in splendour with the gold lace of the men's uniforms.

For a moment she wanted to cry. He could see it.

So what?

Kromer was very late in arriving at Timo's. It was half past ten, and Frank had already been waiting over an hour. Kromer had been drinking. You could tell that immediately. His skin was taut, his eyes more brilliant, his movements more than usually ruthless. He almost upset his chair when he sat down. His cigar smelt delicious. It was an even better one than he usually smoked, although he always chose the best he could find.

'I've just been dining with the general in command of this place,' he said in a low voice.

After which he fell silent, to allow time for the full weight of his announcement to sink in.

'I've brought you your knife back.'

'Thanks.'

He took it without so much as a glance, and stuffed it into his pocket. He was too much preoccupied with himself to pay much attention to Frank. All the same, remembering their talk of the evening before, he did ask out of politeness:

'Used it?'

When Frank had returned to Timo's that night he had intended to show Kromer the revolver he had just acquired by right of conquest. He had since shown it to Sissy. There were plenty of other folk he was going to show it to. Yet there he was, hardly knowing why, giving the answer:

'I didn't have the chance.'

'Just as well, perhaps ... Tell me ... You wouldn't know where I could find some watches?'

Whatever Kromer talked about he always put on an air of handling mysterious affairs, of great moment.

He was like that with everybody. With his acquaintances, the people he dined with, the fellows he cracked a bottle with. He rarely mentioned names. He would whisper:

'Somebody very highly placed ... Understand? Very, very highly placed.'

'What sort of watches?' Frank asked.

'Antique watches, as old as possible. I could do with 'em by the dozen – by the shovelful. You don't follow, eh?'

Frank drank plenty too. Everybody drank. For one thing, there was the excellent reason that they spent the greater part of their days in dives like Timo's. Then, too, drinks of decent quality were scarce, hard to come by and madly dear.

Unlike most people, Frank did not get excited when he drank, he talked no louder and his hands remained still. On the contrary, his complexion became paler, duller, his features sharper, his lips so thin that they seemed no more than a pencil stroke on the whiteness of his face. His eyes became tiny, burning with a hard, cold flame as if he were intent on hating the entire human race.

Which was perhaps not far from the truth.

He had no liking for Kromer. No more than Kromer had for him. Kromer found it easy to look cordial, to be hail-fellow-well-met: but he cared for nobody. Yet he was perfectly willing to soft-soap those who admired him. His pockets were always full of a variety of oddments, monstrous cigars, cigarette lighters, ties, silk handkerchiefs, which he would hand to you in a negligent sort of way just when you least expected it.

'Take it,' he would say.

Frank would sooner trust Timo than Kromer. Besides, he had noticed that Timo didn't trust Kromer very far.

Kromer was evidently a dealer. Sometimes you heard about his deals, for he would relate them to you in detail; that was when he needed your help – and he would give you a pretty fair cut of the takings. He spent a lot of time hob-nobbing with the occupiers. That was a paying occupation too. What was he out for? To what lengths would he be capable of going, if it came to the point and his interests were at stake?

No, Frank was definitely not going to tell him about the revolver. He would rather take up the subject of watches: the word had stirred his memory.

'It's for the very chap I've just been talking about, the general. D'you know what he was doing only ten years ago? Working as a labourer in a lamp factory. Now he's forty, and a general. We drank four bottles of champagne, just between the two of us. All of a sudden he told me about his watches. He collects them. He's crazy about them. He says he's got several hundred.

' "This town of yours," he said to me, "used to be full of substantial citizens, high-ranking officials and people living on their own money. It's the sort of place where you should be able to find masses of antique watches. You know what I mean – silver or gold watches, with one or more cases. Sometimes they strike the hour. There are even some with little figures that move . . ." '

As Kromer talked, Frank could see in his mind's eye old Vilmos and his watches – old Vilmos in the room that was always in semi-darkness, lit only by the light passing between the slats of the shutters, old Vilmos winding his watches one by one, putting them to his ear, making them strike, setting tiny automata in motion.

'You could make what you liked out of it,' said Kromer. 'Given his situation, you understand . . . It's his hobby. He's crazy about it. He'd read somewhere that the King of Egypt owns the finest collection of watches in the world, and he'd give his right arm to have his country declare war on Egypt.'

'Fifty-fifty?' Frank asked coldly.

'Do you know where to find some watches?'

'Fifty-fifty?'

'Have I ever tried to chisel you?'

'No. Only I should need a car.'

'That's not so easy. I could ask the general for one, but I'm not sure that that would be very clever.'

'No . . . a civilian car. Just for two or three hours . . .'

Kromer did not press for details. At bottom he was much more cautious than he liked to appear. As Frank was proposing to get him the watches, he would sooner not know where they came from or how he was going to obtain them.

All the same, he was curious. What most roused his curiosity was Frank himself – his manner of taking a decision, so coldly, so calmly.

'Why don't you knock off the first car you find parked at the kerbside?'

That was obviously the simplest plan, and at night, with only twenty miles or so to do in all, there was very little risk. But Frank did not want to have to admit that he couldn't drive.

'Just find me a wagon with someone reliable, and I'm pretty certain I'll be able to get you your watches.'

'What have you been doing today?'

'Been to the cinema.'

'With a little girl?'

'As usual.'

'Did you turn her over?'

Kromer was a vicious creature. He ran after girls from the gutter, especially the really poor ones, because they were easier game, and he always picked them very young. He loved talking about these exploits, with dilated nostrils and thickened lips, using the coarsest words and delving into the most intimate details.

'Do I know her?'

'No.'

'Will you introduce me?'

'Perhaps. She's a virgin.'

Kromer squirmed on his chair and moistened the butt of his cigar.

'Keen on her?'

'No.'

'Then hand her over.'

'I'll see.'

'Is she young?'

'Sixteen. Lives with her father. Now, think about this car.'

'You'll have your answer tomorrow. Come to Leonard's about five.'

That was another bar which they used, up in town. Leonard, because of the locality, had to close at ten.

'Tell me what you did at the cinema . . . Timo! . . . Another bottle, old stuff . . . Come on, tell . . .'

'Same as always . . . Stocking, suspender, then . . .'

'What did she say?'

'Nothing.'

He was going home. There was a fair chance that his mother would have kept Minna for the night. She didn't much like letting them out for their first few days: sometimes they never came back.

He would go and find her and it would be just the same, in effect, as if it were Sissy. He wouldn't be able to tell the difference in the dark.

4

The street was the most brightly lit in the town. Even so there were great pools of shadow. Frank walked along it, his hands in his pockets, his overcoat collar turned up and his breath showing in the cold. The date had been fixed for half an hour's time.

It was Thursday. It had been Tuesday when Kromer had spoken to him about the watches. On Wednesday, when Frank had met him at Leonard's, Kromer had asked:

'Not changed your mind?'

Some people, born in earlier age, would have found them an odd spectacle – the two of them so young, conferring with so much gravity. But the things they were settling were serious enough, God knows! Frank saw his reflection in a mirror on the café wall – calm, fair-haired, wearing a well-cut overcoat.

'Have you fixed the car?'

'I'll introduce the driver to you in five minutes. He's waiting over there.'

'Over there' was another bar, a lower class of place, much rowdier, but still capable of serving reasonable drinks. A man of twenty-three or twenty-four got up. He was very lean and wiry, and, despite his leather jacket, looked like a student.

'This is him,' said Kromer, indicating Frank.

Then, to Frank:

'Karl Adler. You can trust him. He's good.'

They had a drink, because you always had a drink.

'What about the other fellow?' Frank asked in a low voice.

'Oh, yes! Will there . . .'

He hesitated. He didn't like speaking openly, and there were some words which people preferred not to use, which some indeed had superstitiously dropped from their vocabulary.

'Will there be any rough stuff?'

'I don't expect so.'

Kromer, who knew everybody, looked round him, picked out a face through the smoke, and disappeared for a moment out into the street, dragging someone with him. When he came back, he had a man with him, a man with the rough-hewn features of a son of the people. Frank did not catch his name.

'When do you reckon you'll be through? He has to be back at his mother's by ten. After that the janitor won't open the door. His mother's ill, and she often needs him during the night.'

Frank almost decided to give up the whole scheme, not on account of this second fellow, but because of the first, Adler. He hadn't opened his mouth the whole time they'd been left alone together. Frank couldn't be sure, but he was ready to swear he'd met Adler with the violinist from the first floor. Where, he hadn't the faintest notion. Only an association of ideas. Yet it was enough to worry him.

'When do we meet?'

'As soon as possible.'

'Tomorrow? What time do you suggest?'

'Evening at eight. Here.'

'Not here,' Adler interrupted. 'I'll have the wagon ready waiting in the street behind, just opposite the fishmonger's. All you have to do is jump in.'

When they were alone together again, Frank asked Kromer once more:

'Are they safe?'

'Have I ever introduced you to anyone who wasn't?'

'What does this Adler do?'

A vague gesture.

'Don't worry.'

It was very odd. You doubted a chap and trusted him all in one breath. Perhaps it was because everyone had more or less of a hold on everyone else, and because everybody, if only he would think for a moment, had something on his conscience. So you never betrayed anyone else for fear of being betrayed yourself.

'What about the little girl? Have you thought any more about her?'

Frank made no answer. He didn't tell Kromer that on that same Wednesday afternoon – it was Tuesday when he'd taken her to the cinema – he had seen Sissy again. Not for long. Nor immediately after Holst had left – he'd watched Holst through the window going to the tramstop.

He had waited until four o'clock. Finally he had shrugged his shoulders and said to himself:

'We'll see.'

He had knocked on the door as if he had just happened to be passing. He had no intention of going in, because of the old idiot lying in wait behind his fanlight. He simply said:

'I'll wait for you downstairs. Coming?'

He didn't have to wait long. She came all right. She ran the last few yards of the pavement, with an automatic glance at the windows of the block, then, probably just as automatically, she clutched his arm in hers.

'Herr Wimmer has said nothing to my father,' she announced at once.

'I was sure he wouldn't.'

'I can't stop long today.'

They never could stop long the second day.

It was hardly dusk yet. He led her into the entry. It was she who offered her lips, who asked:

'Have you thought about me, Frank?'

He didn't fumble her. He just slipped his hand inside her blouse for a second. Yesterday, at the Lido, he hadn't thought about her breasts, and he had no idea what they were like. The thought had struck him during the night, while he was in bed with Minna, who was almost flat-chested.

Was it that – just curiosity – that had made him knock on Sissy's door and ask her to come down?

He had seen her again today at the same time. Today it was his turn to say:

'I can only spare a few minutes.'

She didn't dare ask any questions, much as she would have liked to. She pulled a little face and whispered:

'Do you think I'm ugly, Frank?'

Just like the others! Always the same. Though he would have found it hard to say whether he thought a girl ugly or not.

No matter. He had made no promise to Kromer, but he hadn't definitely said no. They would see. Minna was making out that she was in love with him, and that, now she knew him, she was ashamed of what she had to do with the customers. She had not been lucky with her first one. More complications! Frank had done his best to soothe her down. She was frightened of what might happen to him, into the bargain. She had seen the revolver, and that had put her in a panic.

Today he had had to promise to wake her when he came in, however late it was.

'Anyway, I shan't be able to sleep,' she had assured him.

Already she had acquired the characteristic smell of the women of the house. It was probably the precautions which Lotte made them take, and the soap she supplied them with. In any case the transformation was swift enough. And the whole morning she had walked about the flat in a black lace slip.

He had promised himself that he would keep his appointment with Adler and the other man without seeing Kromer again, but at the last moment he wavered. Not so much on Kromer's account as because he felt the need to clutch at something solid, something familiar. The crowd in the street always frightened him a little. By the light of the shop windows or the gas-jets you could see those faces passing by, too pale, with drawn features; and some of the eyes in them looked aloof, or wild. Most kept their own counsel. The most terrifying were the eyes that had gone dead, and more and more often you met people whose eyes were dead.

Like Holst? That wasn't quite the same. Holst's eyes harboured no hatred, they were not empty. Nevertheless, you felt there was no way of establishing contact with them, and that was humiliating.

He pushed open the door of Leonard's place. Kromer was there with a man who was like neither of them. This was Ressl, the editor of the local evening paper, accompanied, as always, by a bodyguard with a broken nose.

'Do you know Peter Ressl?'

'By name, of course. Everybody does.'

'My friend Frank.'

'How d'you do?'

He held out a very white hand, long and bony. Come to think of it, it was probably Adler's hands, the hands that were to drive him that evening, that had touched Frank's nerves on the raw. They were exactly like Ressl's.

The Ressl family was one of the oldest in the town, and Peter's father had been a very high official.

They had lost all their money even before the war, but it was in their town house that the general staff had been quartered. Not a month passed without fresh works being carried out there for these guests.

It was rumoured that Counsellor Ressl, who was to be seen brushing past the houses like a ghost, had never addressed a single word to them, and that anyone else in his situation would long since have been hanged or shot.

Peter was a barrister by profession, but for a long time had been in the cinema business. Then quite suddenly he had taken on the job of editor of the evening paper. He was probably the only man in the whole country who had managed to get permission to cross the frontier, for reasons which remained a mystery. Thus he had been to Rome, Paris and London. The dark suit he was wearing this evening came from London, and he was openly smoking English cigarettes.

He was a nervous type, in bad shape. It was said that he took drugs. Another story was that he was homosexual.

'I thought you had an important engagement,' said Kromer, very proud of being seen with Ressl, but rather worried at Frank's arrival just then. 'What are you drinking?'

'I just came to say how-do as I passed.'

'Have a drink. Barman!'

A few minutes later, just as Frank was leaving, Kromer brought something out of his pocket and slipped it into his friend's.

'You never know . . .'

It was a flat bottle, full of spirit.

'Good luck. And don't forget about the little girl.'

They had not really said a word to each other. The car turned out to be a small truck. Karl Adler was waiting in the driver's seat, his foot on the clutch pedal.

'But where's the other chap?' asked Frank, worried.

'In the back.'

Then he saw the red circle of a cigarette in the blackness of the truck body.

'Which way?'

'Straight across town.'

As you passed, you clung to snatches of familiar scenes. They even went by the Lido cinema, and for a moment Frank thought of Sissy, sitting under her lamp, busy painting flowers while she waited for her father to come home.

The fellow at the back came from the lowest of the low. He had big hands, and his skin was deeply encrusted with black. His face, if it had been thoroughly washed, would have been very like Kromer's, only more open and honest. He was not in the least moved. He had no idea what they were going to do, but he asked no questions.

No more did Karl Adler. Only he had an ungracious way of looking straight ahead. All he showed Frank was a profile with an expression of studied indifference, an air of altogether superior disdain.

'And now?'

'Left.'

As no vehicle could be driven without a permit from the occupiers, and the occupiers were very difficult to convince, Adler was forced to work for them. Plenty of people were playing a double game. Only recently, a man had been shot who had been seen every day in company with high-ranking officers. He had been so notorious that the children had spat on the pavement when he went by. Now people said he was a hero.

'Left again at the next crossroad.'

Frank smoked, and passed cigarettes to their mate in the back, who must have been sitting in the spare wheel. Karl Adler had said he didn't smoke. That was his loss.

'When you see a pylon, bear right and climb the hill.'

They were already nearing the village and Frank could find the place blindfold. He might have called it 'his' village, if there had been anywhere on earth he could have been said to belong to. It was here he had been brought up, here that Lotte, nineteen years old when he was born, had put him out to nurse.

There was a fairly stiff climb, past what were known as the lower houses, the majority of which were small farmsteads. Then the road widened out to form a sort of village square, paved with great round cobbles over which cars rattled and jolted. The church was behind the pond – so-called, for it was actually no more than a big puddle. Beside the church was the cemetery, where the sexton – was it still old Pruster? – struck water with his spade less than three feet down.

'I don't bury 'em. I drown 'em!' he would say when he had the drink in him.

The headlights picked out a pink house with life-size angels painted on the gable-end. There were pink houses, green houses, blue houses, yellow houses, almost all of them with a little niche, holding a china figure of the Virgin. Every year there was a festival at which candles were lit in front of all these little statues.

None of this touched Frank. When Kromer had first talked about the watches, he had made up his mind that none of these associations were going to mean anything to him.

On the contrary, it was a golden opportunity. He owed these people nothing, nor anyone else either. It was easy enough to give sweeties to a child and talk to him in a silly, babyish voice.

He had lived here until he was ten, and his mother had come to see him almost every Sunday, at any rate in the summer. He remembered her white straw hats. She was the most beautiful woman in the world. At each of these visits his foster-mother would fold her red hands across her belly, quite weak with admiration.

Lotte had not always come alone. On several occasions, perhaps four or five, she had brought a man with her – a different one each time. They had all had rather a drawn air, and Lotte would say, with an anxious look at them:

'And here's my Frank.'

Each time it had somehow failed to come off. By the time she sent him to the high school in town as a boarder, Frank had understood the situation only too well, and had begged her not to come to see him on visiting days, even though she never came empty-handed.

'But why not?'

'Nothing.'

'Have your young friends been saying anything to you?'

'No.'

She had wanted to make a doctor or a lawyer of him. It had been her great ambition.

Fortunately, the war had come, and the schools had closed down for several months. When they opened again, Frank had passed his fifteenth birthday.

'I'm not going back to school,' he had declared.

'Why, Frank?'

'Because I'm not.'

He'd never been able to discover whether he reminded his mother of anyone, but, even when still quite young, he had learnt that a certain frown of his invariably silenced her. She would seem frightened, and give way to whatever *he* wanted.

His 'wooden' frown, she called it.

Since then, life had been so difficult that Lotte had not bothered any more about his education. She had fallen into the habit of saying:

'Later on, when it's over.'

And so it had gone on. And then, he had been a man. It was

not so long since he had shot out at Lotte in the middle of an argument – coldly, his eyes very small – the word:

'Whore.'

Now, he was equally cool as he ordered Adler:

'Stop!'

A little short of the village square. There was a road to the right where the truck could be parked without attracting attention. Anyway, there was no one about. Lighted windows were few and far between. The villagers liked their shutters tightly closed. It was difficult to realize that life was going on behind them. The school windows too were dark, those fine windows so many of whose panes he had smashed with his ball.

'Coming?' he said to the chap in the back.

And the answer came, in a common, friendly voice:

'Call me Stan.'

Then, slapping his empty pockets, he added:

'Your pal told me not to bring anything with me. That right?'

Frank had his revolver. That was all that was needed. Adler was to wait for them in the truck.

'Can I depend on you?' asked Frank, seeking his face.

Adler replied, condescendingly, as if the question disgusted him:

'That's what I'm here for.'

The snow crunched more loudly than in town. They could see gardens behind the houses, pine trees, hedges bristling with ice. Vilmo's house was to the right, on the square but standing back a little.

No light was showing, but the occupied rooms were at the back.

'All you've got to do is to see to it that I can get on with the job.'

'Right.'

'It's possible we may have to scare them.'

'I get you.'

'We might even have to push them around a bit.'

'OK.'

It was years since he had been there, but his feet could not fail to tread in the self-same path they had followed so long before. Perhaps the most vivid recollection of his childhood was Vilmos the clockmaker, with his watches and his famous garden.

Before he even reached the door, he seemed to recognize the smell of the house. It had always been a house of old people, for Vilmos the clockmaker and his sister had been ageless.

Frank took a dark handkerchief out of his pocket, and tied it round his face. Stan tried to protest.

'It's different for you. You're not known here. But if you want . . .'

Frank handed him another handkerchief identical with the first. He had thought of everything.

He still remembered Fräulein Vilmos's cakes, cakes such as he had eaten nowhere but in her house. They were thick and tasteless with patterns in pink or blue icing. She kept them in a box decorated with coloured pictures of the adventures of Robinson Crusoe.

And always she insisted on calling him:

'Cherub.'

Vilmos must be at least eighty, his sister in her seventies. He found it difficult to be clear about it, because you had different ideas about people's ages when you were little. To him they had always been old. Vilmos was the first creature who had ever disclosed to him that you could take all your teeth out of your mouth at one go, for he wore a denture.

They were misers. The two of them, brother and sister, were each as miserly as the other.

'Shall I ring?' asked Stan, who was much shaken at the thought of being on his feet in an empty square flooded with moonlight.

Frank rang himself, surprised at finding the bell-pull so low down, where formerly he had had to stand on tiptoe to reach it. His revolver was in his right hand. He had his foot ready to slip inside the door, the same as when he had first called on Sissy. Footsteps approached from a distance, as in a church. That brought back memories too. The passage was long and wide, with dark walls and mysterious doors like those of a vestry. It was paved with grey flagstones, and two or three of them were always loose.

'Who's that?'

It was Fräulein Vilmos's voice. She was not afraid of anything.

'A message from the priest,' he replied.

He heard the chain drawn back and pushed forward his foot, holding the revolver close to the pit of his stomach. To Stan, who suddenly appeared awkward, he said:

'Inside!'

Then to the old woman:

'Where's Vilmos?'

How tiny she was! And how white her hair! She clasped her hands together, and stammered in her cracked voice:

'But, my good sir, you know perfectly well he died a year ago.'

Frank recognized the passage, the dark brown paper got up to look like Cordova leather, with the pattern of gold threads still visible. The shop was on the left, with the workbench over which Vilmos used to crouch, a black-framed glass in one eye.

'Where are the watches?'

Then he added, growing more tense:

'The collection . . .'

Then, pointing the revolver:

'It'll be the better for you if you're quick about it.'

Perhaps he had been on the verge of failure. He had not foreseen that Vilmos might be dead. With the old man the thing would have been much easier to carry off. He would have been so scared, he would have handed over his watches at once. But the prim little old lady was made of sterner stuff. She had seen the revolver all right, but you could sense that she was looking for a way out, that she had decided not to surrender, that she would fight to the finish, to the last ditch.

Then there was another voice. It was Stan, whom Frank had forgotten. He said thickly:

'Couldn't we help her recover her memory?'

He must be used to this sort of thing. Kromer had not chosen a novice. Perhaps he had done it deliberately, not having confidence enough in Frank.

The old woman had her back close to the wall. A scraggy lock of yellow hair hung over her face. Her arms were spread apart, the palms of her hands pressed against the imitation Cordova leather. Frank repeated, almost like an automaton:

'The watches . . .'

He hadn't had much to drink, yet everything seemed to be happening as in a drunken haze. It was all blurred and muddled, with just a few details standing out with exaggerated clarity: the lock of hair, yellowish grey in colour, the hands flattened against the wall, the heavy blue veins in those hands, the hands of an old woman . . .

Frank, who was always so cool, turned too abruptly to consult with Stan, and the handkerchief slipped off. Before he could pick it up, or turn away his head, she recognized him and cried:

'Frank!'

Then she added – how absurd it sounded!

'Little Frank.'

He repeated, his voice grating:

'The watches.'

'I know you'll find them in the end. You always managed to get your own way. But don't do me any harm. I'll tell you . . . Oh God! Frank! It's little Frank!'

She seemed reassured and, at the same time, more frightened than before. She had lost her immobility. You could feel that her wits were beginning to work again. She started to trip down the passage, towards the kitchen, where he could see the wicker easy chair with a big orange cat curled upon the red cushion.

It sounded as though she were talking to herself, or reciting prayers, as she jerked her bony limbs along in the ancient clothes that were so much too big for her.

Perhaps she was merely trying to gain time? She was glancing covertly at Stan, wondering perhaps whether he would not more easily be moved to pity.

'What can you want with them? When I think how happy my poor brother was to show them to you, how he made them strike in your ear one after another, and how I always had sweets for you . . . Look, the box is still on the mantelpiece, but it's empty

now . . . You can't get sweets now . . . You can't get anything
. . . We'd be better of dead.'

She was crying – in her own way, perhaps, yet she was crying.
Possibly it was just another trick.

'The watches!'

'He moved them from one place to another so often, what
with all these troubles . . . There now, he's been dead a year, and
you never even knew! Nobody knows anything anymore . . . I'm
sure, if he were here . . .'

What was she sure of? It was ridiculous. It was time to get it
over. Adler must be growing impatient, and he was quite capable
of going off without them.

'Where are the watches?'

She was still strong enough to move a log on the hearth, and
he felt she did it deliberately, just to have her back turned to him
when she spat out venomously:

'Under the flagstone . . .'

'Which flagstone?'

'You know perfectly well which one. The cracked one. The
third . . .'

Stan remained in the kitchen to keep an eye on the old woman
while Frank looked for a tool to prise up the flagstone in the
corridor. She offered him some coffee. Frank heard vaguely what
she was saying.

'He used to come and visit us nearly every day, and I always
had some cakes for him in this box.'

Then, more softly, she added, as though she weren't speaking
to a man with the lower half of his face masked by a handkerchief:

'My God, he can't have become a thief! And he's armed. Is
his revolver loaded?'

Frank found the watches, in their boxes and cases, protected
by several layers of sacking. He called, in a sharp voice:

'Stan!'

Now they had only to make their getaway. It was all over.
The old woman stammered foolishly:

'Don't you think he'll have a cup of coffee?'

'Stan.'

She clung on to them, followed them along the passage.

'Lord, Thou hast seen everything. To think that I . . .'

All they had to do was quit the house and get back to the truck waiting a couple of hundred yards away. Even if she could scream loud enough to warn the neighbours, it wouldn't matter, because there wasn't a car in the village with any petrol, and the telephone did not work at night.

He half-opened the door, and saw the square bathed in moonlight, without a trace of life. He said to his companion:

'Go on ahead . . .'

Stan knew what that meant. The old woman had seen Frank with his face unmasked. She knew him. Sometimes you could rely on the occupiers' protection. At others they dropped you flat, for no obvious reason, and the police did not fail to reap the benefit. It was no good getting to know them better every day. Their conduct always retained a touch of the unpredictable.

In fact, no one could be trusted.

Stan took a few steps outside with the sack full of watches hanging at arm's length. The hardened snow could be heard crackling under his feet.

The door shut behind him. He must have heard a muffled report. Then the door opened once more, and he saw a square of yellowish light, which began to narrow again before disappearing completely.

Footsteps caught up with his. In the shadows a hand took over the sack.

Then, just before they reached the truck, while the two of them were still alone together, Stan said:

'An old maid!'

There was no echo to his voice, and they got back into the truck. After holding out his cigarettes behind him, without turning round, Frank lit his own and gave a curt order:

'Back to town!'

Now he had a bad few minutes to get through, but he felt

sure it wouldn't last long. It was only in the truck that it seized him. Up to then he had mastered his nerves.

Now suddenly they gave way. Almost. The others must not notice anything wrong. It was a sort of interior tremor or spasm. He had put out all his strength to stop his fingers from trembling, and there was a sort of hard bubble of air trying to burst its way out of his chest.

He lowered the window. The icy air on his forehead did him good. He inhaled greedily.

It took no more than the sight of the street-lamps, as they neared the town, to start him calming down. And he had not touched the flask that Kromer had pushed into his pocket.

The attack was nearly over. It was purely physical. He had had the same experience, though less acutely, with the sergeant.

He was satisfied. It was something that had to be gone through once and for all, and now, there it was. With the Eunuch, it hadn't counted. That incident had had no meaning. He had, as it were, merely been acquiring technique.

Oddly enough, it now seemed to him that he had just accomplished an inevitable act, an act of whose necessity he had long had a presentiment.

'Where shall I drop you?'

Did Adler suspect what had happened? He couldn't have heard the report. He had asked no questions. He had simply pushed aside the sack, which had got in the way of his driving, and which now lay between their feet.

Frank was on the point of answering:

'At my place.'

Then mistrust got the upper hand again.

'At Timo's,' he said. 'Not too close.'

Then he thought again, and decided not even to go straight to Timo's. It was no good putting the watches straight into Kromer's hands, just like that. In the house at the back, where the tarts lodged, his booty would be more secure.

Before they got into town, he thrust his arm into the sack and felt the cases. There were some he recognized. He took one of them out, and slipped it into his pocket.

He was all right – as right as rain. He was delighted at the thought of meeting Kromer. He was delighted at the thought of a drink.

The truck scarcely stopped, then went on without him. He made his way along the alley and pushed into one of the girls' rooms. She was not there, but he would find her in Timo's bar. He slid the sack under the bed, after hiding in it the revolver which there had been no time to clean.

It was almost a solemn moment. He recognized the lights, the faces, the aroma of wine and spirits, Timo, who waved to him from the bar.

He walked slowly, a squat little figure in his overcoat, his features pleasantly relaxed, a light flame dancing in his eyes. Kromer was not alone. He never was alone. Frank knew the two men with him, and he was not at all keen to talk to them just yet.

He leaned over Kromer.

'Will you come with me a minute?'

They went to the toilets at the back, and there, without a word, Frank placed the case in Kromer's hand. He had made no mistake, dark though it had been in the truck. It was the big blue case containing a watch with a porcelain dial, with the engraved figures of a shepherd and shepherdess.

'Only one?'

'I've got fifty more, but first you're to talk to him. We must know where we're going.'

Had this evening left its mark on him? Already in the truck, Adler had pointedly avoided turning his way, and their shoulders had not once so much as brushed together.

Kromer was different, put out. He did not dare to ask any questions and his eyes turned away, returning to Frank's face only in little covert glances.

At other times, when they were discussing a piece of business, Kromer was the boss, as he made only too clear.

But now he did not argue. He hurried back into the bar, saying almost submissively:

'I'll try to see him tomorrow.'

Then, as he sat down again at his table:

'Have a drink.'

Frank had forgotten to give him back the flask he hadn't used, and now he handed it over, looking Kromer full in the face.

Did Kromer understand?

Then he went home to bed with Minna, and made love to her so furiously that she was scared.

She understood too. Everybody understood!

F rank spent the entire day in the kitchen, with his feet in
the oven, unshaven, unwashed, reading a cheap edition of
Zola. Did his mother suspect anything? On other days she
always urged him to get dressed about midday because there was
only one bathroom and that was wanted in the afternoon for the
customers and the girls.

But today she said nothing. She must surely have heard the
noise that he and Minna had made the night before, and now
Minna was glooming round the place with a worried, hangdog
look on her face; she spent the time, either staring out of the
window as if watching for the police to arrive, or else gazing into
his eyes, quite disappointed that his only worry was the cold he
thought he had taken.

As for Frank, he dosed himself with aspirin, put drops up his
his nose, and then buried himself in his book again with an air
of determined concentration.

No doubt Sissy was waiting for him. Several times Frank
caught himself looking at the alarm clock on top of the stove,
especially after Holst had gone to work, but he didn't budge.
There were the usual comings and goings in the flat, voices
behind doors, all the familiar noises. Never once did he muster
up the curiosity to climb on the table and peep through the
fanlight. Minna, quite naked, her eyes haggard, her hand on her
belly, had come to get a hot water bottle, without getting so
much as a glance from Frank.

However, he did finally get dressed after nightfall. He walked past Holst's door. He could have sworn that it creaked, that Sissy was just behind it, waiting to let him in. But he went calmly on his way, smoking his cigarette, which tasted of menthol.

It was past seven before Kromer arrived at Leonard's. He tried to conceal his excitement.

'I've seen the general,' he said.

Frank did not raise an eyebrow.

Kromer whispered an enormous figure.

'Fifty-fifty, and I'll look after the two chaps,' he said.

Kromer was already trying to recover his previous relationship with Frank, to resume the status of an important and busy man of affairs.

'I want sixty per cent,' Frank said firmly.

'All right.'

Kromer was thinking that he'd still be able to do Frank down. Frank would not see the general and would not know what he actually paid.

'On second thoughts, no. I'll take fifty as we agreed. Only, I must have a green card.'

Kromer himself hadn't got a green card. If Frank had said that, it must have been because a green card was the hardest thing on earth to get hold of. All you had to do when you'd got it was just to show one corner. A man like Ressl must have got one, though he kept it well tucked away. In the vast hierarchy of passes, there were first of all the car permits, then the all-night passes, and finally the passes which got one into the prohibited sectors.

But the green card, with its photograph and finger-prints, and the signatures of the local commanding officer and the head of the political police, simply enjoined all those in authority to allow the bearer freedom 'to accomplish his mission'.

In other words, no one was entitled to search you. When the patrols saw a green card, they would immediately be on their guard, and would start making random excuses, looking vaguely disquieted.

Strangely enough, Frank had never thought of a green card before this meeting with Kromer. The idea had struck him quite suddenly, while they were arguing about the percentage and he was wondering how far he dared push his demands.

Equally strange was it that Kromer, after a moment of stupefied astonishment, did not burst out laughing or start a flood of protests.

'I can always ask.'

'Your general can do it if he wants to. He can take it or leave it. If he wants the watches, he'll know what to do.'

He would get his green card, of that he was certain.

'What about the little girl?' asked Kromer.

'Nothing fresh. It's going on all right.'

'Have you had her yet?'

'No.'

'Will you leave her to me?'

'Perhaps.'

'She's not too thin? Is she clean?'

Why was Frank now almost certain that the story of the girl strangled in the barn was pure invention? Not that he cared. He despised Kromer. And it was amusing to think that a man like Kromer was going to be put to a lot of trouble to get him a green card, a thing Kromer would never have dared to ask for for himself.

'Tell me, who is this friend of yours, Karl Adler?'

'The fellow who drove the truck? He's a radio engineer, I think.'

'What does he do?'

'He works for them, logging illicit transmitters. You can depend on him.'

'That's what you say.'

Kromer kept on coming back to his obsession.

'Why don't you ever bring her along?'

'Who?'

'The little girl.'

'I've told you already, she lives with her father.'

'That needn't stop you.'

'We'll see. Maybe I'll fix something.'

People probably thought of him as tough. Even his mother

was scared of him. Yet he could suddenly fall into a dream, as he did now, gazing with real tenderness at a splash of green. It was nothing. Just the bottom of a decorative panel, on the wall of Leonard's bar. It was a picture of a meadow; each blade of grass was distinct and every daisy had its full complement of petals.

'What are you thinking of?'

'I'm not thinking.'

That was how his foster-mother had been in the habit of questioning him. So had his mother in her turn every time she came on her Sunday visits.

'What are you thinking of, my little Frank?'

'Nothing.'

He would answer sharply, because he hated being called 'my little Frank'.

'Look! If I get you your green card . . .'

'You *will* get it.'

'OK. Well, let's think. We can pull something big, can't we?'

'Possibly.'

That evening he was certain that his mother knew. He had come in early, because he really had the beginnings of a cold, and he was always frightened of being ill. He found them sitting in the main room, the one they called the salon. Fat Bertha was busy darning stockings, Minna was sitting with a hot water bottle on her stomach and his mother was reading the paper.

All three were sitting quite still, so still and silent in the quiet flat that you might have thought they were a painting, and would have been surprised to see one of them open her mouth.

'You already?'

The newspaper was bound to carry the Fräulein Vilmos story. They would not have splashed it, because outrages of that kind happened every day. But, even if there were only three lines at the foot of the back page, Lotte wouldn't miss them. She never missed any item about people she had known personally.

She must have understood part of the truth and guessed the rest. Even the noise he had made with Minna the night before must have come back to her memory, and for her, knowing men as well as she did, details like that had an exact meaning.

'Had supper?'

'Yes.'

'Wouldn't you like a cup of coffee?'

'No, thank you.'

She was frightened of him. She prowled apprehensively round him, realizing that he had really always been like that, though less flagrantly and openly.

'You're snuffling.'

'I've got a cold.'

'Why don't you have a hot drink and let me cup you?'

He would be glad of the drink, but not the cupping. He had a horror of these little glass hemispheres which his mother had a craze for sticking on her lodgers' backs at the least sign of a cough, and which left round pink and brown blotches on the skin.

'Bertha!'

'I'll go,' said Minna hurriedly, with a grimace of pain as she got up.

The room was warm and peaceful; Frank's cigarette smoke collected round the lamp, the fire purred sleepily in the stove. There were four fires purring in the flat while outside a fine snow had begun to fall, drifting slowly down in the dark outside the windows.

'You're sure you don't want anything to eat? We've got some liver-sausage.'

The words themselves meant nothing. Their sole purpose was to establish contact. He realized that it was his voice Lotte wanted to hear, as if to find out whether it had changed.

All because of the old Vilmos woman!

He sat there smoking, slumped in an armchair covered in claret-coloured velvet, his legs stretched out towards the fire. The odd thing was that he sensed in his mother a sort of feeling of guilt. He felt sure that, if she had heard his footstep early enough, she would have hidden the paper away. Was it deliberately that he had climbed the stairs on tip-toe, missing out some of the steps?

The fact was that he had not been thinking of Lotte at all,

but of Sissy, whom he had been afraid of seeing peep through the Holsts' half-open door.

At that time of day she was alone with her saucers. Did she go to bed while waiting for her father to come home? Did she stay awake, all by herself, right up to midnight?

He had to admit to himself that he was afraid of seeing the door open, of having to go in, of finding himself alone with her in the badly lit kitchen, with perhaps the remains of a meal on the table.

In the evenings she would no doubt pull out the folding-bed. And the bedroom door would be left open to let in the warmth.

The picture was altogether too sweet and sickly. It was too melancholy, too ugly.

'Why don't you take your shoes off? Bertha!'

It was Bertha who came to take them off for him. Sissy too would have done it, without hesitating to go down on her knees.

'You look tired.'

'It's my cold.'

'You ought to get a good night's sleep.'

He went on reading between the lines. It was as if he were automatically translating from a foreign language. Lotte was advising him to sleep alone, and not to make love that night. There was one thing she didn't know, or at any rate didn't know yet, which he himself only had a foreboding of. And that was that he didn't want any of them, not Minna, nor Bertha, not even Sissy.

A little later, Lotte supervised the making of his bed.

'Will you be warm enough?'

He was not going to sleep there. Tonight he would sleep in anybody's bed, even in an old woman's, because he needed someone close to him.

It was surprising how Minna, who had been quite inexperienced when she arrived, had learned everything in three days. She stretched out her arm so that he could rest his head on her shoulder. She was careful not to speak. She petted him gently, like a nurse.

*

71

His mother knew. There was no longer any doubt of that. The proof was that by the morning the paper had disappeared. There was another little sign too which he noticed, and which she would certainly have refused to acknowledge. When she gave him his usual good-morning kiss, she was unable to repress a slight shudder. She was vexed at herself and at once became over-affectionate.

He was certain he would get the green card. For anyone else that would have represented an extraordinary success, a goal you could hardly have dared to dream of, because it put you in the same position as an underground leader in the other camp.

He could have been one.

He had tried to join at the beginning, while they were still fighting with tanks and artillery, but they had packed him off to school again.

For a long time he had hung round a tenant on the fifth floor, a forty-year-old bachelor with a big brown moustache, who engaged in mysterious activities and who had been the first to be shot.

Had the violinist been shot already, or deported? Were they torturing him? Probably nothing would ever be known, and his mother would go to pieces little by little, just like so many others they had seen. For a time she would go on queueing, knocking on office doors, only to be turned away wherever she tried. Then, they would see her no more, and forget all about her, until one fine day the janitor would decide to call in a locksmith.

They would find her in her bedroom, dry as a mummy, dead the last eight or ten days.

He felt no pity. Not for anybody. Not even for himself. He neither asked pity, nor would he accept it, and that was why he was so irritated with Lotte; she gazed fondly after him, her eyes full of anxiety and tenderness.

What he would find really interesting would be a talk with Holst some time, a good long talk, just the two of them together. This desire had long been working in him, even before he was yet aware of it.

Why Holst? He had no idea. Perhaps he never would know.

He refused to think that it might be because he had never had a father.

Sissy was a fool. That morning Bertha, while doing the housework, had found an envelope with Frank's name on it under the door of the salon. Inside it was a single sheet of paper, with nothing on it but a pencilled question mark and the signature 'Sissy'.

That was because he had made no sign to her the evening before. She was probably in tears, imagining that her life was over. Just because of that, just because of her persistence, he decided not to see her. He would go to the cinema, alone if need be, to pass the time until his appointment with Kromer.

But she was even more persistent than he had reckoned. He had scarcely set foot on the stairs – and he had been careful to make no noise – when she appeared with her hat and coat on, all ready to go out. Evidently she had been waiting, behind the door, ready dressed, perhaps for hours.

He had to wait for her on the pavement, while the snowflakes dropped on his lips and melted.

'Don't you want to see me any more?'

'Of course I do.'

'You've been avoiding me for two whole days.'

'I don't avoid anybody. I'm very busy.'

'Oh, Frank!'

Had she too thought of the old Vilmos woman? Was she quick enough to see the connexion with the news in the paper?

'Why don't you trust me?' she said reproachfully.

'I do trust you.'

'You never tell me a thing of what you're doing.'

'It's not women's business.'

'Frank, I'm frightened.'

'What of?'

'Frightened for you, Frank.'

'What's it matter to you?'

'Don't you understand?'

'Of course I do.'

Night was beginning to fall. The snow was still dropping in

very fine flakes. It was the same as with summer weather building up for a storm. Too much of this sort of thing, and you found yourself praying for a good sharp fall of snow to clear the sky and bring the sun through again, even if only for a moment or two.

'Come on.'

They linked up, arm in arm. Girls always liked that.

'Your father's said nothing to you?'

'Why?'

'He suspects nothing?'

'It would be awful if he did.'

'Think so?'

She was shocked at Frank's scepticism.

'Oh, Frank!'

'He's a man like any other, isn't he? He's made love too, hasn't he?'

'Be quiet.'

'Is your mother dead?'

She hesitated, flustered by the question.

'No.'

'Are they divorced?'

'She left.'

'Who with?'

'A dentist. Don't let's talk about it, Frank.'

They had passed the tannery, and reached the old basin, which had once been a harbour, before the barrage had been built. Now there was scarcely any water, and the old boats which had been left there, God knows why, were rotting away, some with their keels in the air.

The place where they were walking was, in summer, a green turfed slope, on which the local children came to play.

'Was he good-looking, this dentist?'

'I don't know. I was too little.'

'Did your father ever try to see her again?'

'I don't know, Frank. Don't let's talk about daddy.'

'Why not?'

'Because.'

'What did he do, before?'

'He wrote books and articles in the reviews.'

'What sort of books?'

'He was an art critic.'

'Did he go to museums?'

'He knows every museum in the world.'

'What about yourself?'

'Some of them.'

'Paris?'

'Yes.'

'Rome?'

'Yes. And London, Berlin, Amsterdam, Berne . . .'

'Did you stop at good hotels?'

'Yes. Why do you ask?'

'What do you do, you two, when you're all alone?'

'Where?'

'At home, when your father has finished driving his tram.'

'He reads.'

'What about you?'

'He reads aloud. He explains it to me.'

'What does he read?'

'All sorts of books. Poetry, very often.'

'Do you like it?'

How much she wished they could talk of something else! She could feel him growing rigid with distaste. It was no good her weighing more heavily on his arm and twining her ungloved fingers in his. He pretended not to understand.

'Come on,' he said at last, his decision taken.

'Where do you want to take me to?'

'Somewhere quite close. Timo's. You'll see.'

It was far too early. There was no music. The only people there were regulars who had deals on with Timo or among themselves. There were no women. And the colours of the walls and the shutters were harsher than they would be later. It was rather like going into a theatre in the daytime, in the middle of a rehearsal.

'Frank . . .'

'Sit down.'

'I'd much rather you took me to the cinema.'

Because it was dark there, eh? Only, he just didn't want the darkness. Nor the sour taste of her mouth. Nor her suspender to follow up with his hand.

'Doesn't he get bored, never seeing anyone?'

It took her a moment to understand that he was still talking of her father.

'No. Why should he get bored?'

'I don't know. Were you well off?'

'I suppose so. For a long time I had a governess.'

'Does it pay – driving trams?'

She sought his hand under the table and said, in a suppliant tone of voice:

'Frank!'

Without worrying about her, he called:

'Timo! Come over here. We want something special to eat. Hors-d'œuvres to begin with. Then chops, with fried potatoes. But first let's have a bottle of Tokay – you know which.'

He leaned over her. He was going to speak to her about her father again. The telephone rang. Timo answered, wiping his hands on his white apron. He looked at Frank.

'Yes . . . yes . . . I'll get it for you . . . Not too dear. No. But you can't have it for nothing . . . Who? No, I haven't seen him today . . . By the way, your friend Frank is here . . .'

He covered the mouthpiece with his hand, and said to Frank:

'It's Kromer. Want to speak to him?'

Frank got up and took the receiver.

'Is that you . . . Successful? Good . . . Yes . . . I'll let you have them this evening . . . Where are you now? At home? Dressed? . . . By yourself? It would be a good idea if you were to look in on our friend Timo straight away . . . I can't explain . . . What? That's more or less it . . . No, not today. You must be satisfied with looking on . . . A long way off. No! If you play the goat, the whole thing will be scuppered . . .'

When he sat down again, Sissy asked:

'Who was that?'

'A friend.'

'Is he coming here?'

'Of course not.'

'I thought you asked him to come.'

'Not now . . . later this evening . . .'

'Listen, Frank . . .'

'What, again?'

'I want to go.'

'Why?'

The waiter brought them thick chops and fried potatoes on a silver dish. It must have been months, probably years, since she had eaten fried potatoes, let alone grilled chops with the bones trimmed with paper frills.

'I'm not hungry.'

'That's too bad.'

She didn't dare say she was frightened, but he could sense her fear.

'What is this place?'

'A restaurant. A bar. A nightclub. It's everything you wish. It's Liberty Hall. It's Timo's.'

'Do you come here often?'

'Every day.'

She did her best to chew the meat, lost heart and laid down her fork. Then, as if she were half fainting, she breathed:

'I love you, Frank.'

'Is that a disaster?'

'Why do you say that?'

'Because you talk about it with such a tragic air, as if you were talking about a disaster.'

Looking straight in front of her, she repeated:

'I love you.'

And he badly wanted to answer:

'That doesn't go for me.'

Then he thought no more about it, for Kromer came in with his overcoat, his cigar, and his habitual air of being the principal person present. Without appearing to recognize Frank, he made his way to the bar, and hoisted himself with a little sigh of pleasure on to one of the high stools.

'Who's that?' asked Sissy.

'What's that to you?'

Why had she an instinctive fear of Kromer? He looked at them, at her, at her especially, through the smoke of his cigar; and, when she lowered her eyes to her plate, he seized the opportunity to wink at Frank.

She begun to eat automatically, possibly to keep a hold on herself and avoid meeting Kromer's eyes. And she ate to such effect that she left nothing but the bones. She even ate the fat. She wiped her plate with a piece of bread.

'How old is your father?'

'Forty-five. Why?'

'I should have said he was sixty.'

He could sense the tear that had sprung to her eye, a tear which she did her best to hold back. He could sense her anger struggling with another feeling, her impulse to leave him flat, to sweep out by herself. Would she find the way out?

Kromer had become thoroughly worked up, and was signalling to Frank with more and more eloquent glances.

Then Frank nodded his affirmative.

The bargain was struck.

That was that!

'There's coffee cake.'

'I'm not hungry any more.'

'Two coffee cakes, Timo.'

All this time Holst was out with his tram, driving in front of him – as if it were fastened to his belly – the big staring headlight, with its yellow glow blotching the snow – the snow seamed with the twin black scars of the glistening rails. His little tin box would be placed close to his levers. Perhaps he would take a bite at his bread and scrape every so often, and chew it slowly, standing there in his shapeless felt boots tied round his legs with string.

'Come on,' said Frank. 'Eat up.'

'Do you really think you love me?'

'You dare to ask me such a question?'

'If I asked you to go away with me, would you come?'

She looked straight into his eyes. They were now at her flat, where he had escorted her. She still had her coat and hat on. Old Wimmer must be getting ready to listen behind the fanlight. He was sure to butt in. They hadn't much time.

'Would you like to go away, Frank?'

He shook his head.

'Suppose I asked you to sleep with me?'

Deliberately he had chosen an expression that would shock her.

She went on looking him full in the face. It was as though she longed with all her being for him to see to the very depths of her clear eyes.

'Do you want that?' she asked, slowly and distinctly.

'Not today.'

'Whenever you want me.'

'Why do you love me?'

'I don't know.'

Her voice betrayed a hint of hesitancy, and her look was less open. What had she nearly answered? Other words had been on the tip of her tongue.

He wanted to know and yet he dared not press her. Perhaps he was mistaken. He could have sworn – it was silly, because there was nothing to make him think it – he could have sworn that she was on the point of saying:

'Because you're unhappy.'

And that was not true. He could not allow her, he could not allow anybody, to think anything of the sort. Anyway, why did she bother about him?

Her neighbour had begun to move. They could hear his breathing behind the door. He made to knock – then hesitated. He knocked.

'Excuse me, Fräulein Sissy. It's me again . . .'

She couldn't repress a smile. Frank left, growling a vague good night. He did not go home. He took the stairs two at a time, and made his way to Timo's.

'Tonight?' asked Kromer, his mouth watering at the thought.

Frank looked at him grimly and then let fall, sharply, the one word:

'No.'

'What's the matter with you?'

'Nothing.'

'Changed your mind?'

'No.'

He ordered a drink, though he didn't want it.

'When?'

'Before Sunday evening anyway. On Monday her father starts his early shift again, and he'll be home by late afternoon.'

'Have you told her?'

'There's no need for her to know.'

'I don't understand.'

Kromer was a little frightened.

'Do you want to . . . ?'

'Not at all. I've got my own scheme. I'll explain it when the time comes.'

Frank's eyes had grown very small. His head ached. His skin was moist, and he felt a nervous tremor, as when one is sickening for influenza.

'Have you got the green card?' Frank asked.

'You'll have to come to the office with me tomorrow to fetch it.'

Good! They got down to the subject of watches.

What need was there for him to prowl up and down in the street just before midnight, to watch Holst come home?

But he didn't sleep at Lotte's. He did not warn her, but made do with Kromer's divan.

Part Two
Sissy's Father

1

Minna was ill. She had been put in the camp-bed which was usually kept for Frank, and was shifted from room to room according to the time of day. There was no room in that household for a sick person. Nor could they let her go home to her people, or call in a doctor.

'It's that Otto again!' Lotte said to Frank.

His real name was Schonberg, and his first name was not Otto. Nearly all the customers had their particular nickname, especially the regulars like Schonberg. He was a grandfather. Thousands of families depended on him for their livelihood, and those who met him in the street greeted him in fear and trembling.

'Every time he promises me he'll be more careful and the very next time he starts all over again.'

So there was Minna, with her red rubber hot water bottle, Minna, being pushed around from room to room and spending the best part of the time in the kitchen, with a look of shame on her face, as though it were her fault.

Then there was the business of the green card, which involved comings and goings all over the place, and then, at the last moment, masses of papers and photographs in quintuplicate instead of in triplicate as Frank had brought them.

'How is it that your name is Friedmaier, like your mother's? You ought to use your father's name.'

This had seemed suspicious to the red-haired clerk, with his skin like a thick orange. He too was afraid of taking responsibility. Kromer had had to telephone the general from the worried clerk's own office.

Frank got his card in the end, but what hours the business had taken! All this time he looked as if he had influenza on him, though without the temperature. Lotte would often look at him covertly. She wondered what was the matter suddenly, to make him so fidgety.

'You'd much better rest,' she said; 'stay in bed for a day or two.'

Then again, Frank had set himself to find a replacement for Minna for Saturday, which was always the most important day of the week at Lotte's. He knew where to look. He knew several girls.

All of which took up a great deal of time. He was on the go continuously, and yet it seemed as if those two days would never come to an end.

The stained snow, in rotten-looking heaps smeared with black, and with rubbish embedded in their surface. The white powder, which occasionally peeled in little flakes off the crusted sky, like plaster off a ceiling, did not suffice to cover all this filth.

He went to the cinema again with Sissy. Everything had now been settled between Kromer and himself, and the details fixed. But Sissy, of course, knew nothing of all this.

On the same day he asked his mother:

'Are you going out on Sunday?'

'I expect so. Why?'

She went out every Sunday. She would go to the cinema, then to a restaurant to eat cakes and listen to the orchestra.

'Do you think Bertha will be going to her people?'

Lotte's establishment was shut on Sundays. Bertha would certainly go and visit her people. They lived in the country and thought she was in service with a respectable family.

There would only be Minna left in the flat. There was nothing to be done about that.

As soon as they were seated at the cinema – it was on the Friday – Sissy asked, with the air of a little girl begging a favour:

'Please, will you let me do just as I want?'

She moved her chair a little, drew back Frank's arm, took off her hat, and then buried her head in the hollow of his shoulder.

Her first sigh told such a story of simple content that she seemed to be on the point of purring like a kitten.

'You're not too uncomfortable? You don't mind?'

He made no reply. Perhaps she kept her eyes shut the whole time, and on this occasion it was he who saw the film.

He did not touch her that afternoon. He was embarrassed at the thought of kissing her. It was she who glued her lips to his, abruptly, just once, when they had nearly reached the house, and just as she was leaving him she said very quickly, dashing away:

'Thank you, Frank.'

It was too late. Everything had, in a way, already begun. On the Saturday the military police took it into their heads to search the flat where the violinist and his mother lived. Frank had just gone out when they arrived. When he got back, he could feel, even from the outside, that the building had an indefinably different look. In the porch a plainclothes man was stationed near the janitor, who was doing his best to appear unconcerned.

When Frank reached the first-floor landing – he had gone out to telephone Kromer – he found three or four uniformed men engaged in stopping the housewives from going upstairs to their own flats and in preventing the other tenants from going out.

Everyone was silent. It was depressing. In the corridor you could catch glimpses of other uniforms; the violinist's door – had he been brought along to be present at the search? – the violinist's door was open, and there were noises coming out of it as though furniture was being staved in, and from time to time an old woman's voice, cracked with weeping, raised in entreaty.

Frank coolly fetched out his green card, which he had not yet used, and everyone saw it, everyone knew what it meant. The soldiers stood back to let him pass. Behind him the silence grew even more oppressive.

He had done it on purpose. Then, the day before he had bought Minna a dressing-gown. He had not bought it in a shop;

it was a long time since the shops had been able to show padded satin dressing-gowns. Besides, he would never have bothered to push open a shop door to buy it.

He had already been carrying all his money in his pockets – his share of the proceeds of the watches – enough to feed an average family, two or three average families, for years and years. It was still there, and he didn't know where else to put it.

As often happened, someone had been unpacking some goods in a corner of Timo's, and Frank had bought the dressing-gown. He had half an idea that he was buying it for Sissy. Not exactly though, because the whole thing was already settled, right down to the practical details. You couldn't explain a thing like that. Of course, he would give it to Minna, but that wouldn't stop him thinking of Sissy. Lotte would be wild. She would say it looked as if this was intended to make up to Minna for the accident she had had with that brute Otto.

It was the first time he had ever bought anything – anything personal – for a woman, and, mad or not, Sissy was there in the background.

Well, there had been all that. There had been the replacement for Minna on the Saturday – she had worked for Lotte before, and a bad lot she was too. What else had happened?

Nothing. This constant influenza, which would neither clear up, nor come out into the open, this persistent headache, this uneasy feeling throughout his body, too vague to deserve the title of illness. The sky – white as a sheet, whiter and purer than the snow – which seemed to have frozen solid and which occasionally let fall a fine shower of icy dust.

On Sunday morning he tried to read, then stuck his face against the frosted window-pane and stared out at the empty street so long, staying so still, that Lotte, who was growing more and more disturbed about him, grumbled:

'You'd better have your bath while the water's hot. Bertha's waiting her turn. If she goes first, there'll only be lukewarm water left for you.'

The bedrooms were not in use on Sundays, so they wanted to

put Minna in the bed in the little room for the day. Lotte was surprised to hear her son say sharply and decisively:

'No. She can have the bed in the big room.'

Lotte had a premonition that something was afoot. She knew he was going to receive a visitor. Probably she guessed that it had to do with Sissy. That was just why, thinking to please him, she had kept the big bedroom free. She gave up.

'Just as you wish,' she said. 'Are you planning to stay at home?'

'I've no idea. In any case, I'd sooner you didn't come home too early.'

Minna was ridiculously grateful for the dressing-gown, which she insisted on wearing in bed that day. She believed it meant he cared a bit for her. Just for that, he threw Bertha over the foot of the bed before he had his bath – as always in the morning she had only her wrap over her fat, childish figure – and made love to her.

It did not last five minutes. It was as though he were in a fury of rage, as though he were avenging himself. His cheek did not so much as brush against hers. Their heads did not touch. When it was over, he left her without a word.

All this time a heavenly smell of cooking was wafting through the flat. In the end everyone had washed and dressed. They ate. Lotte was dressed very much as when she used to come and see him in the country, and she had scarcely aged at all. He had a vague suspicion that it was because of him that she had set up her manicure business and ceased to receive customers herself.

She was quite wrong to worry.

Bertha, who had two trams to catch, was the first to leave. Then Lotte powdered her nose, looked at herself in the mirror, and hung about for a bit for no particular reason, still anxious.

'I think I shall have dinner in town.'

'I'd be glad if you would.'

She kissed him once on each cheek, then a second time on the cheek she had kissed first. He hated that because it reminded him of his foster-mother. It was an obsession with some people. He counted mechanically, half under his breath:

'. . . two . . . three!'

So she went off, and waited in her turn for the tram at the corner of the street. He knew that Minna would be embarrassed at having to spend the whole day in the big bed – it was Lotte's bed at night – and would never be able to work up an interest in the Zola novel he had lent her.

She waited for him to come and see her, to talk to her, though she scarcely dared to believe that he would. She too had seen him through the window, in company with Sissy. She too had heard him knock at the Holsts' door.

She was not going to let herself be jealous; at any rate she would not show it. She realized that she was not a virgin, that she had come to Lotte's of her own free will, that she had nothing to hope for.

Nevertheless, after an hour or so, she tried a little stratagem. She began by breathing heavily, then she whimpered and let her book fall on the carpet.

'What's the matter with you?' he came and asked.

'It's hurting.'

He took the hot water bottle, refilled it in the kitchen, put it back on her stomach, and then, just to show how little he wanted conversation, put the book back on the counterpane.

She did not dare call him back. She heard no movement from him. She wondered what he was doing. He couldn't be reading, for, with all the doors open, she would have heard him turning the pages. He was not drinking. He was not asleep. The only thing that happened was that he would occasionally go to the window, and stay there quite a long time.

She was frightened on his account, and yet was quite unaware that that was the surest way to harden him against her. He was old enough to know what he was doing. What he was doing was what he wanted to do. And he did it in cold blood. That afternoon he even went to examine himself furtively in the mirror, to make sure that his features were completely unruffled.

Wasn't it he who had stood in the alleyway and deliberately attracted Holst's attention, although there had been no need to do it and, but for that, his act would have gone unwitnessed?

Then again, about the old Vilmos woman, had he tried any trick or blind?

He would accept pity from no one. Nothing that could resemble pity. For he must not ever become such a coward as to feel pity for himself.

That was what they would never understand – Lotte, Minna, or Sissy. Very soon it would be out of the question, so far as Sissy was concerned.

What had she been thinking of as she leaned her head on his shoulder the whole length of the film? Once or twice she had lifted her head a little and asked:

'Am I making you tired?'

His arm had been numb, but not for the world would he have admitted it to her.

Kromer would not understand either. He had already ceased to understand Frank. Deep down, he was anxious much more than he was prepared to admit. Anxious about everything and nothing. It was Frank that was worrying him. When Frank had got his green card safely shoved in his pocket, they had scarcely got outside the military police bureau before Kromer had asked:

'What are you going to do with it?'

Frank savoured the malicious pleasure of answering:

'Nothing.'

Kromer did not believe him. He tried to guess at Frank's intentions, his plans. He was not much more reassured in the matter of Sissy.

'You really haven't touched her?'

'Just enough to be certain she's a virgin.'

'Doesn't that mean anything to you?'

And Kromer, with a wink and a forced laugh, said:

'You're too young.'

Kromer was so uncomfortable that Frank spent a good part of the afternoon wondering whether he would come. The man was all worked up. He must have spent the night turning over in bed and thinking of Sissy. But he was the sort of man to get cold feet at the last minute and go and drink himself silly at Leonard's or some such place instead of coming as arranged.

'Why haven't you told her the truth?' he had asked Frank.

'Because then she would have jibbed.'

'You think she's in love with you? Is that what you mean?'

'Perhaps.'

'And when she finds out?'

'I suppose it'll be too late.'

At bottom they were all somewhat in fear of him, because he had set his course for the ultimate limit.

'What if her father turned up!'

'He's not allowed to desert his tram.'

Yes, the trams ran on Sundays.

'And if a neighbour . . . ?'

Frank had preferred not to mention Herr Wimmer, who knew too much, and who indeed might very well take it into his head to interfere.

'The neighbours are out on Sunday,' he had replied firmly. 'If it came to the worst, a sight of my green card could make them shut up.'

Which was, generally speaking, true. But before now fools had been known to get themselves jugged for less than that – for the sheer pleasure, for instance, of being seen by their fellows shouting an insult after some passing soldiers. They were almost always people of the Herr Wimmer type.

The old man had not yet said anything to Holst. Perhaps he wanted to spare him worry, thinking himself clever enough to keep watch over Sissy himself. Or again, perhaps because he was convinced that she was sensible enough not to get into trouble. Old men were like that – even the ones who had fathered children before marriage. They forgot all about it at once.

Minna sighed afresh. Night had come on. He went softly in to turn on the light for her, draw the curtains and fill the hot water bottle for the last time.

He would have preferred it if she had not been there, if there had been no witness. And yet again – was it not desirable that someone *should* know, someone who would say nothing?

'Will she come?'

Frank did not answer. His main reason for choosing the back

bedroom had been that it had a door giving direct on to the corridor. Furthermore, you could also get to it through the kitchen.'

'Will she come, Frank?'

That was a lapse of taste. When his mother was there, she always called him Herr Frank. He was annoyed at her behaving more familiarly when they were alone, and replied irritably:

'It's none of your business.'

She seemed to ask pardon and then, almost at once, could not stop herself asking:

'Is it the first time?'

Oh no! Not that, of all things! No sentimentality, if you please! He had a horror of this pity which girls felt for other girls who had not yet gone the way they had gone themselves. Would she be asking him next not to hurt Sissy?

Fortunately, at that moment Kromer rang the bell. In spite of everything, he had come. He was even ten minutes early, which was a nuisance, because Frank didn't in the least want to talk. Kromer was fresh from his bath. His skin, too pink and too taut, reeked of perfume.

'Alone?' he asked.

'No.'

'Your mother?'

'No.'

And then, louder, with deliberate brutality:

'There's a girl in there whose belly has been bashed in by a dirty old man.'

For a moment Kromer would have retreated, but Frank had taken care to shut the door behind him.

'Come in,' he said. 'Nothing to be afraid of. Take off your overcoat.'

He noted with suspicion that Kromer, instead of smoking his habitual cigar, was sucking a cachou.

'What'll you drink?'

Kromer was afraid to drink, lest it might impair his capacity.

'Come into the kitchen. That's where you'll wait. In our house the kitchen is the holy of holies.'

Frank grinned like someone who had been drinking. Nevertheless, the glass he clashed against Kromer's was his first that day. A good thing Kromer knew nothing of that. He would be completely scared.

'There. It'll all go off just as I've told you.'

'Suppose she switches the light on?'

'Have you ever known a young girl to want the light on at a time like that?'

'Suppose she talks to me, and I don't answer?'

Frank said firmly:

'She won't talk.'

Even those ten minutes were dreadfully long. He watched their slow passage on the dial of the alarm clock over the kitchen stove.

'Now you must get your bearings so as to find your way in the dark. Come with me. Here's the bed, immediately on your right as soon as you've gone through the door.'

'I see.'

He must be got to take another drink, otherwise he would falter. And he must not falter at any price. Frank had worked out the whole plan like a piece of clockwork, with the meticulous care of a child.

Some things cannot be explained, and it is useless trying to make anyone else understand: this thing just had to happen. After that he could rest easy.

'You're sure you can find your way?'

'Yes.'

'On the right, immediately inside the door.'

'Yes.'

'I'll turn the light off.'

'But what about you? Where will you be?'

'Here.'

'You swear you won't go away?'

To think that only ten days before he had looked on Kromer as an older man, as a man much stronger than himself, as – in short – a man, while he had regarded himself as nothing but a boy!

'You're getting all worked up over nothing!' he said contemptuously to screw Kromer up to the sticking point.

'No, no, old chap. It's you I'm thinking of. *I* don't know the house, and I want to avoid . . .'

'Shsh!'

She came. Like a mouse. And at that moment Frank's senses were so sharpened that he was able to hear Minna get up, barefoot and without noise, to come and listen at the door in her dressing-gown. So, even in bed, Minna had heard the Holsts' door open and shut again. What had fetched her out to look, no doubt, was the fact that the sound had not been at once followed by steps on the stairs, as usually happened.

Who could tell? Anything was possible. Perhaps Minna had seen another door which was not quite shut and which creaked a little – old Wimmer's. Frank was convinced that old Wimmer was on the look-out.

But Minna could not know about that. On reflection, Frank was sure she didn't know about it. Otherwise she would have been frightened on his account and would have come running to warn him.

Sissy had walked along the corridor, her feet scraping a little on the roughened floor. She had knocked – scratched, rather – on the door of the little bedroom.

He had turned out the lights. If they had spoken out loud, Kromer would have been able to hear them from the kitchen.

She said:

'I've come.'

In his arms she felt quite rigid.

'You asked me to come, Frank.'

'Yes.'

He shut the door behind her, but there was still the one into the kitchen, which she could not see and which remained ajar.

'You still want to?' she asked.

They couldn't see anything, except for a faint reflection between the window curtains from the gas lamp on the street corner.

'I do,' he answered.

He didn't have to undress her. He just began and she went on by herself, without a word, standing close against the bed.

Perhaps she despised him without being able to help loving him. He didn't know. He didn't want to know. Kromer could hear them. Frank said, and how stupid they sounded, the words which he could scarcely get out:

'It would have been too late tomorrow. Your father starts his morning shift.'

She must be almost naked – she was naked. He could feel the softness of clothes and undergarments beneath his feet. She was waiting. Now came the hardest part: to get her to lie down on the bed.

She felt for his hand in the dark. She murmured, and it was the first time she had spoken his name in that tone – how lucky that Kromer was the other side of the door!

'Frank!'

Then Frank said, very quickly and very softly:

'I'll be back in a minute . . .'

He brushed against Kromer as their paths crossed. He almost had to push him into the room. He shut the door again at once, with a haste he would have found it hard to explain. He stood there, waiting, motionless.

There was no town any more, no more Lotte, no more Minna, no more trams at the corner of the street, no more cinema, no more universe. There was nothing left any more, only a mounting emptiness and a feeling of anguish that made the sweat stand on his forehead and forced him to press his hand against his heart.

Someone touched him, and he almost cried out. He restrained himself with a great effort. He knew it was Minna, Minna who had left ajar the door of the big bedroom, from which came a little light.

Could she see him? Had she seen him, when she came in, before her hand had roused him, like a sleepwalker wakened at a touch?

He kept silent. He was angry with her, so angry he could wish her dead for having failed to say one of those foolish phrases which girls knew so well how to use.

But no! She stayed at his side, as rigid and as white as he was, in the patch of light which was too feeble for features to be distinguished, and it was only a long time afterwards that he realized that it was on his wrist she had laid her hand.

It was as though she were taking his pulse. Did he look ill? He was not going to allow her to think of him as sick, to go on looking at him; he was not going to allow her to see what nobody had the right to see.

'*Frank!*'

Someone had shrieked his name. Sissy had shrieked. It was Sissy who had shrieked his name, *his* name; it was Sissy running barefooted, battering at the door on to the corridor, Sissy calling for help or trying to get away.

Frank did not move, perhaps because Minna, whom he had no love for, whom he despised, who was nothing but a tart, less than nothing, was still holding him by the wrist in a foolish sort of way.

Now there was an uproar in the bedroom, just as when the military police were searching the violinist's flat. The two of them were moving back and forth on their bare feet, chasing and struggling, and they could hear Kromer's voice, the voice of one trying not to get panic-stricken.

'At least put some clothes on,' he was pleading. 'Please, you must! I swear not to touch you again . . .'

'The key . . .' she cried.

It would all come back to him later. For the present he was beyond thought or movement; he was going to the ultimate limit, as he had sworn to do.

In spite of everything, Kromer had had enough wit to snatch the key. It was true they had the light on now. A thin streak of luminous pink was visible under the door – was it Sissy who had switched on the light? Had she accidentally come on the little bulb-switch hanging at the bed-head?

What were they doing? There were violent movements. It was as though a fight was going on, with dull, inexplicable, thuds. Kromer repeated, like a worn-out gramophone record:

'Not until you've put something on . . .'

She did not speak of Frank again. She had called his name just once; she had cried it aloud, with all her strength.

If any of the neighbours were in, they couldn't fail to hear. It was Minna who thought of that. Frank still did not budge. There was only one question he wanted to ask, which he would ask, no matter how – on his knees, if need be – so vital had it suddenly become.

'Has Kromer . . . ?'

Something broke inside him.

She was gone. The door had banged. They had heard her footsteps in the corridor. Minna let go of his wrist, and rushed into the bedroom. She thought of everything, even remembering to open the door on to the landing.

Kromer did not appear at once. Knowing him as he did, Frank was sure that he would be anxious to restore his clothes to order. At last he pushed open the door.

'Well, old man,' he said. 'I shan't forget this.'

Frank did not stir.

'What's the matter?' asked Kromer.

'Nothing.'

'If only you'd warned me there was a switch at the head of the bed, I could have managed it.'

Frank did not, would not, stir.

'I took great care not to answer when she spoke. I felt her hand groping in the dark, but I never imagined it was because she was going to switch on the light.'

Frank had not asked his question. His eyes were pinpoints, his gaze hard, so hard that Kromer was almost frightened and wondered for a moment whether he had not let himself be caught in a trap.

That didn't make sense. There was no rhyme or reason in it.

'In any case, you can boast . . .'

Minna came back and turned the switch, flooding them with white light which made them blink.

'She's gone downstairs like a mad thing. She didn't try to go home. One of the neighbours, Herr Wimmer, tried to stop her as she went by. I'll swear she didn't even see him.'

So! Now it was done.

Kromer could take himself off. He was scared stiff. He did not think of leaving. He was mad with rage.

'When shall I be seeing you?' Kromer asked.

'I don't know.'

'Coming to Timo's this evening?'

'Perhaps.'

She had gone, and Herr Wimmer had tried to stop her.

She had gone downstairs at a run.

'Look here, young Frank, it seems to me that you . . .'

He broke off: just as well for him. He was no one's young Frank any more. He never had been. They had just imagined whatever they wanted.

Now, he had paid his footing.

He asked, with the vacant look of one who has not been listening:

'What?'

'What do you mean?'

'Nothing. I just asked you: what?'

'And *I* was asking you if we should see you at Timo's this evening.'

'And *I* answer: what?'

He couldn't stand any more. The sensation over his heart was becoming really intolerable, as if he were going to die.

'Well, old man . . .'

'Yes – go.

Oh to sit down quickly, to get quickly to bed! Let Kromer be off. Let him go and tell Timo and his friends as much as he liked.

Frank had done what he wanted. He had rounded the cape. He had seen what was on the other side.

He had not seen what he expected to see. No matter!

Let him go! In God's name, let him go!

'What are you waiting for?'

'But . . .'

Minna had gone into the bedroom. She ought never to have presumed so far; she was quite incapable of understanding matters like this. Now she came out with a black stocking in each hand.

So Sissy had gone off without her stockings, her feet uncovered except for her slippers.

And Kromer did not understand either. If they kept on, the two of them, Frank would go mad, would throw himself on the floor and begin to gnaw at something, anything.

'Get out, for the love of God, get out!'

Would nobody realize that he had reached the other side of the turning, that he had nothing in common with any of them any more?

2

In the garden of his foster-mother, Frau Porse, there had been one tree, a lime tree. One evening, just at dusk, when a low sky seemed to be pressing down on the earth and drawing everything into itself like a fog, a dog had begun to bark, and they had found a stray cat in the tree.

It was winter. The water butt under the gutter was frozen. From the back of the house you could see the village windows lighting up one by one.

The cat was crouched on the lowest branch, about fifteen feet from the ground, from where it looked steadily down.

It was black and white, and belonged to no one in the village. Frau Porse knew all the cats.

When the dog barked, they had just poured hot water for Frank's bath into the tub which was set on the kitchen floor. It was not actually a proper tub, but the sawn-off half of a barrel. The windows were steamed over. In the garden they could hear the voice of Herr Porse, who was a roadmender, saying, with the air of certainty which he brought to everything, especially when – as was usually the case – he had had a drink or two:

'I'll bring it down with a shot from my gun.'

Frank had caught the word 'gun'. The shot-gun hung on the white wall over the hearth. Already half undressed, Frank had put on his shirt and trousers again.

'Try to catch it first. Perhaps it's not so badly hurt as all that.'

The cat could still be seen clearly enough to make out the red

99

stains on the white patches of its coat, and one eye hanging out of its socket.

Frank had lost track of what happened next. In a moment there were half a dozen people, ten people, let alone the children, all with their noses in the air. Then someone came along with a lantern.

They tried to lure the cat by putting a saucer of milk on the ground in full view, after taking the precaution, of course, of chaining the dog up in his kennel. But the cat would not budge. From time to time it gave a plaintive miaow.

'Listen how the poor thing calls!'

'It's calling all right, but not us.'

The proof of that came when someone climbed on a chair to try to catch it, and it leapt on to the next branch above.

All this went on for a long time, an hour at least. More neighbours arrived, and it was only by their voices that they could be recognized. One young man climbed up into the tree, but every time he reached out his arm, the cat climbed higher, so that in the end all they could see from below was a dark round mass.

'To the left, Helmut . . . At the end of the big branch . . .'

The astonishing thing was that, as soon as they gave up trying to catch it, the wounded animal began to cry all the more. You could have sworn that it was indignant at being left.

Then they went off to fetch ladders. Everyone busied themselves on that errand, full of excitement. The roadmender chattered incessantly of getting his gun, and had to be shut up.

They did not get the black and white cat, but had to go home with it still in the tree. They left some milk, a mess of cat's food with meat in it.

'It knew how to get up. It'll know how to get down again,' they said.

Next day the cat was still in the lime tree, almost at the very top, and it went on crying all day. Again they tried to catch it. Frank was forbidden to go and look, on account of the eye hanging out of its head. Even Frau Porse was almost ill at the sight.

He had never known the end of the story. They had assured him on the third day that the cat had gone away. But was it true? Or had they just told him that to spare his feelings?

What had just happened was almost exactly the same, except that this time it was not just a stray cat, but Sissy.

In the end Frank went into the back bedroom alone, almost solemnly, shutting the doors behind him with great care, rather as he would have entered a room in which someone was lying in state.

Keeping his eyes lifted from the sheets, he put the bedspread back in place, and was perhaps going to throw himself on the bed when his eye caught a small object lying on the night table.

A few minutes earlier he had had Sissy's stockings in his hand, stockings of black wool with the fine darning in the feet which girls are taught in convents.

It was not curiosity that made him pick up the handbag from the night table. He simply wanted to touch it. He could do that, since he was alone. And then a thought struck him. He remembered how often Lotte had to ring the doorbell when she came home with the explanation:

'I've left my key in my old handbag again.'

Sissy too had a key, the one for the flat opposite. And where would she have put it, if not in her bag? She had not thought of it when she ran away. At that moment nothing was further from her mind than going home. She hadn't even seen Herr Wimmer when he tried to stop her as she went went by.

So her key was here, in the bag, with a handkerchief, some ration books, some paper money, some small change and a pencil.

'Where are you going, Herr Frank?'

It was not yet six o'clock. He could clearly see the black hands on the dial of the alarm clock in the kitchen. Minna had not gone back to bed but was sitting by the stove. She was calling him Herr Frank again, and following his movements with a timorous look.

He did not realize that he was still holding a little black bag of American cloth, that he had neither hat nor overcoat on, and thus dressed he was opening the door.

'At least put your coat on, if you're going out.'

A sick person no longer feels his sickness when he has someone to care for who is even worse. Minna had forgotten her trouble. She would have gone with Frank, if she had not known that he would never allow it.

'You'll be back directly, won't you? You're not well.'

The door opposite was shut. There was no thin streak of pink light showing beneath it. Frank went downstairs with a determined air. It was as though he knew just where to find her.

At the end of the Grünestrasse there was a street to the right, the one in which Timo's place was, with the old dock behind. It led to the street over the bridge, and by then you were almost in the middle of the town. There were lights, shops, passers-by.

But if you turned left, as Frank had done on one occasion with Sissy, there was nothing to see except the backs of houses, and featureless stretches of waste ground. Part of the basin had been filled in, but part had been left. Building had started for a teachers' training college, but the war had brought the work to a standstill. Now it was just a roofless skeleton, with jutting steel beams and unfinished walls. Two rows of trees, still thin and stunted, with ironwork to protect them, traced the line that an avenue was one day to follow. But it was cut across with trenches, and ended abruptly in a sand pit.

Night had fallen. There was one forgotten-looking gas-lamp for the whole of this part of the world, while across the water, the lights formed an almost unbroken festoon in front of the houses, and the trams passed to and fro.

He knew he would find her there, but he wanted to avoid frightening her. He had no intention of speaking to her. Merely to give her back her key. Holst would not be home until midnight, and she could not stay outside all that time with only her slippers on her feet, and no stockings, and no money.

He passed quite close to someone just at the corner of the street — a man, Herr Wimmer for certain. Momentarily he shrank back in fear, for, if the man had taken it into his head to strike him, he would have felt bound not to retaliate.

Herr Wimmer too must be looking for Sissy. He had probably followed her for a while and then lost track of her on the waste ground.

For the space of a second, the two almost touched each other. It was a little easier to see just at that spot. Even though the moon was not visible, it was there behind the clouds, and there was enough light to distinguish outlines.

Had Herr Wimmer seen the bag which Frank still had in his hand? Had he thought of the key? Had he understood what the younger man had come out to do?

In any case, he had let him pass. Frank cast about in all directions, moving very fast, stumbling over the heaps of hardened snow. Then he stopped short to look around him.

He wanted to call Sissy's name, but that would certainly be the best way of ensuring that she did not come, of making her plunge even deeper into the obscurity of these wastes, or else, like the black and white cat, go to earth in some hole.

Occasionally he would hear movement. He would rush towards it, only to draw blank. Then he would hear footsteps in another direction, and begin to run towards them, to find it was Herr Wimmer following a track parallel with his own.

Several times his feet crashed through sheets of hard ice, and he went in up to his knees.

There she was! He saw her. He recognized her silhouette, but he didn't dare rush forward, or speak, or call out. He simply held out the bag at arm's length, much as they had shown the saucer of milk to the cat.

But she had already started off again. She disappeared in a patch of shadow and then, and only then, he took the risk of crying, in a voice which made him feel ashamed in this desert of silence.

'The key!'

He caught another glimpse of her crossing a patch of white and ran, stumbling, repeating:

'The key!'

He did not want to speak her name, for fear of scaring her. Perhaps he should have handed the bag over to Herr Wimmer, who might have succeeded in getting up to her. He had not thought of that. Nor had Herr Wimmer. But was the old man really any more likely to succeed than Frank? Frank had lost sight and sound of him. A man of his age ought not to be floundering about on a piece of ground sown with pitfalls. She was not far away – a hundred yards at the most. But the lad who had climbed the tree in Frau Porse's garden had several times had his hand within an inch or two of the cat. Possibly the cat had hesitated which course to choose, and then at the last moment made the leap on to a higher branch.

The river was frozen, but the sewer outflow, which prevented ice from forming over a wide stretch of water, was not far away.

He tried once again, twice. He wanted to cry with discouragement.

It became an obsession – the key. The worn, shiny little bag, with a handkerchief, some ration books, a little money – and a key.

Then, as he was not far from her and she couldn't help seeing him, he picked out the best-lit spot and stood quite still. He remained there at his full height, with the bag stretched out at arm's length, and cried out once more, at the top of his voice, heedless of the ridiculous spectacle he made.

'The key!'

He waved the bag. He wanted to be sure that she saw it, that she understood. As conspicuously as possible, he laid it on the snow in full view, repeating:

'The key . . . I'm leaving it here . . .'

For her sake, it was better for him to go. She would be suspicious and full of mistrust so long as he was prowling about in the neighbourhood.

He floundered off, feeling quite sick. He literally dragged himself away from the waste ground, forcing himself to go back to the tramlines, to the black path between the banks of snow which was the pavement of his own street.

Timo's was only a couple of steps away, but he didn't go there. He passed the dark mouth of the little alley by the tannery without even noticing it. When he got in, the janitor observed him from behind his curtain, and no doubt he already had the news. By that evening, next morning at the latest, the whole block would know.

He climbed the stairs. There was no light in Herr Wimmer's flat. Evidently he was not back yet.

All these events began to merge in a grey chaos, disconnected and featureless. Hours followed hours. They were certainly the longest he had ever lived through. Sometimes he wanted to cry out when he looked at the alarm clock and found that the hands had not moved.

Yet from all those long hours nothing was to remain in his memory but a few fragments, odd scraps standing out like a heap of ashes in the hearth.

His mother coming home, her perfume at once pervading the room. She looked at him for just one second, then turned immediately to Minna. It was Minna that she beckoned to come with her into the big bedroom. Did they suppose he couldn't hear them whispering together? Let Minna tell the whole story! She certainly would not wait for his permission. She would feel herself bound to tell, for his good as well as her own. From now on, the two women would try to protect him!

'I wish you'd have something to eat, Frank – just a little something.'

Lotte was expecting him to say no. Yet he did eat. He couldn't remember what, but he did eat. His mother went to re-make the bed in the back room. Minna did not go back to bed. She put on an innocent air. She sat down in one of the armchairs in the salon, and she watched.

Was it Holst they were afraid of? Or the police? Or old Wimmer?

He smiled contemptuously.

'You can go to bed now, Frank. Your room is ready. Unless you'd rather have the big room, just for tonight?'

He did not go to bed. He couldn't have said what he did,

what he thought of. At certain moments – and this was all he remembered of it afterwards – things came to life under his eyes, just as they had done when he was tiny. The reflection on a copper ashtray, for instance, which turned into a face looking at him – or a tapestry-covered stool in front of the stove, on which his mother was wont to put her feet when sewing.

Those hours seemed as though they could never pass; yet they did pass. The women took off his shoes, and he let them put on his slippers. They talked about Bertha, who was not due back until next morning, and who was to try to bring back with her a piece of pork and some sausages.

Herr Wimmer came in alone about eight. Other tenants on the various floors came home, and the janitor would certainly have given them the news as they came in.

Perhaps Sissy was already dead?

The road-mender had gone on repeating that it would be better to finish the cat off with one good shot from his gun. There were probably people in the block who were thinking the same thing about Sissy. Others, if they had dared, would have been only too glad to have put a bullet in Frank.

That didn't worry him.

'Why don't you go to bed?'

Then, since both knew what he was waiting for, Lotte added: 'We'll listen. I promise to wake you if anything happens.'

Had he burst out laughing? Anyway, he had wanted to.

This thing must end one way or another; with the cat it had lasted two days at least. Had the black and white beast really gone off into the blue, with one eye hanging out of its head?

It was more likely that the road-mender had got out his gun in the end, while Frank was at school, and that they had preferred to tell him a lie.

How long the minutes were before midnight! Even longer than those which preceded five o'clock, and which were now so far away that they belonged to another world.

The two women were the first to start when steps sounded on the stairs, but they made a show of going on with what they were doing, the one with her sewing, the other with her Zola novel, though she would no doubt have been hard put to it to say what it was about.

The main door downstairs had banged. It was Holst. It could only be Holst, and someone went to stop him in the passage. The janitor would be on the lookout, waiting to tell him the news. How came it that immediately footsteps could be heard on the stairs? They were still faint. As far as the first floor the noise was scarcely audible. From the second floor on, Frank recognized the muffled tread of the felt boots, keeping step with another pair of feet.

He stopped breathing. Minna nearly got up to open the door and look, but Lotte motioned her to stay where she was. All three sat listening. The other step was a woman's. The tap of high heels could be distinguished. Then they heard the key turn in the lock. And then one word, in Holst's gentle voice:

'Come.'

It was not until much later that Frank was to learn that Sissy had waited for her father at the corner of the entry, at the spot where he himself had one night flattened his back against the wall. Would he also learn that she had been about to let her father pass? That Holst had already been out of sight of the corner where she was crouching, when with her last strength she had cried:

'Father!'

They went in. The door shut again.

'You can go to bed now, Frank. Be sensible.'

He guessed what she had in mind. His mother was afraid that Holst, once he got his daughter to bed, would come and knock on their door. She would sooner face him herself. If she dared – though Frank's impassive look awed her – she would advise him to go and spend a few days in the country, or at some friend's place.

But God knows, things went simply enough. Old Wimmer did not quit his lair. But he must certainly not have gone to bed either. Through his fanlight he could hear everything.

Did Holst get to bed that night? For a long time there were noises in his flat. They must have had a little wood or coal left, for he lit a fire. There was the sound of the poker being used, and water being put on to boil.

The light never went out. Twice Frank opened his door a fraction. The first time was at half past one, the second a little after three o'clock. Each time the pink line still showed under the door opposite.

Frank didn't sleep either. He stayed in the salon, where the two women, despite his opposition, insisted on setting up his camp-bed for him. They tried to get him off with hot drinks, without success. He drank everything they brought him and remained clear-headed. His head had never been so clear in his life. He was almost frightened, as though this phenomenon was somehow supernatural.

The women undressed. Frank's mother gave Minna the attentions she needed. He heard the whole of their highly technical conversation, full of references to feminine interiors and fresh mention of the name of Otto.

They probably thought he was asleep. Lotte was quite surprised, when she came to turn off the light, to hear her son's clear voice say firmly:

'No.'

'Just as you like. All the same, try to get some rest.'

It was about five o'clock when Holst opened his door and went to knock on Herr Wimmer's. He had to knock more than once. They talked in low voices in the corridor, and then Herr Wimmer had probably got dressed. He in his turn went to knock on Holst's door, and Holst let him in at once.

Holst left. Frank had no difficulty in guessing why. He had gone to fetch a doctor. It was still too early to move about the streets without a permit, but Holst wouldn't care. He could have tried to telephone from the janitor's lodge. But he hadn't – and Frank would have done just as he did. Doctors did not readily put themselves out, especially when they were rung up.

He would have to go a long way. There were no doctors left in the district, except a bearded old man who was always drunk and had lost everybody's trust, and whose only patients now were public assistance cases.

Holst would have to cross the bridges. Evidently he found someone in the end, because about six o'clock a car stopped in the street outside. Could it be an ambulance? Suppose they were going to move her elsewhere? Frank ran to the window, trying to see, but could make out nothing but two headlamps.

Only two men mounted the stairs. If they were going to take Sissy away, there would have been orderlies with a stretcher.

He put out the light, to prevent Holst knowing that he was awake, and perhaps from a sort of shame, because keeping the light on would have looked provocative. Whatever it was, it was not fear. He was not frightened of Holst. On the contrary, he would do nothing to keep out of his way.

The doctor stayed a long time. The stove was refuelled, the fire poked. No doubt more water was put on to heat. Had Sissy gone to pick up her bag where he had put it down? Had she understood his manoeuvre? If not her father would have endless trouble to go through to get new ration books.

The doctor was there a full half-hour. It would have been better if Herr Wimmer had cleared off. He stayed and stayed. It was not until ten to seven that he went back to his own flat.

So much for those interminable hours. After that, Frank went to sleep. He slept so deeply that he did not notice when they moved his bed into the kitchen, and set it up against the stove, with a hot water bottle at his feet.

The kitchen did not give directly on to the street. The only daylight came through the fanlight. Nevertheless, as soon as he opened his eyes, he knew something had changed. The stove was purring away, within reach of his hand. He had to raise himself to look at the alarm clock, which said eleven. In the next room he could recognize Bertha's voice and her country accent.

'You'd much better stay in bed, Frank,' said Lotte, hurrying in. 'We didn't want to wake you to put you in a proper bed, but I'm sure you're feverish.'

He was not feverish: that he knew. It would be too easy to go sick. They could stick as many thermometers as they liked in his mouth, or the other end for that matter.

Snow was falling, thick and silent, so thick that the windows of the building opposite were scarcely visible, and even in the kitchen the quality of the air had changed.

'Why will you never let anyone take care of you?'

He did not even answer.

'Come with me, Frank.'

Since he was up and had his dressing-gown on, she led him into the salon. The carpet was rolled back – they were in the middle of doing the housework. She shut all the doors.

'I don't want to blame you. You know I've never done that. I simply ask you to listen to me. Believe me, Frank, you'd better not show yourself outside today, nor for several days to come perhaps. I sent Bertha out to do the shopping. They almost refused to serve her.'

He wasn't listening and she understood the glance he shot in the direction of the Holsts' flat. By way of reassurance, she added hurriedly:

'I'm sure it won't be anything serious.'

Did she think he was in love, or suffering from remorse?

'The doctor called this morning. He ordered oxygen cylinders. She's caught a chill. Her father . . .'

Well! Why did she pause? Why didn't she go on?

'Her father . . . ?'

'He never leaves her. The tenants have clubbed together to take them a bit of coal.'

They had two tons in the cellar, but nobody would touch that coal.

'People won't think about it any more when she's better. Even if it turns out to be pneumonia, as they're saying, even that never lasts more than three weeks. Listen, Frank. Listen seriously for once. I *am* your mother.'

'My God!'

'This evening, better still tonight, since you've got a piece of paper you've chosen not to tell me about, but everyone else has seen . . .'

The green card! So she too was impressed. She was ready to procure young girls who were scarcely of age for the pleasure of the occupying officers, yet she was shocked that her son was in possession of this famous green card. However, seeing he'd got it, he might as well make the most of it.

'You'd better go away for a few days and not show yourself round here. It's happened before. You've got friends. You've got money. If you are short, I can give you some.'

Now why did she say that when Minna must have told her about the thick wad of notes in his pocket? No doubt his mother had also had a look at it while he was asleep. That too would frighten her. There was too much of it. You couldn't suddenly get yourself all that money without risks.

'I'll find you a quiet room, if you'd rather. The friend I went out with yesterday will let me have one any time I like to ask her. She wants nothing better than to put you up. I'll come and see you, look after you. You need rest.'

'No!'

He was not going to leave the block. He knew perfectly well what his mother was thinking. This time he had gone too far. She was panicky, that was the truth. So long as she kept quietly to her petty traffic in girls, even if officers were among her clients, people would despise her, but would not dare say anything. They were content to ostracize her, to avert faces when she climbed the stairs, to leave her more than her share of space if by any chance she happened to go queueing.

Now things had become more serious. The affair contained a touch of sentiment which had worked on the tenants' feelings. A young girl was ill, perhaps was going to die, and she was poor into the bargain.

Lotte was frightened, and that was that.

And Lotte, who could behave so amicably towards an Otto, towards officers who had had dozens of people shot or tortured, was angry with him, with *him*, because he had got hold of a green card she would never have dared dream of for herself.

If only he hadn't shown it to anyone!

The whole block was against them. Their victim was at their door, right at their door. Feelings had already been stirred the day before when the violinist's flat was searched. Now the story was going round that his poor old mother had been struck several times with a stick to make her keep quiet.

Even if people did not associate them directly with that incident, their minds were over-excited. It would be a long time before anyone in the block forgot that, while mothers of families were prevented from passing, while their children waited for them without a fire, Frank alone, a mere whippersnapper, had coolly got past the police barrier merely by showing his green card.

Lotte was also frightened of Holst.

'I implore you to listen to me, Frank.'

'No.'

It didn't matter about her and the girls. He would stay. He would not run away at nightfall, as they were pressing him to do. He would not seek asylum with Kromer or any of his mother's friends.

'You always get your own way.'

'I do.'

Yes, now more than ever. Henceforward he would have everything his own way without caring about anybody. Lotte had better realize that, and the others too.

'All the same, go and get dressed. Someone might come.'

It was not a customer who rang the bell a little later, just before midday. It was Chief Inspector Kurt Hamling, frigidly polite as ever, with his customary air of paying a neighbourly call. Frank was under the shower when he came, but all the doors were open – as usual in the morning – and he could hear every word that was said.

His mother's traditional:

'Won't you take of your galoshes?'

Today this was not just concern for the inspector's comfort. It was snowing in real earnest, and soon there would be a pool of mud on the carpet in front of the chair where the inspector was sitting.

'No, thank you. I just dropped in.'

'A drink?'

He never said yes, but he accepted tacitly. He observed:

'The weather has turned milder. We shall have a clear sky in a day or two.'

It was impossible to be sure which weather, or which sky, he was speaking of, but Frank, who was not afraid of him, pulled on his bath robe, and deliberately joined them in the salon.

'Well! I didn't expect to find your Frank here.'

'Why?' asked Frank aggressively.

'I heard you were in the country.'

'Me?'

'People talk a lot, you know. And we have to listen. It's our job. Fortunately, we only listen with one ear, else we should finish up by arresting everybody.'

'A pity.'

'What is?'

'Your listening with only one ear.'

'Why?'

'Because I should love to be arrested. Especially by you.'

Lotte protested:

'Frank, you know you can't be arrested.'

She must have been really frightened, for she added, with a defiant look at the chief inspector:

'Not with the papers you've got.'

'But I mean just that,' he insisted.

'What do you mean?'

'Just exactly what I said.'

He poured himself a drink, and clinked glasses with Kurt Hamling. Both of them, it seemed, were thinking of the door opposite.

'Your health, Herr Inspektor.'

'And yours, young man.'

Why did he hark back to his idea?

'I really thought you were in the country.'

'I never had any intention of going there.'

'A pity. Your mother's a good woman at heart.'

'You think so?'

'I know what I'm saying. Your mother's a fine woman, and you'd be wrong to doubt it.'

Frank sneered:

'I doubt so many things, you see.'

Poor Lotte, signalling to him in vain to be quiet! She was out of her depth. The plane on which they seemed to be doing battle was far above her head, but, even if she could not always follow, she had intuition enough to realize that it looked like a declaration of war.

'How old are you, my boy?'

'Apart from the fact that I am not your boy, my answer is that I am eighteen and shall soon be nineteen. Now it's my turn to ask a question. Unless I'm mistaken, you're a chief inspector?'

'That's my official title.'

'How long have you been that?'

'I was promoted six years ago.'

'How many years have you been in the police?'

'Twenty-eight next June.'

'Yes, I could be your son, you see. I ought to respect you. Twenty-eight years doing the same job – it's a long time, Herr Hamling.'

Lotte was about to open her mouth to order her son to be quiet. Really, this was going too far and was bound to end up in trouble. However, Frank refilled the glasses quietly, and handed one to the inspector.

'Your health!'

'And yours!'

'To your twenty-eight years of faithful service!'

They had gone terribly far. It would be difficult to keep up that tone much longer, and yet it would be even more difficult to withdraw.

'*Prosit!*'

'*Prosit!*'

It was Kurt Hamling who retired.

'My dear Lotte,' he said, 'I must go. There must be dozens of people waiting for me at the office. Take good care of the boy.'

He went off, broad of back and square of shoulders, his big galoshes stamping wet prints on each step of the stairs.

He did not realize that he had just done Frank the biggest service imaginable — for several minutes, Frank had stopped thinking about the cat!

3

The scene with Bertha took place on the Thursday. It was nearly midday, and Frank was still asleep, for he had not come in till nearly four in the morning. That was the third time since Sunday. And the fact that he was still in bed so late, that it interfered with the housework, although not the cause of the upset, may have had a great deal to do with it. Afterwards, he didn't think to inquire about it.

He had had a lot to drink. He had taken it into his head to pilot round the nightclubs two couples he did not know, paying for their drinks, each time fetching his thick wad of notes out of his pocket. When the patrol had pulled them in for singing in the street, he had shown his green card and they had let him alone.

There was a new girl at the flat. He had not had to look for her: she had just arrived on her own, with calm assurance. Her first name was Anny.

'Have you worked at this business before?' asked Lotte, looking her over from head to foot.

'Do you mean, have I been to bed? You needn't worry about that. I've had more than my share.'

And, when Lotte had questioned her about her family, she had replied:

'Which would you rather I told you? That I'm a general's daughter or a high-ranking official's? Anyway, even if I have got a family somewhere, they won't come and worry you. I can promise you that.'

Compared with the others, with all the girls they had ever had, she had an air of breeding. She was quite small, slender and rounded at once, with brown hair and a golden skin without the slightest blemish. She reminded you of a piece of goldsmith's work. She was not yet eighteen, and she was already something of a shrew.

When she saw the others doing the washing-up, for example, she went and sat down in the salon and started reading one of the heap of magazines she had brought with her. She carried on in the same way again in the evening, and next morning she said to Lotte:

'I suppose you're not expecting me to act as a skivvy into the bargain?'

Minna began work again, although it still hurt her. But it was nearly always the new girl that the customers chose. Which was odd, too. Full of curiosity, Frank had climbed on to the table. She preserved a surprising dignity. It was the men who seemed to feel degraded, to see themselves in a hateful or a ridiculous light. Frank could guess at what she was saying, without a smile, and without any bitterness either, with the indifference of a great lady.

'Would you like me to turn on the other side? Higher? Lower? There! And now?'

While they were engaged with her, she would look at the ceiling with the lovely eyes of a wild creature. That was how she caught Frank's eye; she must have seen him dimly through the glass. For a long time he wondered if she really had seen him, for she had not flickered an eyelid or shown the least surprise. With her thoughts far away, she just went on waiting until the man was relieved.

A little later she asked:

'Is it madam who sets you to watch?'

'No.'

'Are you a peeper?'

'No.'

She shrugged her shoulders. Because of her, Minna and Bertha had to share a bed, and Frank was again using his camp-bed in the kitchen. On the Tuesday evening he went to Anny's bed, and she said firmly:

'If you've just come for your own amusement, get on with it. I suppose I have to do this with the son of the house. But don't imagine you're going to spend the night in my bed. I loathe sleeping with anybody.'

Minna tried to strike up a friendship with her, but she spent her whole time reading. As for Bertha, she was reduced more and more to the status of a servant and avoided speaking to the newcomer, waiting on her with a bad grace – for Anny insisted on being waited on as though it were a matter of course. She even had to be helped to wash and dry her hair.

Frank was asleep when the quarrel began. As usual each morning, they had pushed his bed – with him in it – into the back room. Much later he heard voices raised, and recognized Bertha's accent – Bertha, whom he had never before known angry. The words she was uttering formed no part of her usual vocabulary, which was restrained, almost refined.

'I've had enough of this joint, and I won't stop here a day longer. Besides, with all the filthy business that's going on, it can't last much longer, and I want to be well out of it when trouble comes.'

'Bertha!' commanded Lotte in a sharp voice. 'I beg you to be quiet, d'you hear?'

'You can shout louder than that, while you're at it, but I won't advise you to try. There's plenty of people in the block watching out for you and ready to do you in if only they dared.'

'Bertha, I order you . . .'

'Order away! Why only yesterday, at the market, a kid no bigger than that spat in my face – and it wasn't for me, it was for you. I can't think why I don't pass it on to the right address.'

Would she have done that? Probably not. It was her way to store up grudges over a long time, and, now that the sluices were down, the whole lot was pouring out in a thick flood. She had not seen Frank come into the kitchen behind her, barefooted and in his pyjamas. So she was dazed with surprise, while she was talking about the spitting incident and looking at Lotte, to receive a sudden slap, a slap from a quarter where she thought nobody was.

When she saw Frank, she clenched her teeth.

'It's you, is it, you young pup? Just try that again . . .'

Lotte did not have time to get between them, before two more slaps cracked out as sharp as a ringmaster's whip. In a second, Bertha, crimson in the face, hurled herself at him, clutching at him as best she could, while he did his utmost to fend her off.

'Bertha! . . . Frank! . . .'

Minna had taken refuge in the salon, while Anny, who was smoking a cigarette in a long ivory holder, was leaning against the doorpost, an interested spectator of the set-to.

'A little puppy, yes, that's what you are . . . A dirty little beast who thinks anything goes because his mother keeps a brothel . . . indulging in filthy tricks that would make the cheapest of girls blush . . . Let me go, you! Let me go, or I'll scream at the top of my voice, and rouse all the neighbours. You'll need more than your revolver and your blasted bits of paper to throw them of once they're after you . . .'

'Frank! . . .'

He let go. His scratched cheek was bleeding a little.

'Just wait till they've got you cornered. You won't have to wait long. There won't always be foreign soldiers in the country to protect you, you and your sort . . .'

'Come and settle up, Bertha.'

'I'll come when I please, madam. You'll be in a proper fix tomorrow, all of you, when there's no one to make your coffee or empty your chamberpots! When I think I even had to bring you pork from home!'

'Come, Bertha.'

Bertha turned one last time to Frank, her eyes blazing, and by way of farewell spat in his face:

'Coward! . . . Dirty little coward! . . .'

And yet, when he had gone to bed with her, she had always been the most tender, with a tenderness that was almost maternal.

*

It was not likely that Bertha would say anything. Lotte was worried. She should have remembered that this was not the first such incident. A score of times similar scenes had flared up without anything happening afterwards. She had tried to listen when Bertha went downstairs with her bundle, to find out if she stopped to gossip with any of the tenants or the janitor. It wasn't likely, because Bertha was in as bad odour as they were themselves. After all, it was *her* the urchin had spat at. Besides, she was the one people could most easily get at.

They saw her waiting for the tram at the street corner, perhaps already regretting what she had done.

Lotte regretted it even worse. Bertha might not excite the men much, but all the same she gave them their satisfaction in the end, and the advantage of having her was that she did practically all the housework.

Minna would try her hand at it, but she was not strong, and she had not yet recovered from her injury. As for Anny, the utmost to be expected from her was that she would make her own bed in the morning.

And then there were all the errands, the queues which inevitably meant contact with the people of the neighbourhood, sometimes with tenants from the block.

'You ought not to have slapped her. However – what's done can't be undone . . .'

She noted her son's pale colour, the rings under his eyes. Frank had never drunk so much. He had never gone out so much, without saying where, his face hard, and the loaded revolver always in his pocket.

'Do you think it's wise to go about like that?'

He did not bother to shrug his shoulders, let alone answer. He had formed a new habit which was rapidly becoming a mannerism – when people spoke to him, he would look through them as though he couldn't see them, and would go on doing whatever he was engaged in as though he hadn't heard a word.

Not once had he the luck to meet Holst on the stairs, although he was up and down them five or six times a day – far more frequently than when things were normal. Probably Holst had asked the tramway company for leave so that he could look after his daughter. Frank thought that he would be obliged to go out, if only to buy medicines and food. But they had managed otherwise. First thing in the morning old Wimmer knocked on his neighbours' door, and it was he who undertook their errands. Once, when the door had been left ajar, Frank had seen him, wearing an apron and doing the housework.

The doctor came once a day, round about two o'clock. Frank managed to be about when he left. He was quite young, looking more like an athlete than a doctor. He did not appear worried. True, the patient was neither his daughter nor his wife. Would Holst fall sick too? That had occurred to Frank. Then, on Wednesday, just as he was catching the tram, he had turned automatically to look up at the window and had caught sight of Holst's face between the curtains. Nothing could happen, of course, and yet Frank had been quite shaken by this renewal of contact. They had remained calm and grave, the two of them, without hatred, and there was nothing between them but a great void.

His mother would have been even more worried if she had come to know that he had deliberately taken to paying daily – sometimes twice daily – visits to the little café by the tram stop, the one where you went down the steps on entering. That was bordering on provocation, for he had nothing to take him there. As soon as he came in, the regulars shut up and began ostentatiously gazing elsewhere. The proprietor, Herr Kamp, who was nearly always sitting at their table – they were great card players – got up reluctantly to serve him.

On Monday Frank paid for what he had had with a high denomination note which he peeled off his wad.

'I'm sorry,' said Herr Kamp, pushing it back. 'I haven't got enough change.'

Frank left the note on the bar, and contented himself with throwing over his shoulder as he left:

'Keep the change.'

He could have sworn, on the Tuesday, that the regulars were waiting for him, and that caused him a little shiver. That happened to him quite often now. One day something was bound to happen, though he couldn't foresee just when or what. It might well take place in this quiet, old-fashioned little café! Why had the patrons looked at Herr Kamp so knowingly, with smiles they scarcely troubled to hide?

The proprietor had brought his order without a word, and then, just as Frank was going to pay, he had picked up an envelope placed conspicuously between two bottles on the shelves behind the bar, and handed it to him.

As soon as he touched it, Frank realized that it contained banknotes and coin. It was the change from the large note he had left the previous day.

He said thank you, and left. But that would not stop him from coming again. Then he almost fell out with Timo. It was two o'clock in the morning. He had had a lot to drink. He saw a man in a corner with a woman. He didn't like the man's face. Frank, who was at the bar, showed his revolver to Timo, and said:

'When that chap leaves, I shall shoot him.'

Timo looked at him stonily, all trace of friendship gone.

'Are you mad?'

'No, I'm not mad. He's got an ugly mug, and I'm going to shoot him.'

'You be careful I don't shoot my fist into *your* face.'

'What d'you say?'

'I say I don't like the way you're behaving lately. Go and play that sort of game somewhere else if it amuses you, but not at my place. I warn you, if you touch that chap, I'll have you pinched at once. Point number one! Next, from now on, you will kindly leave that toy of yours elsewhere, otherwise you don't come in here. Point number two! Now, I've got a bit of advice for you – don't drink quite so much. It makes you get above yourself, and you're too young for that.'

To tell the truth, Timo came to apologize a little later. This time, he appealed to Frank's sense of reason.

'Perhaps I spoke a bit strongly just now, but it was for your own good. Even your friend Kromer thinks you're getting dangerous. I don't want to know anything about your affairs. All I know is that for some time past you seem to have imagined you're a big man. Do you really think it's clever to show off your wad of notes to anyone and everyone? Do you suppose people don't know how that sort of stuff is got hold of?'

Frank showed him his green card. Timo did not appear impressed. Embarrassed rather. He made him put it back in his pocket.

'That's another thing you'd better not flash too much.'

He returned to the charge for a third time. All conversations with Timo took place in snatches, because his patrons were continually calling him from every corner.

'Listen, son. I know you'll say it's only jealousy on my part, but I shall have done my duty. I don't pretend those papers of yours are worthless. Only, there are ways and ways of using them. Besides, there are things that are more complicated . . .'

He did not care to explain.

'What, for instance?'

'Oh, what's the use of talking about it? One always says too much. Now, look. I'm on good terms with *them*. Some of them bring me things for sale, and they deal straight with me. They let me alone. I see a great many of them, of every sort and kind. Perhaps that's why I can guess one or two things.'

'Such as?'

'I'll give you an example. About a month ago, there was a high-ranking officer at the third table over there, a colonel, good-looking, still young, fresh coloured, his chest covered with decorations. There were two women with him, and I don't know what he was telling them – I was busy elsewhere. Anyway, they were all laughing very loud. At one point he took his wallet out of his pocket, probably intending to pay. The women seized hold of it and started to play with it. They were tight, all three of them. They passed papers and photographs across the table. I was at the bar. It was then I saw a fellow get up, a chap I'd taken no notice of, an ordinary sort of chap, a civilian, the sort you're constantly meeting in the street. He wasn't even well dressed. He went over to the table and the colonel looked at him in an embarrassed sort of way, still trying to smile. This chap said just one word to him, and our high-ranking officer got straight up and sprang to attention. He took his wallet back from the woman. He paid his bill. I could have sworn I'd just seen him go down like a pricked balloon. He left his girl friends flat, without a word of explanation, and he went out with the civilian.'

'What's that got to do with me?' growled Frank.

'Well, it seems that next day he was seen at the station, leaving for an unknown destination. Don't you see? Some of them seem to be powerful, maybe are powerful just now. But never – get hold of this – never as powerful as they'd like you to believe. However powerful they may be, there are others more powerful still. But those others are usually quite unknown.

'You work with an office where everyone shakes hand with you, and you think you're safely provided for. Only, at the same time, in another office – no connexion with the first – somebody is starting a card index under your name.

'If you want to know what I really think, they've got several sectors. And just because you're well in with one sector, you can't go running risks in another.'

Frank remembered all this the next morning, and it bothered him all the more because he had a hangover. Every morning he promised himself to be more careful, but he started off again at once, just because he had to have a drink to steady his nerves.

What struck him most was a connexion between Timo's lecture and a phrase Lotte had used, to which he had paid no attention at the time.

'You can tell Christmas is coming,' she had said. '*The faces are beginning to change.*'

By which she meant that her clientele was changing, at least that part of it which consisted of occupiers. Every time this happened, she passed an unpleasant week or two, having to live in a state of constant suspense. Every three months, or six – it usually coincided with the big festivals of the year, though that was probably only by chance – there were changes among the staff, civil as well as military. Some went home to their own country, and others came from there, new men with different manners and unknown characters. She had to start all over again. Every time a new one rang the bell, Lotte felt she had to go through her little act of running a manicure salon, and she did not feel reassured until the customer mentioned the first name of the colleague who had sent him along.

Without knowing just why, Frank wouldn't have liked his general to leave. He called him 'his' general though he did not know him, had never seen him. It was Kromer who knew him. There was something childlike and reassuring about the general's passion for watches. Frank was like his mother. He felt happier with people who had a passion. For instance, when you knew the practices Otto was addicted to, you couldn't be frightened of him any more. In fact, Otto was one of those whom Frank could one day make use of. He would be sure to pay heavily rather than have certain of his actions made public.

The sun could be seen once more, and it was thawing nicely. The latest snowfall had not yet had time to get dirty, and in some districts the unemployed taken on by the city council were still busy heaping up the shining stuff along the pavements.

Frank felt that Kromer was avoiding him. It was true that Frank in his turn was avoiding Kromer. So what was he worrying about? And why say that he was worrying when he was perfectly calm, when it was he himself, of his own free will and fully aware of what he was doing, who was doing his utmost to draw down misfortune on his head?

Going to Kamp's, for instance. There must certainly be members of the underground, and of the resistance leagues, among those who frequented the little café. They were in the queues which he passed well knowing that his good clothes and shoes alone constituted a provocation.

He had twice met Karl Adler, who had driven the truck to the village that night when he had called on Fräulein Vilmos. It was really rather odd – twice in four days, quite by chance, and both times in unexpected places. The first was on the pavement opposite the Lido, the second in a tobacconist's up in town.

Whereas formerly he had never met him. Or rather, since he did not know him, they could have rubbed shoulders a hundred times without Frank's noticing.

This was how you began to imagine things!

Was it deliberately, out of caution, or from a sort of integrity, that Adler pretended not to recognize him?

None of this mattered, anyway. And if it did, if it meant that there was a deep-laid plot, Frank would still be delighted. Nevertheless, there was a little thing that bothered him. Opposite the cinema Adler was not alone. He had a man with him who lived right in their own block.

This was someone Frank had caught odd glimpses of on the stairs. Frank knew he lived on the second floor, towards the left, and that he had a wife and little daughter. He would be twenty-eight or thirty. He was a thin fellow, in poor health, who wore a straggly beard the hairs of which were too fair and too long. He wasn't a workman. Had he an office job? Perhaps. On second thoughts that couldn't be it, because Frank noticed that they did not meet at regular times, and he didn't look or move like a commercial traveller.

Probably he was a technician, like Adler. If so, it would be natural for the two to be acquainted.

You never knew who belonged to a network, or a league. Often it was the people who appeared the most inoffensive, and the fair-haired man from the second floor, with his wife and little girl, was the very type of tenant to pass unnoticed.

But why should those people want to execute him? He'd done them no harm. In reality, the ones they most often shot were their own members who had turned traitor, and Frank couldn't betray people he didn't know. They despised him all right, that was certain. But, like his mother, he had much more to fear from the wrath of the neighbours, a wrath founded on envy, and concerned simply with coal, warm clothing and enough to eat.

And Lotte was frightened only of the people in the neighbourhood. Frank having been let alone till now, she realized that she need not worry any more because of Fräulein Vilmos. Even Kurt Hamling's attitude, the odd little phrases he had let drop, suggested only a purely local danger. Otherwise, there would have been no point in his advising Frank to go and spend a few days in the country or with friends.

Frank had not succeeded in meeting Holst, as he would have wished, but they had seen each other from a distance. Holst, who must know Frank's steps as well as Frank knew his, had heard him come in and out ten times a day, and could easily have attacked him on the landing.

Frank was not frightened. There was no question of being frightened. The thing was infinitely more subtle. It was a game he had made up, just as, when a child, he used to make up games which he alone could understand. This used to happen most often in the morning, in bed, while Frau Porse was getting his breakfast, and best of all when the sun was shining. For example, he would shut his eyes and think:

'Fly!'

Then he would peep between half-open lids at a single spot on the hangings which he had selected beforehand. If there was a fly on that spot, he had won.

Now, he might have said:

'Fate!'

For he wanted fate to take notice of him. He had done everything possible to force it to do so, and he continued to challenge it from morning to night. The day before he had said to Kromer with studied negligence:

'Ask your general, will you, what he'd like, apart from watches.'

He was in no need of money. Even at the pace he was going, what he had would last for months. There was nothing he needed. He had bought himself an overcoat even more conspicuous than the one he had had before, a light beige one in genuine camel hair. There were not five others like it in the city. It was not really quite heavy enough for the time of year, but he wore it out of bravado. For the same reason he had the revolver constantly in his pocket although its weight made it a nuisance, and although it might one day stand him in bad stead, despite his green card.

It was not that he wanted to become a martyr, nor merely a victim. But as he passed through his own neighbourhood, especially at night, he enjoyed the thought that at any moment a bullet might fly from some shadowy corner.

Nobody was interested in him. Not even Holst seemed to be, and yet Frank had done enough to attract his attention.

Sissy must loathe him. Anyone else in Frank's shoes would have left the block after what had happened.

Fate was lying in wait for him somewhere. But where? Instead of waiting for fate to reveal itself at its appointed time, Frank ran after it, casting about everywhere in his search. He was crying out in fact, just as when he stood on the waste ground, holding at arm's length the bag with the key in it:

'Here I am. What are you waiting for?'

As if he had not enemies enough, he went out of his way to create new ones. Wasn't that his reason for slapping Bertha? And now, when Minna ventured to show a little tenderness, or even ordinary consideration, he would do his best to hurt her feelings by answering:

'I loathe people with sick stomachs.'

He would bring chocolates for Anny, who thought neither of offering them to the others nor even of saying thank you. He loved looking at her. He could have gazed at her body for hours, but he got no satisfaction out of making love to her. The second time he had gone to her bed, she had sighed peevishly:

'What, again?'

Her body was a work of art, but her body was all she had. Moreover, it seemed lifeless, devoid of magnetism. She would dispose it where and as required, with the air of saying:

'There it is. Look at it, pet it, do what you have to do, but be quick about it!'

It was on Thursday that Bertha left. On Friday, about half past three, Frank was in the street when he noticed the second-floor tenant standing in front of a shop window. It was only later that Frank realized that this contained a display of corsetry. An hour at least had passed by then. He had gone with a lad he vaguely knew called Kropetzki, to eat cakes at Taste's. Ressl, the editor, was there too. Here Ressl was really at home. This was the refined setting which suited him, and Frank had seldom seen a woman better dressed or more thoroughbred looking than the one who was with him.

Ressl honoured Frank with a little wave of greeting. Frank and his friend listened to the music, for Taste's was the one place where chamber music was still played at five o'clock in the afternoon. This led him to think of the violinist, for here in the orchestra a long, thin man was playing the violin.

Had the violinist been shot? People were always panicking, but more often than not those who had been rumoured dead walked in at their own front door again one fine day. Some people also spoke of torture, but torture was not common. Unless, of course, the others, the ones who said nothing, were keeping quiet from caution?

The thought of torture chilled the blood in his veins, and yet, if it came to the point, he would not be frightened by torture. Could he hold out against it? He was convinced he could. It was an idea that had occurred to him so often that it was quite familiar. Even before it had become customary, for, when he was tiny, one of his amusements had been to stand in front of the mirror and cause himself pain, burying a pin, for instance, in his flesh and watching his face for flinching and tremors.

They wouldn't torture him. They wouldn't dare. The other side used torture too, at least so people swore.

Why should they torture him when he had nothing to tell them?

In a few days it would be Christmas. A hollow Christmas once again. Except when he was quite small, he would never have known a Christmas that was not hollow. At seven or eight years old he had gone into town at that season of the year, and the streets were more brightly lit up than a ballroom, men in lined overcoats, women in furs, were hurrying along the pavements, and the window displays seemed about to topple over into the street, so crammed were they with things to buy.

There would be a little tree in the salon at Lotte's, as in other years. It was put there mainly for the customers. Who would be left in the flat? Minna no doubt had some family. Even if the girls didn't bother about their relatives for the rest of the year, they did remember them when the big festivals came round. As for Anny, no one knew where she came from. Perhaps she would stay? Most likely, she would ask nothing more than the chance to stuff herself and then bury herself in her magazines.

Even Kromer went home for Christmas, a journey of twenty odd miles!

Sissy would still be in bed. Holst would spend his last farthing, if he had one, or would sell off some old books, to decorate a tree for her. They would ask old Wimmer to stop; he had now found his vocation, and was acting as their maid of all work.

'What are you thinking of?' asked his friend.

Frank jumped.

'Who? Me?'

'Who else?'

'Nothing. I'm sorry.'

'You looked as if you wanted to strangle the orchestra.'

What? He wasn't even looking at them. He'd forgotten them.

'I say, I want to ask a favour, but I daren't.'

'How much?'

'Oh, it's not what you think. It's not for me. It's for my sister. You're said to be lousy with money.'

'What's the matter with your sister?'

And Frank reflected ironically that, whatever was up with her, she hadn't passed through Lotte's school.

'It's her eyes. If she doesn't have an operation, she'll go blind.'

He was a lad of Frank's own age, but a soft timid creature, born only to be crushed. The snivelling type.

'How much will it cost?'

'I don't know exactly, but I think if you could lend me . . .'

Frank flicked over his wad of notes like a conjuror. It had grown into a game.

'If you say thank you, you're an even bigger ass than I thought.'

'Frank – I – '

'You heard me. Let's scram.'

Was it sheer chance that the fellow from the second floor was just a little way up the street, still stuck in front of a shop window, but this time one displaying dolls? He had a little girl. Christmas was coming. Quite natural, his answer would be, for him to be window shopping.

Suppose Frank were to march up to him and demand squarely what he was after, were to show him, if need be, his green card, or shove the revolver under his nose?

As a matter of fact, Timo's lecture had had its effect. Frank went on his way, then turned round. The fellow was not following. Only Kropetzki was clinging to him, and it was the hardest thing in the world to shake him off. If fate was watching for him, it was not for that night. He was able to dine in town, meet Kromer – he was preoccupied, almost aloof – go drinking in three different night spots and get into a long argument with a man he didn't know – all without any results.

Nor did anything happen between Timo's and home, even while he was passing the mouth of the alley by the tannery. It would be funny if fate chose just that corner to lie in wait! It was the sort of idea that came to you at three in the morning, when you had drunk a lot.

There was light showing at the Holsts'. Perhaps it was time for compresses, or drops, or God knows what attentions. He listened at the door. His footsteps had certainly been heard. Holst knew he was on the landing, and Frank deliberately made quite a long pause, pressing his ear against the panel of the door.

Holst did not open it, did not stir.

Old goat!

There was nothing left except to go to bed, and, if he had not been so tired, he would have made love to Anny, simply to infuriate her. As for Minna, she made him feel sick. She was so stupidly in love. She almost certainly cried when she thought of him. Perhaps she prayed. And she was ashamed of her injury!

He went to bed alone. There was a little fire left in the stove and for quite a long time he stared at the little pink disc of the poker-hole.

Old goat!

And it was in the morning, when he had yet another hangover, that it happened. He had searched for fate in every corner, and fate was in none of the places where he had hunted.

Yet another trick of chance: there wasn't a drink in the house, the two decanters were empty. Lotte had forgotten for several days to warn him that their stock had run out.

He would have to go to Timo's. On that sort of business it was better to see Timo in the morning. Timo didn't like selling his liquor, even at a stiff price. He argued that he always lost on the deal, that good bottles were worth more than bad money.

Frank wanted a drink. Lotte's hair was done up in curlers. She had put on a loose smock to do the housework with Minna, while Anny did not budge even when they swept under her legs. There she was, impassive as a goddess, plunged deep, not in a dream or in contemplation, but in her magazine, and she was letting the ash of her cigarette fall on the floor.

'Don't buy too much at once, Frank.'

It was odd. He had been on the point of leaving his revolver in the flat, not because of what Timo had said to him, but simply because it weighed heavy in his pocket. If he did not do so, it was because that would have appeared to him like cheating.

He didn't want to cheat.

He met Herr Wimmer coming upstairs with some provisions, a string bag containing a cabbage and some swedes – and Herr Wimmer made no sign, passing close to him without a word.

Old goat!

He remembered afterwards that he had stopped on the second-floor landing to light his first cigarette – and very nasty it tasted, as it always did when he had drunk too much the night before – and that he had looked mechanically along the corridor to his left. He had seen nothing. The corridor was empty, except for a pram at the end. He heard a baby wailing.

He reached the ground-floor corridor, and was going to walk past the janitor's lodge. Just at that moment, the lodge door opened.

He had never thought this was the way it would happen. Indeed, he still did not realize that anything was happening.

The janitor had his usual look, his everyday cap. At his side there was a man, ordinary enough and yet with a vaguely foreign look, wearing an overcoat that was a bit too long.

Just as Frank passed, the foreigner touched the brim of his hat, as if to thank the janitor, fell into step with Frank and overtook him before he had got half-way across the pavement.

'You will kindly follow me.'

That was all. He displayed something in the hollow of his hand, a card in a cellophane holder, with a photograph and some seals. What sort of card? Frank had no idea.

He said, very calmly, a little stiffly:

'Very well.'

'Hand it over.'

He had no time to wonder what he was to hand over. The man at once plunged his hand into the correct pocket, whisked away the revolver and slipped it under his overcoat.

If anyone had been looking just then – Frank had no idea if anyone was – the little scene must have been quite meaningless.

There was no car at the kerb. They walked side by side in the direction of the tram stop. They waited for the tram like anyone else, without even looking at one another.

4

I t was the eighteenth day. He was holding out. He would go on holding out. He had discovered that it was entirely a question of holding on: provided he did that, he would have them defeated. Was it really a matter of defeating them? That was another problem, which he would solve in his own good time. He had thought much. He had thought too much. Thinking could be dangerous too. He had to force himself to keep to a strict discipline. When he thought that he would defeat them, that meant that he would get out. And the phrase 'get out' did not apply only to the place where he was.

It was astonishing how, *outside*, one used words without caring about their real meaning. He was not over-educated, it was true, but there were so many like him – they were the majority – and he now realized that he had always been content to use words which were only approximations.

This question of the meaning of words had occupied him for two days. Perhaps it would come back to him afresh.

Anyway, this was the eighteenth day, and that constituted an absolute certainty. He took care to ensure that this certainty should be absolute. He had selected an almost blank space on the wall. Each morning he scratched a stroke on it with his thumb-nail. It was harder than you might think. Not the scratching of the stroke, even though his nail was already worn down to the quick. No – the difficulty was to stop at one stroke. To be sure that he had scratched it. It was a plaster wall, which made the task simpler. But it had not been easy to find a clean patch, because of all the others who had been there before him.

At the same time – and this was another of his discoveries – you had to avoid becoming too pernickety: you mustn't start asking yourself questions, because here you tended to doubt, and he had realized that, once you began to doubt, you were lost.

He would get to the bottom of the problem alone, provided he kept to his disciplines, and did not let himself wander off into reverie. You became very strict about some questions. For instance, his last morning outside he did not know the date. Or rather, he knew it without quite knowing it. He wasn't sure. So that, even though he could guarantee the eighteen days he had been here, he would not dare swear, to a day, to the date of his arrival.

That was how you lived.

More than likely, it was the 7th of January. Or could it be the 8th? So far as concerned 'before', he had no incontrovertible point of reference. Here, he could guarantee his scratches on the wall.

If he could stand it, if he didn't let himself go, if he concentrated hard enough – though without concentrating too hard – it would not take him long to understand, and then everything would be over. It reminded him of a dream he had more than once dreamt. There were several of these recurrent dreams, but the clearest was that of flying. In it he raised himself in space. Not out of doors, in a garden or street, but always in a room, in the presence of witnesses who did not know how to fly. He would say to them:

'See how easy it is!'

He would lay his hands flat on empty air, and press. Taking off was slow and difficult. He had to exercise a powerful effort of will. But, once in the air, he had only to make slight movements, now with his hands, now with his feet. His head brushed against the ceiling. He could never understand why the others were so astounded. He would smile down on them, condescendingly.

'You see – it's easy, I tell you. Just a question of will power.'

Well, here the situation was much the same: if he willed with enough concentration, he would understand. The conditions were difficult, of course. He had very soon realized that he must guard against getting out of step.

One little example: his arrival. They were his last hours, his last minutes *outside*. Or *before*. He used either expression without distinction. He ought to preserve an almost mathematically precise recollection of that brief time. He did. He watched over it like something precious. But at the price of constant effort. Every day he was in danger of changing details of the picture. He was tempted to do so, and would constrain himself to rehearse each several occurrence, linking each image with the next.

Thus, it was just not true that Kamp had come out on to his doorstep, or that the regulars in the little café had burst out laughing. He had been on the point of adding this touch. He had very nearly believed in it. But the truth was, he had seen no one, no one at all, before the tram, lurching as usual, had pulled up in front of them. He and his escort had not looked at each other to see whether they should get on in front or at the rear. It was as if the man knew Frank's ways, and wanted to humour him, for they had got on in front.

Frank was still smoking his cigarette, the other had the last quarter of a cigar in his mouth. He might have thrown it away, might have wanted to go and sit inside. But Frank had never sat in the inside of a tram, except when he was tiny and was made to. For no reason at all, sitting inside distressed him.

The man had stayed on the forward platform.

That particular tram, after crossing the bridges, went almost straight across the upper town, its route terminating in a working-class neighbourhood on the edge of open country. They had passed nearby the military offices, and the man had not got off. It was not until three blocks further on that he motioned to Frank and they went to wait for another tram, at a circular yellow stop-sign.

The sky was brilliant. That morning the town seemed to be glittering with all its window panes, with all its snow, with every one of its white roofs. Was it he who was altering the picture?

Yet there was one detail he could be sure of. While they were waiting for their second tram, he had dropped his cigarette-end in the snow. Usually the snow was hard, covered over with a crust. The tobacco ought to have gone on burning for quite a time. But the cigarette had gone out, as though swamped by the moisture of the sun-warmed snow. If he were less strict about exactitude, he would say that it had sunk into the snow with a little sputter.

That was the kind of detail he was paying attention to now, because such things gave him his bearings. Without them he would have let himself wander off into thinking and believing anything.

The second tram they took followed a kind of circular boulevard across districts which were no longer strictly part of the town, but were not yet in the suburbs. More than once women with their shopping bags had boarded the tram for a short ride. Frank gave some of them a hand, and the man did not object.

Just for a moment he went so far as to wonder whether the whole thing wasn't a trick. Was Kromer responsible? Or Timo? Or was it Chief Inspector Kurt Hamling taking a little revenge?

He had been right to keep that thought to himself. He was satisfied, in general, with the way he had borne himself, even now when he had time to examine every last detail under a magnifying glass. Others, no doubt, would have asked questions, or waxed indignant, or again would have indulged in uncouth joking. With simple dignity he had modelled his attitude on that of his escort, who must, however, be a subordinate official, a mere inspector, with no special instructions about Frank.

They had probably given him the order:

'Bring in that young man.'

And then added:

'Careful. He's armed.'

It was habit that had told him at once which pocket Frank kept his revolver in. As for his own attitude, the thing Frank was proudest of was that he had not begun nervously chain-smoking. When he threw away a cigarette, he made the mental resolution:

'Two tram stops before I light another.'

They got off in a very open part, a new district, which the people who lived in town hardly knew. The bricks were still pink, the paintwork was fresh, and just opposite the tram stop, were some spacious buildings with a courtyard in front and a high ironwork gate.

It was a school. More probably a college. At the gate there was a box with a sentry, but there was nothing sinister about the place. Just opposite, Frank had noticed a little café in the same style as Herr Kamp's, only newer.

'We may have to wait a bit. We are early.'

These were the first words the man had uttered since that single sentence when he first accosted Frank. He had spoken them rather anxiously, as though he were afraid of being found at fault. Frank thought how on other days he did not go out so early, and how his sole reason for doing so that morning had been that there was nothing to drink in the flat.

Did Lotte know already? Or Holst? Or Sissy?

He was quite calm. He had been calm throughout. Reflect as he might afterwards on his behaviour, he was still satisfied with himself. There was nothing awe-inspiring about going into the courtyard of a school, even when there was a box with a sentry at the gate.

They went to the right and climbed some steps, the man going in front till they came to a glass-panelled door which he opened so as to let Frank go through first.

It was hard to say what this little building had been before. Perhaps the porter's lodge? There was a bench; and the room was cut in half by a desk which looked like a counter. Woodwork and furniture were painted pale grey. The man went towards an adjoining room, where he said a few words, and then came back to sit down beside Frank.

He looked no more cheerful than Frank did. On the contrary. He was a sad, over-conscientious type. He did his duty joylessly, or even against his convictions. Between his lips he still had his cigar butt. It was wet with saliva and was beginning to smell nasty. He made no protest when Frank crushed out his cigarette on the floor and lit another.

He was what Frank called one of the 'lesser' men, a type like Kropetzki, born to be whipped. There must be more important personages in the next room. Its door was open, but only the upper part was visible because the counter blocked the view. Frank and his escort had arrived at a slack period. He had scarcely lit his cigarette when he heard the dull thud of a fist striking a face. No groans followed. There was just the voice of the striker, or someone else, asking:

'Well?'

Frank was sorry he couldn't see, but didn't dare get up. He had just waited for the blows which followed each other rapidly but brought forth from the man who was struck nothing but, once, a feeble moan.

'Well, swine?'

Frank had sat unmoved. He was sure of that. He had had eighteen days to think about it, and he was only the more honest with himself on that account.

What the incident had aroused in him was curiosity. At first he had asked himself:

'Is it true that they take all their clothes off?'

Quite soon, in all likelihood, it would be his turn. Why did he start thinking of Minna's injury? Because the story was that they struck you in the genitals with blows of knee or foot. That made him go pale. Yet the man in the other room was unflinching. In the intervals of silence, his breath could be heard, wheezing slightly.

'You still say it wasn't you?'

A blow. With a little practice, you should be able to tell by the noise which part of the body had been struck.

A shower of blows this time. Then a faint groan. Then nothing.

Nothing but a few words in a foreign language uttered in a tone of reprimand.

Had all this been organized specially for his benefit? He must find out. It was difficult to believe, certainly. He no longer thought like the people outside. But he did not yet think like his neighbours in the classrooms. He did his best to remain clear-headed, to observe a mean in everything. He was convinced he would succeed. They would not get him down.

Especially because it might be a test. It would not do to talk like that to Lotte, or Kromer, or even Timo. *He* had made progress since he had last seen them. They had not. They went on with their petty lives, went on reasoning in the same old fashion, and so they could not advance.

He felt like smiling when he recalled what Timo had said to him about the green card and the sectors.

Was Frank now in a sector, or not?

Was it an important sector?

If Timo were to pass along the street, and notice the barred gate with its sentry, he would still suspect nothing. Things had to be seen from inside, and he, Frank, was inside. That he *was* inside would have to be admitted.

For his own part he was quite prepared to admit that there had been some truth in Timo's lecture. Timo didn't realize it: he was talking at large, as people did talk outside. The green card existed. If it had been created that was because it had its own importance. If it had its importance, it was no less important that it should not be sullied.

Formerly, to become an ordinary freemason – and that was just what all officials were – you had to undergo tests.

That was what Timo had failed to understand, what neither he, nor the others, nor yet Frank himself had thought of. It was not because of that idea that Frank was calm – otherwise he would have despised himself – but he spent a certain time each day in entertaining it, making cross checks and going more deeply into certain aspects of the question.

Why, he wondered, had the same thing not happened to him, in the office to which he had been brought, as to his predecessor. *He* had been carried out by two men, one taking his head and one his feet, for he was out – perhaps more than out. They must have gone too fast and too hard. The chief was not pleased. The word he had uttered in a flat voice, banging on the table with a paper knife, must mean:

'Next!'

Frank's escort got up and slipped his cigar-end into his waistcoat pocket. Frank got up too, behaving perfectly naturally.

Had he been convinced at that point that a few minutes later he would step out a free man, and would take the tram in the opposite direction?

He was no longer sure. These were questions he had put to himself too often, which grew more and more complex each day. There were some he kept for the morning and others for the afternoon, for sunrise or sunset, for before or after his soup. It was in fact a discipline, which he compelled himself to keep to with great severity.

'Come!'

Had the man said, 'Come'? Probably not. He had said nothing. He had merely motioned to Frank to go round the counter, or had even shown him the way by going first.

And then things had become almost farcical. The chief before whom he appeared did not look at all like a chief, no more like a chief than Herr Wimmer. He was not in uniform. He was dressed in grey. His jacket was too tight, his collar was too high, and his tie was badly knotted. His clothes sat on him like a straitjacket.

He was a little, middle-aged man like those in the offices where ration books or coal coupons were given out – like any sort of minor official. He wore spectacles with lenses as thick as magnifying glasses, and he appeared to be waiting for lunch-time with some impatience.

Now here was another cardinal question, at the bottom of the whole problem: *Had there, or had there not, been a mistake?*

Timo had seemed to suggest that they were like the rest of the world, that one of their offices might well be entirely ignorant of what was happening in the office next door. At the food office people got two books in mistake for one without asking, while others failed to get a lost book replaced.

This was serious. He must not let himself get excited, but it was necessary to contemplate that possibility as scrupulously as the others. Nor must he forget to allow for the fact that it was lunch-time, that the chief was hungry and that he had just given way to a display of temper when he saw the previous prisoner pass out.

Yet it was impossible to make any exact deduction from his behaviour. Had he deigned to look at Frank? Did he know him? Had he a file in front of him?

While Frank was waiting next door, on the grey bench, there must have been five of them in the office, since there were now three left, the chief sitting at his desk and the two others on their feet. One of them was young, younger than Frank. He was badly dressed.

So, two standing, one sitting.

Frank at once held out his card across the desk. He had been holding it in readiness for the past half hour. He had been feeling it in his pocket throughout the journey by tram. If Timo was right, the old chief might have shrugged his shoulders, or sneered.

As it was, he took the card, and without so much as a glance at it, laid it close by him on top of a heap of papers. Meanwhile the other two were going through Frank's pockets methodically, but without brutality.

Nothing was said to him. He was asked no questions. The man who had fetched him in stood in the doorway, without appearing to keep any special watch on him.

The old gentleman must be thinking of other things, looking through a file which had nothing to do with Frank's case. Without showing any curiosity he allowed the contents of Frank's pockets to pile up in a corner of his desk, including the wad of bank notes.

When the search was finished, he raised his head, as if to ask:
'Is that the lot?'

The policeman remembered one more detail, and came and laid the revolver on the desk.

'Is that all?'

Then at last, with a gentle sigh, he took a long schedule, a sheet of paper in a special format, with printed words and blanks to be filled in.

'Frank Friedmaier?' he asked, without seeming to care one way or the other.

He wrote in the name in stiff upright characters, and then a quarter of an hour went by during which he noted down in a special column every one of the objects which had been turned out of Frank's pockets, not overlooking so much as a box of matches or a stump of pencil.

They did not treat him roughly. No one took any interest in him at all. If he had rushed to the door and run away as fast as he could, probably only the sentry would have shot at him, and probably he would have missed.

Was it really so ridiculous to think of this as a test? Why should they give green cards to people they didn't know and weren't sure of?

Why had he not been hit, like the other man? And had the other man really been hit? Such things ought not to happen in an office open to anyone passing by.

He had done some thinking in eighteen days. Terrible, deep thinking. Not only about that. He had had time to think about Christmas, the New Year, Minna, Anny, Bertha. They would all have been surprised, Lotte included, if they had known all he had discovered about them.

Thinking was not easy, though, because of his neighbours. For here, as in Grünestrasse, there were neighbours. Exactly, Herr Holst! Absolutely, Herr Wimmer! The difference was you couldn't see them, and for that very reason had even less confidence in them here than in the neighbours anywhere else.

They had tried to get him from the very first day, but he had been mistrustful. He mistrusted everything. He was on the way to becoming the most mistrustful man alive. If his mother were to come to see him, he would wonder if she had not been sent by *them*.

The neighbours tapped on walls, on water pipes, on radiators. The heating system was out of action, but the old radiators were still in place.

It must not be forgotten that he had been consigned, not to a real prison, but to a school, a college which, according to all he had seen of it, must be quite a high-class institution.

His neighbours had sent him messages at once. Why?

He was not so feather-brained as not to have noted the general layout of the place, or to deduce therefrom that he was a privileged prisoner. How many were there to his right? Ten at least, so far as he could estimate. To judge from their accents – for he sometimes caught odd words when they passed along the iron gangway – they were mostly workmen and country folk.

Probably they were what the newspapers called saboteurs. Genuine or bogus. Or bogus mixed with genuine.

He was not going to let himself be caught.

He had not been beaten. He had been treated civilly. He had been searched, but it had been done tactfully. Everything had been taken from him, cigarettes, lighter, wallet, papers. His tie too had been removed, together with his belt and his shoelaces. Meanwhile, the old gentleman had gone on filling up the schedule in his abstracted way. When it was finished, he had passed Frank the schedule and a pen, pointed to a dotted line and said, with scarcely a trace of foreign accent:

'Sign here.'

He had signed, without thinking twice. He had signed mechanically. He did not know what he had signed. Had he been wrong? Or was this not, on the contrary, a way of demonstrating to them that he had nothing on his conscience? He had not signed for fear of a beating. He had simply realized that this was an indispensable formality, and that it would be useless to rebel.

This point, too, he had pondered deeply, and he had no regrets. If there was anything he regretted, it was having opened his mouth to say:

'I should like . . .'

He had had no time to say more. The old gentleman had motioned with his hand, and Frank had been taken away, across a second courtyard, this one paved with bricks, so far as he could judge from the tracks worn in the snow. What had he been going to say? What was it he would have liked? A lawyer? Certainly not. He was not so simple as that. To communicate with his mother? To disclose the general's name? To notify Kromer, or Timo, or Ressl, who had remembered him at Taste's and had given him a slight sign of recognition?

It was a good thing he had not had time to go on with his sentence. He must get out of the habit of uttering useless words.

He had not yet known that everything he saw had its importance, would each day become a little more important.

The thought came:

'A school.'

And there was a ready-made image.

Whereas, in certain cases, the most trivial details became one day so precious that you couldn't forgive yourself for not having been more observant.

There was a big interior court, which must have seemed all the bigger to him because at the time it was flooded with sunshine. A two-storeyed building in new brick ran its whole length, and there were evidently no interior staircases, because, as on board ship, you saw outside staircases of iron and suspended corridors rather like gangways which gave access to all the classrooms.

How many classrooms were there? He didn't know. He merely had an impression of vastness. On the other side of the court was another building, the school hall or the gymnasium, lit by tall windows like those of a church: this feature was rather reminiscent of the tannery. Then there was the playground, part of which he had been able to watch these eighteen days, with black wooden forms and desks, all the furniture of a school, piled up as high as the roof.

In spite of the bars across the windows, it still was not a real prison. For one thing, scarcely any warders were to be seen. At the most he had noticed, in passing, two soldiers in the courtyard armed with tommy guns.

It was only at night that the place became a little more impressive, with the searchlights playing over the grounds.

As the windows were without blinds, the light made sleep impossible, or woke you up with a start.

In fact, the absence of sentries must mean that there was a watchtower on the roof, with the searchlights, and machine-guns and grenades. At certain hours footsteps were to be heard clattering on an iron staircase which could lead nowhere else.

In any case, in one way or another, and for whatever reason, he was not treated like the ordinary prisoners. He had not been mistaken when he noted the courtesy – cold, but courtesy none the less – of the old gentleman in spectacles.

To his right, then, there were ten of them at least, sometimes more – you could never be certain, because changes were taking place the whole time. To his left there were three, or perhaps four, and one of them was sick or mad.

This was not a cell: it was a classroom. What had it been used for when the school was still going? For classes which brought only a few pupils together, last-year classes, most likely. For a classroom it was small, but for a cell it was huge, not at all in scale with a single occupant. It bothered him: he didn't know where to put himself. His bed seemed tiny. It was an iron bedstead, an old army cot, with planks in place of the missing springs. He had not been given a mattress. His bedclothes amounted to one harsh blanket reeking of disinfectant.

That disgusted him more than if the blanket had smelt of sweat, more than if it had been impregnated with the odour of human bodies. These whiffs of chemicals made him think of a corpse. The bedclothes were certainly disinfected only when someone had died between them. And men must have died in this room. Certain inscriptions had been carefully effaced. You could still see hearts with initials, as on trees in the country, and flags of which the markings were no longer distinguishable. But the most numerous mementoes were the strokes which had marked the days, with a transverse line for the weeks.

It had been difficult for him to find a clean spot apart for his personal reckoning, and already he was nearing his third transverse line.

146

He did not answer the messages. He had made up his mind not to do so, not even to try to understand them. In the daytime a soldier patrolled the length of the gangway, and from time to time pushed his face against the windows. At night they relied on their searchlights, and the tread of boots was hardly ever heard.

Night fell early, and soon after pandemonium broke loose. Walls and pipes reverberated. He understood nothing. It would have required only a slight effort and a little patience. It must be like a simplified morse code.

He declined, once and for all, to be interested. He was alone. So much the better. They had done him the favour of leaving him alone, and there must be a meaning in that. It didn't matter if the meaning was that his was a more serious case. Besides, he had already had enough experience to doubt that.

From the room to his right, to which newcomers were continually being brought, men were taken out to be shot, if not every day, at any rate several times a week. It was the room for the hodge-podge. They seemed to fish in it as in a fishpond, at random.

That sort of thing happened before daybreak. Did they manage to sleep? Often, there were some who groaned, or, right in the middle of the night, let out a great cry. Probably the young ones.

Two soldiers – always two – came up from the courtyard, and their footsteps re-echoed on the iron staircase, then on the gangway. At the outset, Frank wondered each time if his turn had come. Now, he did not stir. The steps halted outside the classroom door. Perhaps some of the men shut up in there had studied in that very room.

Then everyone began to bawl a patriotic song, and after that you could see in the paling darkness two or three figures walking in front of the soldiers.

If it was deliberate, the operation was calculated to a nicety. The time was so well chosen that Frank had never once been able to make out the features of a passing face. Just the silhouettes. Men walking with their hands behind their backs, without overcoat or hat, despite the cold. And their jacket collars were always turned up.

Presumably they were taken to a last interview in another office, for quite a lapse of time followed, and dawn was breaking just as their steps crossed the courtyard. It took place near the playground. If it had been two or three yards nearer, Frank could have seen the whole thing from the window. As it was, he could never glimpse more than the head and shoulders of the officer in charge of the firing party.

Then he could go to sleep again. For they let him sleep. He did not know how things went in the other classrooms. Quite differently, no doubt, for there was always noise to be heard from early on. *He* was left in peace till his morning meal was brought – an unsweetened brew of acorns, with a small piece of soggy bread.

How pleased that bitch Bertha would be! All the same, he got used to it. He drank up to the very last drop. He ate everything. He was not going to let himself be downed. He had settled his plans on his very first day.

He allowed himself to think about this subject or that only at its appointed time. He had a complete routine in his head. It was sometimes difficult to conform to the time-table. His thoughts had a tendency to get mixed up. When that happened, he would give himself time to relax by staring at a black mark fairly high up on the wall, where the crucifix must have hung when this was still a school.

'Bertha is a stupid whore, but she had nothing to do with this.'

However, as it was not the appointed time, not the turn of Grünestrasse, he took up his speculations at the point where he had left off the evening before.

Sometimes Sissy and Holst intruded themselves. Sissy, for example, coming to pick up the bag with the key in it, whereas in reality he did not know whether she had picked it up, nor even whether she had seen it. It was of no consequence, but it was forbidden by the rules he had prescribed. As for Holst, he had become, so to speak, Enemy No. 1. He was the one who materialized most often, with his grey felt boots, his overcoat, his tin dinner box, and his drooping frame. Yet, most curiously, Frank was quite incapable of remembering his face. It was no more than a blur. Or, to be more precise, an expression.

An expression of what? If he was not careful, he would let himself wander off on this train of thought for minutes and minutes, at any rate for too long, for there was nothing here by which to measure time – had it been absolutely necessary, he would have had to take his pulse.

What could you call the look they had exchanged when Holst was at his window and Frank was waiting for the tram?

Was it nameless?

Well, there was no word for Holst's expression either. It was a mystery, a riddle. And when you were in Frank's situation, you had no right to pore over riddles, even if doing so seemed momentarily to help.

You had to take up the questions one by one, tirelessly, doing your best to remain cool and lucid, and to avoid letting the prison mentality invade your soul.

There was this.

That had happened.

Such and such and such a one might have acted thus.

Nothing must be neglected, neither details of events, nor people.

Throughout the day he kept his overcoat on, his collar turned up and his hat on his head, and he spent the best part of his time sitting on the edge of the bed. His bucket was emptied only once a day, and it had no lid.

Why was it that another prisoner came to empty it for him? Why did Frank not take part in the exercise, when three at least of his left-hand neighbours did so?

He had no wish to walk round and round the courtyard. He could not see them. He could hear them. He made no complaint. He had never tried to soften his guards, who changed almost daily, and he never groaned, as others probably did, in the hope of getting a cigarette, or at least a pull at the one the soldier was smoking.

There was this.

There was Frank.

Then there was this, and that.

The neighbours in Grünestrasse, Kromer, Timo, Bertha, Holst, Sissy, old father Kamp, old Wimmer, still others, not forgetting the violinist, Karl Adler, the fair-haired man from the second floor, and even Ressl, even Kropetzki. Not one must be left out. He had neither paper nor pencil, but he maintained his list in full, unwearyingly, with marginal notes of anything that could be of interest, however slight.

There was Frank . . .

It would take more than Holst's face, or rather Holst's expression, to divert Frank from the task he had undertaken.

Sissy was probably cured.

Cured or dead.

What mattered was the list, to go on thinking, to forget nothing and yet not attach more than their due weight to things.

There was Frank, son of Lotte . . .

That reminded him of the Bible, and he smiled contemptuously, because it was like a pun. He had not come to prison to make puns.

Besides, it was not a prison he had been put in, but a school, and there must be a meaning in that.

5

Nineteenth day.

He had not been put in prison, but in a school.

He linked up automatically with the previous evening's thinking. It was an exercise. You very soon got used to it. After a time the release worked of itself, and after that the wheels went on turning on their own as in a watch. You did this, then that. You always performed the same movements at the same hours and, with just a little care, thought went on gnawing away.

There was nothing unpleasant about the school as such and, if there were various sectors, as Timo put it, Frank must be in one which really mattered, since executions took place nearly every day. What ought perhaps to have been more disturbing was that the authorities persisted in ignoring him, or pretended to do so.

He had not been questioned and still no questioning took place. He was not spied on. If they had spied on his behaviour, he would have spotted it. He was left alone. They did not bother about his linen, which he had been wearing for nineteen days now. He had never once been able to wash himself properly, because he was not given enough water.

He bore them no grudge. As long as it did not indicate a sort of contempt for him, he did not mind. He was unshaven. Others at his age did not have strong beards, but he had started shaving very young, for the fun of the thing. 'Before', he had shaved every day. His beard was now half an inch long. At first it had been stiff, but now it was becoming soft to the touch.

There was a proper prison in the town, which *they* had taken over, of course, and which no doubt was full. It was not necessarily there that they put the most interesting cases.

There was nothing to show he was being played with. If the warders never spoke to him, he had realized that that was because they did not understand his language. The prisoners who brought him his jug of water and emptied his bucket also refrained from speaking to him. They got about. Some of them were shaved, and some had had their hair cut, which showed there was a barber's in the school. If he was not taken there like the others, why should that mean that he had been forgotten? Did it not just signify that he was in solitary confinement?

Some individual was at the bottom of it all, a denunciation or something of that sort. He reviewed the names, the behaviour, of each one, studying their possibilities. He was always embarrassed at having to sit on his bucket, what with the big window through which everything could be seen from the gangway outside. But he had already ceased to feel ashamed at being unshaven, or at his dirty linen or his clothes, now much crumpled from being slept in.

The others went down for exercise at nine o'clock. They must be sent out so early on purpose, to make sure that they should feel cold, particularly as some of them lacked overcoats. Why not wait till eleven o'clock or midday, when the sun would have had time to take the bite out of the air?

It didn't matter to him, since he did not go down. If he had gone down, he would have missed, a little later on, the scene at the window.

The wheels were turning, his thoughts were nibbling away again, yet that did not prevent the feeling of expectancy from starting up in him as early as nine o'clock. It was really nothing, less than nothing. If he had been in a real prison, it would not have taken place, because any contact with the outside world, however distant, would be strictly prevented. Here, no one must have given a thought to that window. Actually, it was a very careless oversight, for the window could be an important factor.

Beyond the school hall, or gymnasium, on the other side of the courtyard, you could feel there was an empty space – perhaps a street, perhaps a row of houses, small, like most of those in the district, and each one occupied by a single family. Further off again, much further, there rose against the sky the back of a building at least four storeys high, most of it hidden by the school hall. The hipped roof of the hall left one window visible, just one, high up, probably on the top floor, which indicated that the tenants were poor.

Every morning, shortly before half past nine, the window was opened by a woman wearing a wrap – like Lotte – with a light coloured scarf round her head, who shook blankets and rugs out in the air.

From so far off her features were indistinguishable. But she was so active, and her movements were so brisk, that Frank deduced that she was young. Despite the time of year, she would leave the window open for quite a time, while she bustled about, keeping an eye on things inside the flat, her cooking, or her baby. She certainly had a baby, for she nearly always hung things out to dry on a line slung across the window, and they were always tiny things.

Who knows? Perhaps she was singing. She must be happy. Frank supposed she was. When she shut her window, she would be back in her own home, with the household odours once more asserting their rights.

So he was angry that day, the nineteenth, when they came to disturb him at a quarter past nine – or at any rate before the woman had appeared at her window. Ever since his arrival he had been waiting to be fetched. He had thought of it all day and every day. Now, when the summons came at last, he was furious at being disturbed a quarter of an hour too soon.

It was a civilian, accompanied by a soldier, who stopped on the gangway outside his door. He had a brown moustache. He looked something like a schoolmaster. Frank surmised at once that this must be one of the two men who had been beating the man in the office when he himself was waiting in the outer room on the day of his arrival. He was a man who would doubtless strike to order, calmly, without hatred, yet zealously, just as he would have applied himself in an office to doing accounts.

Was that why Frank was being taken downstairs? Neither the civilian nor the soldier gave so much as a glance at his room. They said nothing to him. They simply motioned to him to come out. The civilian walked ahead, and Frank followed. It did not occur to him to look into the other classrooms as he had so often promised himself he would. Better still. It was the hour at which the prisoners exercised in the big courtyard. He could see them, both while he was walking along the gangway and when going down the exterior iron staircase.

But he forgot to observe them. Later, he could remember only a sort of long dark snake. Which meant that they walked in single file, about a yard apart, and the whole formed an almost closed oval with ripples in its outline.

What would it mean if they beat him? That a mistake had been made, that he was suspected of offences he had not committed – for they did not take Fräulein Vilmos seriously. Oddly enough, he had stopped thinking about the sergeant. That business seemed to him so innocuous that he felt positively innocent.

They went – he was taken – towards the little building where he had been received the first day, and he climbed the same steps. This time he was not kept waiting. He was taken straight in to the office of the old gentleman, who was in his usual place, and Frank, on looking round the room, saw his mother.

His first reaction was to frown, and, before looking at her more closely, or speaking to her, he waited for the official's instructions. But the old gentleman appeared as indifferent as ever. He went on writing in his cramped script, and it was Lotte who spoke first. It was a minute or two before her voice found its normal key. It was too flat, the way a voice sounds in a cave.

'You see, Frank, these gentlemen have allowed me to come and see you and bring you some of your things. I didn't know where you were.'

She spoke the last words very quickly. They must have warned her. Doubtless there were subjects which she might broach, others which were forbidden.

Why did he seem to be sulking at her? In reality, he was uneasy. He was on his guard with her. She came from elsewhere. She was altogether too like herself. It was appalling how like herself she was. He recognized the scent of her powder. She had put rouge on her cheek-bones, as she did every time she went out. She was wearing her white hat, with a tiny veil partly hiding her eyes. This was sheer vanity, on account of the fine wrinkles of her 'onion skins', as she called her eyelids. She had spent a full half-hour in front of the glass in the big bedroom. He could see her drawing on her kid gloves, fluffing up her hair on each side of her hat.

'I can't stay long, Frank.'

So a limit had been set to her visit. Why couldn't she say so openly?

'You look well. If only you knew how happy I am to see you looking well.'

Which meant:

'To see you alive.'

Because she had believed him to be dead.

'When did they notify you?'

She answered, her voice low, with a furtive glance at the old gentleman:

'Yesterday.'

'Who told you?'

She evaded his question and said, with simulated keenness:

'Just think – I've been allowed to bring you a few little things. Linen first of all. Now you can have a change of underclothes at last, my poor Frank.'

He was less pleased at that than she had expected. Yet a month ago, he would have put this pleasure above anything else.

She was shocked. Shocked at his appearance. She looked at the crumpled clothes, the turned-up collar of his overcoat, the soiled shirt; she noted the absence of a tie, the unkempt hair, the nineteen-days-old beard, the gaping shoes. She felt sorry for him, and he felt it. But he did not want anybody's pity, least of all Lotte's. She sickened him, with her make-up and her white hat.

Would the old gentleman be tempted by her? Had she tried? At all events, she must have chosen her lingerie with special care.

'I've put everything into a suitcase. These gentlemen will give it to you.'

Her eyes went to the suitcase, where it stood against the wall. It was one he recognized.

'Above all you mustn't let yourself go . . .'

Let himself go in what way?

'Everyone has been very nice. Everything's fine.'

'What's fine?'

He was hard; almost churlish. He blamed himself for being like that, but he just couldn't help it.

'I've decided to give up my business.'

Her handkerchief was rolled up into a ball in the palm of her hand, and she felt ready to cry.

'Hamling advised me to do that. You were wrong to distrust him. He has done all he could.'

'Is Minna still with you?'

'She doesn't want to leave me alone. She sends you lots of messages. If I could find somewhere else to live, we would move, but it's practically impossible.'

This time the look which Frank directed at her became pitiless, almost savage.

'You would leave the block?'

'You know how people are. Now you're not there, it's worse than ever.'

He asked sharply:

'Is Sissy dead?'

'Heavens – no! What are you thinking of?'

She glanced at her little gold wrist watch. For her, time still mattered. She knew just how many more minutes she was allowed.

'Does she go out?'

'No. She's . . . look, Frank, I don't know exactly what's the matter with her. I believe she's depressed. She's not making a good recovery.'

'What's wrong?'

'I don't know. I haven't seen her myself. Nobody sees her, except her father and Herr Wimmer. They say she's neurasthenic.'

'Has Holst gone back to his job on the trams?'

'No. He works at home.'

'What at?'

'I don't know that either. Book-keeping, probably. What little I've learnt I've had from Hamling.'

'He sees them?'

Before, the chief inspector had known the Holsts only by name.

'He has been to their place several times.'

'Why?'

'Now, Frank, how do you suppose I can answer that? You're asking questions as though you didn't know the block. I never see anybody. Anny has left. It seems she's being kept by a . . .' (It must be forbidden to talk about the occupiers here.) 'If Minna had left me too, I don't know what would have become of me.'

'Have you seen any of my friends?'

'Not one.'

She was lost, disappointed. She must have come full of joy, in the same way as people go to visit a patient in hospital, taking grapes or oranges, and he gave her no credit for her good intentions. You would have sworn he was angry with her, that he held *her* responsible for her own disappointment.

He pointed to a parcel lying on a chair near his mother, and asked:

'What's that?'

'Nothing. Some things that were in the suitcase and I'm not allowed to leave you.'

'I don't want you to move to another house.'

She sighed, a little impatient. Didn't he realize that she couldn't talk freely? Oh yes, he knew. But he didn't care. The tenants were making life impossible for Lotte? So what? He forbade her to leave the block, and that was that. Was it for her or for him to decide? Which of the two counted most now?

'Has Holst spoken to you?'

Why did she look so embarrassed when she answered:

'Not personally.'

'He's sent you a message by Hamling?'

'No, Frank. Why do you keep thinking about that? There's nothing to worry about there. My time's up. If I'm to have another chance to come and see you, I mustn't overdo it the first time. I'd like to kiss you, but it's better not. They might think you were passing me a message, or whispering in my ear.'

Anyway, he had no wish to kiss her. She must have been there quite a while before he came down, for they had had time to search the suitcase before he arrived.

'Keep well. Take good care of yourself. Above all, don't worry.'

'I'm not worried.'

'You're acting so strangely.'

She too was in a hurry to get it over. She would go and wait for her tram opposite the gate, and she would snivel the whole way home.

'Good-bye, Frank.'

'Good-bye, mother.'

'Take care of yourself.'

Yes, yes! Of course he would! As if he meant to let himself go into a decline!

The old gentleman lifted his eyes to look at each of them in turn, then motioned to Frank to pick up the suitcase. A civilian took Lotte back across the courtyard, and her steps could be heard, clearly at first, her high heels tapping on the hardened snow. The old gentleman spoke slowly, choosing his words deliberately. He insisted on using the exact expression, and was very careful about his pronunciation. He had taken lessons and continued to practise.

'You must go and get ready.'

He enunciated each syllable individually. He didn't seem to be a bad sort. Just a stickler for accuracy. He hesitated before risking a longer sentence, and rehearsed it mentally beforehand.

'If you wish to be shaved, you will be taken.'

Frank had declined the offer. Which had been a mistake. A visit to the barber's would have enabled him to get to know another part of the buildings. He didn't know why he had refused. He was not particularly keen on being dirty, or playing the role of the bearded prisoner. The truth was – and it would take him days to get at it – that when his beard was mentioned, he had automatically called to mind Holst's felt boots.

There was no connexion. Indeed, he wanted none to be found. He preferred to think of something else.

And now there was no lack of material for thought. He had been allowed to take his suitcase. Once more a civilian went ahead, and a soldier followed, on the way back to his classroom. He almost had the illusion of being led to a hotel room. His door was shut, and he was left alone.

Why had he been ordered to get ready? It was an order, there could be no doubt of that. The moment had come. They were going to take him off somewhere. Would they let him take his suitcase? Would he come straight back to the school? Evidently they had removed the newspaper the things had been wrapped in, and everything was upside down. There were little cakes of pink soap which reminded Frank of Bertha's skin, a smoked sausage, a fairly big piece of bacon, a pound of sugar, and slabs of chocolate. He also found half a dozen of his shirts and some socks, as well as a new pullover which his mother must have bought for him. At the bottom there was even a pair of thick knitted gloves, such as he would never have worn outside.

He changed. He had missed the woman at the window. He was thinking too quickly. This time, it didn't count. He was being hustled, which made him more cross than ever. He had got to the stage of missing his solitude and his own little ways. When he came back, if he did come back, he would have to set all this out clearly in his head. He munched at the chocolate without realizing that this was the first time he had done such a thing for nineteen days; and the chief impression left by Lotte's visit was a feeling of disappointment.

He did not know how else things might have gone, but he

was disappointed. He had not found a single point of contact with her. He had asked her questions and it had seemed – it still seemed – as though her answers bore no relation whatever to what he had asked.

However, she had given him some news, as quickly and directly as she could. Clearly she had not been troubled by the authorities, because up to the day before she still had not known where he was. So the newspapers had not mentioned him. The local police had not taken a hand. If they had, she would have known through Kurt Hamling.

Hamling was continuing to visit the block, but he had crossed the landing, rather as one crossed a river. Now he went to the Holsts' flat. What for? Holst was no longer driving a tram. There was a perfectly simple reason for that. One week in two the job had obliged him to come home in the middle of the night, and while he was away Sissy had been alone. He must have found another job which kept him at work only during the daytime.

Sissy was never left alone. He knew well enough how his mother and people of her kind spoke of such matters. If she had used the word 'neurasthenic', if she had appeared embarrassed, it must be more serious.

Was Sissy mad?

Frank was not afraid of words. He compelled himself to utter that one aloud:

'Mad!'

That was it. With the two men, her father and old Wimmer, taking it in turns to be with her, and the chief inspector who came from time to time and sat in a chair, without taking off his overcoat or the galoshes that left wet patches on the floor.

Frank was to be taken away somewhere. If not, there would have been no sense in telling him to get ready. He was ready much too early. There was nothing left to do, and it was useless to start thinking during this sort of intermission. The only result would be to throw him off his balance. After the chocolate, he nibbled at the sausage. It had not occurred to his mother that he wouldn't have a knife to cut it with. And he had no water left to wash his face. He smelt of smoked meat.

If only they would come quickly and take him away! And, above all, bring him back as soon as possible and leave him in peace.

The same civilian as just now. As a matter of fact, apart from the soldiers who were constantly changing, there were not very many of them. They all had a family likeness. If Timo was right, the sector they belonged to must rank quite highly. Hadn't Timo told him that the man before whom the colonel had quailed looked like a little clerk?

Here, they were all of that sort. Not a cheerful or smart one in the lot. It was impossible to imagine them sitting down to a good dinner, or petting a pretty girl. They might have been born to fulfil the dullest jobs.

Since, again according to Timo, truth and appearance went by contraries, so far as they were concerned, they must be enormously powerful.

The little office again. The old gentleman was not there. Gone to lunch, no doubt. Frank found his tie and his shoelaces on the desk. One of the men pointed to them, and said, with a bad accent:

'You may.'

He sat down on a chair. He was no longer impressed. If these folk had understood his language better, he would have begun to chatter to them about anything that came into his head.

There were two of them waiting, their hats on their heads. As they left, one of the two handed him a cigarette, then a match.

'Thanks.'

A car was waiting in the courtyard, not a police van, nor a military vehicle, but a black and glossy limousine, such as rich people used to own before the war, people who could afford a chauffeur. Very flexible, quite silent, it went through the gateway and turned towards the town, following the tramlines. Although the windows were shut, the atmosphere in the car had just a little tang of the outside air. There were people to be seen on the pavements, shop windows, an urchin hopping on one leg and kicking a half brick along with his foot.

They had not made him bring his suitcase along. Nor sign any papers. He would be coming back. He was convinced that he would be coming back and that he would once more be seeing the woman hanging baby clothes out at her window. Oh! If he had only turned round in time he might have recognized the building she lived in. He must remember that on the way back.

It was a much shorter journey by car than by tram. They were nearing the city centre already. They drove round an imposing building which housed the majority of the military offices. The general's must be in there. There were sentries at all the doors, and barriers prevented civilians from passing along the pavement.

They did not stop in front of the monumental flight of steps, but in front of a low door in a side street. There had been a police post there, but it had been moved. There was no need to motion him to get out. He had understood. For a moment – a brief moment – he remained standing in the middle of the pavement, without moving. He could see people on the other side of the street. He recognized no one. No one recognized him. No one even looked at him. He did not linger. That was certainly not allowed.

He went in, of his own accord. He waited for a second to let his escort precede him through a maze of dark and complicated corridors. There were mysterious inscriptions on the doors, and here and there they met a girl secretary carrying files of papers under her arm.

This was not the place where he would be tortured. There would not have been so many young women in light coloured blouses. They did not look at him as they went by. There was nothing dramatic about the place. These were simply offices, quantities of offices crammed with ever increasing numbers of files, where officers and ncos in uniform smoked cigars while they worked. The mysterious signs on the doors, letters followed by figures, evidently indicated the various branches.

It was a different sector: Timo was quite right. The difference could be sensed at once. Was it a lower or a higher sector? He could not yet say. Here, for instance, he could hear sudden bursts of talk, whispers, laughter. There were well-nourished men who puffed out their chests and buckled their belts before going out. You thought about the women's breasts under their blouses, the softness of their thighs under their skirts. Some of these people undoubtedly made love on the corner of their desks.

Frank himself behaved differently. He looked about him just as he would have done anywhere else, and he was a little embarrassed at having kept his beard. He carried himself almost as he had done 'before'. He tried to see his reflection in the glass panel of a door, and lifted his hand to his tie.

They were there. It was almost at the very top of the building. The rooms had lower ceilings, the windows were small, the passages were dusty. He was taken into an outer office, where there was nobody, where there was nothing to be seen except row upon row of green filing cabinets, and a large deal table covered with dirty blotting paper.

Was he mistaken? It seemed to him that his companions did not feel at home, that they had put on an air at once distant and humble, with perhaps a little dash of irony – or was it contempt? They looked a question at each other before one of them knocked on a side door. The man disappeared, to return at once followed by a stout officer in an unbuttoned tunic.

In the doorway he scrutinized Frank from head to foot, drawing on his cigar with a self-important air.

He appeared satisfied. At first glance, he had seemed rather surprised at finding Frank so young.

'Come here.'

He was genial and gruff at one and the same time. He laid his hand on Frank's shoulder, steering him into the room. The two civilians did not follow, and the officer shut the door. In a corner, near another door, a young officer of lower rank was working by the light of a desk lamp, for that part of the room was badly lit.

'Friedmaier, isn't it?'

'That's my name.'

The officer glanced at a typed sheet of paper which he had ready.

'Frank Friedmaier. Very good. Sit down.'

He pointed to a straw-bottomed chair on the other side of the desk, and pushed across a box of cigarettes and a lighter. This was evidently customary. The cigarettes were for visitors, for the officer himself was smoking an exceptionally light and aromatic cigar.

He had thrown himself back in his armchair, his paunch well forward. His hair was sparse, and he had the high complexion of a heavy eater.

'Well, my friend, what's our story?'

In spite of his accent, he had a thorough mastery of the language, knew all its subtleties, and his familiarity was intentional.

'I don't know,' said Frank.

'Ha! Ha! *I don't know!*'

He seemed delighted with this answer, and translated it for the benefit of the other officer.

'Still, you will have to make up your mind, you know! You've been left plenty of time to think things over.'

'Think over what?'

This time the officer frowned, got up and strode to a table where he picked up a file. He consulted it. This might have been no more than a bit of stagecraft. He sat down again, resumed the same position and flicked the ash off his cigar with his little finger.

'I'm waiting.'

'I want nothing better than to answer your questions.'

'There you are! What questions, eh? I'll bet you don't know.'

'No.'

'You don't know what you've done?'

'I don't know what I'm accused of.'

'There you are! There you are!'

It was a mannerism. He had a droll way of uttering the words at the least provocation.

'You'd like to know what we want to know! Is that it?'

'That's it.'

'Because, maybe, you know other things besides?'

'I know nothing.'

'Nothing at all! You know just nothing at all! All the same it was your pocket this was found in.'

For a moment, Frank had expected to see the revolver jerked out from the desk drawer, into which the officer had plunged his hand. He had gone pale. He felt he was being eyed closely. He watched his interlocutor's hand reluctantly, and was astonished to recognize the wad of notes he had carried round in his pocket and shown off at every opportunity.

'There you are! And *that's* nothing, I suppose?'

'It's money.'

'Yes, it's money. A lot of money.'

'I earned it.'

'You earned it – there you are! When you earn money, there's always some person, or a bank, to pay it over to you. That's correct, isn't it? Now what *I* want to know, quite simply, is – who paid you this money? It's simple. It's easy. All you have to do is tell me the name. There you are!'

There was a sudden silence. Then, after quite a pause, the officer reiterated, more insinuatingly, his cheeks a little pinker:

'Just tell me the name . . .'

'I don't know.'

'You don't know who paid you all this money?'

'I certainly got some of it from several sources.'

'Is that so?'

'I do some business.'

'Really!'

'You pick up a bit here, some more there. Notes change hands. It's hard to keep track . . .'

But suddenly the officer's tone changed, he slammed the drawer to with a sharp noise, and said flatly:

'No.'

He looked furious, threatening. For a second Frank thought he meant to strike him as he moved round the desk, came close to him and again placed his hand on his shoulder. But it was to make him get up, and meanwhile the officer went on talking as if to himself:

'It's just any old money, is it? Money we pick up here and there and stuff into our pockets without bothering to look at it.'

'Yes.'

'No!'

Frank's chest was tight. He didn't know what his interlocutor was driving at. He could sense a vague threat, a mystery. He had been thinking madly for eighteen days, almost nineteen. He had tried to foresee everything, and now nothing was turning out as it ought to have turned out. All at once the whole set-up was different. The school, the old gentleman in spectacles, suddenly came to stand for an almost reassuring world, and yet now he had a cigarette between his lips, and he could hear the click of a typewriter in the next room, the voices of women passing along the corridor.

'Take a good look at this, Friedmaier, and tell me if it's still just any old money.'

He had picked up one of the notes from his desk. He led Frank to the window, one hand still on his shoulder, and held the note up so high that the light shone through.

'Come closer. Don't be frightened. You mustn't be frightened.'

Why did those words seem more charged with menace than the sound of blows he had heard that first day in the old gentleman's office?

'Take a good look. In the left-hand corner. Tiny little holes. Six tiny little holes. There you are! And those little holes form a pattern. And there were little holes like that in every one of the notes you had in your pocket and in every one of those you spent.'

Frank was beyond speech or thought. It was as though a gap had opened in front of him where it was least to be expected, as if the wall had melted away around the window, leaving the two men on the brink of the emptiness above the street.

'I don't know.'

'You don't know, don't you?'

'No.'

'And you don't know what these little holes mean either? There you are! You just don't know!'

'No.'

It was true. He had never heard of such a thing. He had the impression that the mere fact of knowing the meaning of what the officer called the little holes would be a more damning indictment against him than any crime. He wished the officer would look him in the eyes and there read his good faith, his entire sincerity.

'I swear to you that I don't know.'

'But *I* know.'

'What do they mean?'

'*I* know. And that's why I must know where you got the notes.'

'I've told you . . .'

'No!'

'I swear . . .'

'The notes were stolen.'

'Not by me.'

'No!'

How could he be so definite? And now he was saying, stressing each syllable like a hammer blow:

'They were stolen *here*.'

Seeing Frank look round the room in terror, the officer elaborated:

'They were stolen here, *in this building*.'

Frank was afraid he was going to faint. From now on he would really understand the expression 'cold sweat'. He understood other things too. He believed he understood everything.

The little holes had been made in the notes by the occupiers. Which notes? Which reserve did they belong to?

No one knew, no one had ever suspected, and it was already terrifying just to have been let into the secret.

He wasn't the one they were really after! Nor Kromer either. *They* knew quite well that both of them were petty traffickers, and that people of their sort had no access to certain funds.

Was the general already under suspicion? Had they arrested Kromer? Had they questioned him? Had he talked?

All Frank's labours for eighteen and a half days had been in vain. They had all been stupidly wide of the mark. He had been wasting his time on people of no importance, people of his own stature, as if fate were going to make use of such tools.

Fate had chosen a banknote, doubtless one of those he had spent, perhaps at Timo's, perhaps at the tailor's where he had bought his camel-hair overcoat. Perhaps too one of the notes he had given to Kropetzki for his sister's eyes.

'We really must know, mustn't we?' said the officer as he sat down again.

And he pushed the cigarette box across to Frank again.

'There you are, Friedmaier. That's the case.'

Part Three

The Woman at
the Window

1

He was lying on his stomach, asleep. He was conscious of being asleep. That was a thing which – with many others – he had learned recently. Formerly it had only been towards morning, and especially after sunrise, that he had been conscious of being asleep. And, as the effect was heightened when he had been drinking the night before, he had taken to coming home late after drinking too much, solely in order to savour that particular form of sleep.

Nevertheless, that kind of sleep had not been quite the same as this new-found one. Before, he had never slept flat on his stomach. Did all prisoners learn to sleep thus? He had no idea. He didn't care. However, he would gladly have used their complicated system of communication, if he had had the patience and the taste for learning it, simply in order to send them the advice:

'Sleep flat on your stomach!'

It was not just a matter of lying on his stomach. But of flattening oneself, sprawled like an animal or an insect, against the planks that replaced the springs of the bed. Hard as they were, he felt he was going to leave the impress of his body on them, as when one lies on freshly ploughed earth.

He was flat on his stomach, and it hurt. Dozens of tiny bones or muscles hurt him, not all at once, not all together, but in accordance with an order he was beginning to recognize and which he had grown able to orchestrate, like a symphony. There were dark, heavy pains and shrill pains, so sharp they made everything seem light yellow. Some lasted only a few seconds, but their intensity itself was voluptuous, their disappearance causing regret, while others formed the background, blending and harmonizing so completely that it soon became impossible to locate the sensitive spot itself.

His face was buried in his jacket, and this, rolled into a ball, served him as a pillow – his jacket that had been almost new when he arrived. And he had been fool enough, in the early days, to try to keep it in shape by taking it off for the night, so that it did not have now as good a smell as otherwise it might.

The good smell of himself. The good smell of the earth, of the things that live and sweat. He deliberately burrowed his nose into the spot which smelt most strongly – under the arms. He would like to stink, as people outside called it, to stink as the earth stinks, for people outside think that man stinks, that the earth stinks.

He wanted to feel his heart beating, to feel it throughout his body, in his temples, in his wrists, in his toes. To smell the odour of his breath, to feel its warmth. And to mingle images, larger and truer than life – images of things seen, things heard and lived, of other things too that might have happened – to mingle all these, with eyes shut and body inert, yet constantly on the alert for a particular step on the iron staircase.

He had become very good at this game. Why call it a game? It was life. At school they used to say:

'He's awfully good at maths.'

Not Frank, but another boy with a big head.

Frank now was awfully good at life. He knew how to crush himself down on to the planks, bury his face in his jacket, shut his eyes, sink deep, heave ballast overboard, dive and surface at will – or almost. Somewhere days existed, days, hours and minutes. Not here, not for him. He had reached the stage where, when he wanted to reckon, he reckoned in 'dives'.

That seemed mad, but he had not gone mad. He had not lost his footing, and he was more determined than ever not to let himself go. On the contrary, he had made progress. After all, what would be the use of bothering about hours, as they were current outside, in a building where nothing was timed by them?

If a cake was cut in quarters, and you were greedy, you ought to bother about the quarters. But suppose it were cut into slivers, or tiny cubes?

Everything had to be learnt, how to sleep to begin with. To think that men imagined they knew how to sleep! Because they had too many hours to devote to sleep if they chose. There were some who dared to complain of being the slaves of their alarm clocks, when they themselves set the alarm on going to bed, and would even rouse themselves, when they were just dropping off, to make sure that the little knob was properly pulled out.

To be waked by an alarm clock one had set oneself? To be waked by oneself, in fact! And they called that slavery!

Let them learn, first, to sleep on their stomachs; to sleep anywhere, on the ground, like worms and the insects. And, failing the smell of the earth, let them learn to be content with their own.

Lotte sprayed perfume under her arms, and probably between her thighs, and insisted on her lodgers doing the same.

It was inconceivable.

To sleep flat on one's stomach, to measure out, to watch for, to orchestrate one's aches and cramps, to run one's tongue through the gap left by the two missing teeth, and to tell oneself that, if all went well, if the day was propitious, one would see the window open far away there beyond the courtyards – to sleep thus, think thus, brought one very near to truth. It was not yet the whole truth, he knew. None the less it was a comfort to know that he was on the right way.

That signal, it was for the prisoners in the next classroom to go out to play. How else could he put it? Their step was full of joy. They couldn't help it: even those who were to be shot the next day stepped joyously, perhaps because they did not yet know.

They went by. Good. The problem was to know whether the

old gentleman had enough work or not. The old gentleman was much more important than anyone else in the world. He was surely a bachelor. If not, his wife had remained in her own country, which amounted to the same thing. But even when he was busy, he was a man to raise his head all of a sudden and give the order:

'Bring me Frank Friedmaier.'

It was fortunate that he seldom did at this time of day. It was especially fortunate that he did not know, that no one knew, and that was one of the reasons why Frank had taken to sleeping on his stomach. If they knew what he was watching for, if they suspected what joy it brought him, no doubt the school's time-tables would have been turned upside down.

Winter was over. No! It was, of course, still the middle of winter. The hardest frosts were not past, but still to come. They generally came in February or March, and the later they came the fiercer they were; they could last to the middle, even to the end of April.

Put it that the darkest part of the tunnel had been passed. That year, as every now and then did happen at the end of January, there came a false spring. At least, outside, they called it a false spring. The air and the sky were clean and clear. The snow glistened without melting, yet it was not cold. Each morning the water was frozen, but all day long the sun shone so brightly that you would have sworn the birds were about to build their nests. The birds, indeed, must have been fooled too, for some of them were to be seen flying in pairs, chasing each other if they wanted to mate.

The distant window, beyond the gymnasium or school hall, remained open for a longer time. Once Frank had guessed from the woman's movements that she was busy ironing. And another time, it had been splendid, beyond all hoping. She was no doubt taking advantage of one of these milder days to do some spring-cleaning. The window had remained open *for more than two hours*! Had she put the cradle in another room, or tucked the sleeping baby up more snugly? She had beaten out clothes, including a man's clothes. She shook them, beat them like rugs, and every one of her movements was horribly painful, yet soothing, to Frank.

From such a distance she was no bigger than a doll. He would not know her if he met her in the street. That did not matter, since it would never happen. She was no more than a doll. Her features could not be distinguished. But she was a woman, a woman busy about her own home. And with what enthusiasm she went about her work! He felt it, he knew it!

It was for her that he was on the watch each morning. Logically, he ought just then to have been deep in overpowering sleep. At first, he was afraid of missing her. Yet he had missed her only once, when he really was at the end of his tether. Moreover, that was before he had learnt to orchestrate his sleep.

She did not suspect. She never would suspect anything at all. She was a woman – not rich, poor indeed to judge from the place where she lived. She had a husband and a child. Evidently the man went off to work early, for Frank had never caught a glimpse of him. Did she get his dinner ready for him in a tin box, like the one Holst took with him on his tram? It was possible, indeed probable. Immediately afterwards she would start work, in her home, in their home. Sometimes, no doubt, she would sing, or laugh with the baby. For babies didn't only cry, as his foster-mother had tried to make him believe.

'When you were crying . . .'

'That day you cried so . . .'

'That Sunday when you were so very naughty . . .'

Never once had she said:

'When you laughed . . .'

Then the bed, the bed which smelled of the two of them. She did not know the secret. If she did, she would not hang the bedclothes out of the window to air. She wouldn't even open the window. Lucky for him that she belonged *outside*. In her place, Frank would have shut everything up, guarded everything jealously, allowed nothing of their life to escape.

That morning of the spring-cleaning had seemed so exceptional to Frank that he could hardly believe that fate really had reserved such joys for him. Over there, she was celebrating the false spring after her fashion, airing, cleaning, scouring. She had shaken everything, shifted everything. She was lovely.

He had not really seen her, but that didn't matter: she was lovely!

And somewhere in town there was a man, who went off in the morning confident that in the evening he would find this woman waiting for him, and the child in its cradle, and the bed with their two odours.

It mattered little what the man did or thought. It mattered little that at that distance the woman at the window was no bigger than a marionette. It was Frank who lived their life most intensely. Even though, lying on his belly, he dared peep through one eye only, for if *they* perceived what it was that stirred him so deeply, they would change his hours.

He knew them. Wasn't it Timo who claimed to know them? But Timo knew only fragments of the truth, or rather, ready-made truths, such as one reads in the newspapers.

When he was small, his foster-mother Frau Porse used to make him furious by saying:

'You've been fighting with Hans again *because* . . .'

And her *because* was always wrong . . . *Because* Hans was the son of a big farmer. *Because* he was rich . . . *Because* he was the stronger . . . *Because* . . . *Because* . . .

All his life he had seen people being wrong with their *becauses*. Lotte first of all! Lotte who had understood less than anyone.

There was no *because* . . . It was a word for fools. For the people outside, at any rate. With their *becauses*, it would not be astonishing if one day he were awarded a medal he had not deserved, or honoured with a posthumous decoration.

Because what?

Why had he not answered the officer who puffed his cigar smoke into Frank's face when he was being interrogated at headquarters, high up on the top floor? He was no more of a hero than anyone else.

'You had better know, Friedmaier.'

This affair of the notes marked with little holes was no concern of his. He had only to answer:

'Ask the general!'

It was so utterly stupid! A simple matter of some watches. As Frank did not know the general personally, he would have been obliged to add:

'I handed over the watches to Kromer, and it was Kromer who gave me my share of the notes.'

Frank had no pity for Kromer. Even less desire to risk his life for him. On the contrary. For some time now, Kromer had been one of the few men he would sooner see dead, if not the only one.

Well, then, what exactly *had* happened up there in the office?

The officer was facing him, still very much the good fellow, with his light coloured cigar and his pink complexion. Frank had never seen the general. He had no reason whatever to sacrifice himself for his sake. Wasn't it much simpler to say:

'I'll tell you exactly how things happened, and then you'll admit that I have nothing to do with the notes.'

Why had he not done so? No one would ever know. Not even Frank himself. He had discovered explanations two, five, ten days later – all different, and all valid.

The true, the only explanation was that he did not want to be set free, to be returned to the life of everybody.

Now he knew. In reality, whether he talked or not mattered not at all. At least so far as concerned the ultimate result. He would have found nothing to answer to anyone who might try to explain his attitude by saying:

'You knew very well that you were in for it anyway!'

It was obvious. Not that he knew, but that it *had* to be. Only that was a truth he had not admitted until afterwards.

Really he had held out for the sake of holding out. Almost physically. Perhaps, if the question were probed deep enough, it would turn out to be his way of answering back to the officer's offensive familiarity. Frank's reply to him had been:

'I am sorry.'

'You're sorry for what you've done, is that it?'

'I am sorry. Just that.'

'What are you sorry for?'

'I am sorry, for you, that I have nothing to say.'

And he knew. He was aware of everything, of the torture he might expect, of his death, of everything. It was as though he did it deliberately.

He didn't remember very well. It was still blurred. He was ranged like a young fighting cock, facing this extraordinary power planted opposite him, and he behaved like a small boy who wants to be smacked.

'You're sorry, are you, Friedmaier?'

'Yes.'

He looked the officer straight in the eyes. Had he some vague hope of being rescued by the other officer, working away there under the lamp with his back turned? Was he counting on the typists passing along the corridors? Was he still saying to himself:

'That sort of thing *can't* happen here.'

He had kept his end up, anyway. He did not even want to let his eyes blink. He kept repeating:

'I'm sorry.'

He swore to himself not to utter the word 'general' – even under torture – or the name of that cad Kromer. No names! Nothing!

'I'm sorry.'

'Really, you're sorry! Tell me just what you're sorry for, Friedmaier. Think carefully before you answer.'

His next answer was stupid, but he redeemed it later.

'I don't know.'

'You're sorry you didn't know in time that we make little holes in bank-notes, aren't you?'

'I don't know.'

'You're sorry you showed this money to anyone and everyone?'

'I don't know.'

'And now you're sorry you know too much about it. There you are! You're sorry you know too much about it, Friedmaier.'

'I . . .'

'Very soon you'll be sorry you didn't talk.'

All this had taken place in a kind of fog. Neither of them was concerned now with the meaning of the words. They hurled them at random, like stones picked up without looking at the ground.

'You remember now, I'll wager. You're going to remember.'

'No.'

'Yes. I'm sure you remember.'

'No.'

'Yes you do! A great heap of notes like that!'

At one moment he appeared to be joking, and the next his expression became positively savage.

'You do remember, Friedmaier.'

'No.'

'At your age, one always remembers in the end.'

The cigar! Frank remembered particularly that cigar approaching and receding from his face, that other face turning crimson, coming out in blotches, then, suddenly, a certain stillness in those china blue eyes. He had never seen eyes like that, particularly so close to.

'Friedmaier, you're a rat.'

'I know.'

'Friedmaier, you're going to talk.'

'No.'

'Friedmaier . . .'

It was odd how grown-ups went on behaving for the whole of their lives in the same way as at school. The officer had really acted just like a senior in the class, or even like a master tussling with a boy in a temper. He had reached his limit. He panted, almost imploring:

'Friedmaier . . .'

Frank had determined once and for all to say 'no'.

'Friedmaier . . .'

There was a ruler on the desk, a heavy brass ruler.

The officer picked it up, repeating, his self-control almost completely gone:

'My dear young Friedmaier, it is really time you understood . . .'

'No!'

Did Frank want to be hit across the face with the ruler?

Possibly. That was what happened. Brutally. Just when he least expected it, when the officer, perhaps, least expected it too, even though he already had the ruler in his hand.

'Friedmaier . . .'

'No.'

He was not a martyr, or a hero. He was nothing at all. He had understood, perhaps four, perhaps five days afterwards. What would have happened if, instead of 'no', he had said 'yes'?

It would have altered nothing for the others, presumably. Kromer was on the run, Frank was almost certain. As for the general, Frank didn't give a damn for him. Besides it was not the testimony of a young squirt like himself that would affect the fate of a general. He would drop out of circulation, or had already done so. It didn't matter, anyway.

What really counted, as Frank had only discovered afterwards, was that his own fate would have been the same whether he talked or not, except for the blow in the face with the ruler.

He knew too much now. Youngsters who knew as much as he did were just not let loose on the streets again. If they were to announce next morning that the general had committed suicide, there must be no one to go around saying:

'It's not true.'

If officers were being talked about, no one could be allowed to assert:

'They're a lot of thieves.'

At the time, up there, he had not thought of that. He had said 'no'. And he was not sure now that it was because he desired to suffer. Certainly there had been the fascination of torture, the prospect of knowing whether he would withstand it or not, as he had so often wondered.

Lotte said readily of him:

'He turns the place upside down if he so much as scratches himself shaving.'

Lotte didn't matter. She was not in question. Nor was anything that had to do with her. There had been only himself at stake when he had said 'no'. Himself alone. Not even Holst. Even less Sissy.

Let no one ever talk about friendship for Kromer, or about what he owed the general. It was for himself, Frank – no, not even for Frank, just for himself – that he had said 'no'.

To see!

The burly officer, as he finally lost his self-possession, had repeated two or three times:

'Do you understand? Do you understand?'

Frank must have worn that stubborn look of his, the one that made Lotte wild with rage. This was his way of taking his revenge for so many things – it was an account he must balance later – anyway, he had egged on the officer wilfully, almost scientifically.

'You'd better . . .'

'No.'

'You'd better, you know.'

'No.'

And then, whack! The ruler full in his face, right across his face. Frank had felt it coming. Right up to the last minute he could have said 'yes', or, at a pinch, he could have ducked. He did not flinch, and there was the sound of bone cracking.

He desired that blow. He feared it, yet he desired it. He felt the shock of it throughout his frame, from head to foot. He shut his eyes. He thought, he hoped, that he would find himself on the floor, but he remained on his feet.

The most difficult of all – the only difficult thing, in fact, that he had done – was not to put his hand up to his face. Yet he felt as though one eye had started from its socket. Like the cat in Frau Porse's garden! Frau Porse's cat made him think of Sissy. After inflicting what he had inflicted on her, did one have the right to flinch on account of an eye?

The blood was pouring everywhere, down his neck, over his chin, and he had not said a word, had not raised his hand to feel his face, but continued to face the officer, his head raised.

Was it then that he had realized that, whatever might happen in the future, he was lost, but that it did not matter? If so, it was only a fleeting impression. The true discovery, it was away in his corner, lying on his belly, that he had patiently made it.

Not that that altered anything.

He had not thought that performances of this kind took place in their offices. He had not been far wrong. The officer, after delivering the blow, looked uncomfortable and said something like:

'Do what you like with him.'

It was a blunder to have struck with the brass ruler Frank knew now. Such a thing ought not to have occurred in that building. Who knows if the officer had not been punished in his turn, or removed?

Sectors and sectors, as Timo said.

The officer by the lamp, a tall thin man still young, sighed as if to indicate that this was not the first time his colleague had given way to impulses of this sort, then he opened a door to which were attached an enamel washbasin and a towel. Bones or cartilages had been cracked, Frank was sure. He did not know which. When he opened his mouth, he spat out two teeth and let out a cascade of blood.

'Take it easy. It's nothing.'

The second officer was obviously embarrassed.

'When it bleeds, it's nothing,' he said, searching for his words as he spoke.

Notwithstanding, he looked none too pleased about the blood pouring out on the floor, while his chief, planting his cap jauntily on his head, left the office. He seemed to be saying:

'He'll never change.'

The eye had not come out of its socket, but to Frank it felt like that. He could have fainted. It would have been easy. And the officer was rather afraid he would. But Frank wanted to remain tough.

'It won't amount to anything. It's nothing much. You got on his nerves.'

'Really?'

'You shouldn't have done it.'

Was the thin one really more important than the other? Was this just an act to make him talk in spite of everything? The thin officer was tall, rather horse-faced, slow and gentle in his movements. What dismayed him was that the blood would not stop flowing, but went on spurting from nose, mouth and cheek.

Finally, exasperated, he gave up and summoned the two civilians who were waiting outside. They glanced at each other, and then one of them went downstairs.

The rest was settled quickly. The man who had gone downstairs reappeared. They wrapped a sort of coarse, dark scarf round Frank's face. Between them, each holding one arm, they led him to the courtyard, where the car, which they had left outside, had now come to await them.

Were these gentlemen angry with one another? Was there a genuine rivalry between the two sets? The car moved off. Frank felt quite all right, only he had the sensation that his head was quietly emptying itself. It was not a disagreeable feeling. He remembered that he ought to try to spot the block of flats of which he knew only one window, but at the last moment he had not the strength to open his eyes.

He was still bleeding. It was disgusting. There was blood everywhere. He scarcely had time to see the old gentleman, who gave his orders in a few words. The old gentleman was not pleased either.

That was how Frank came to know the sick-bay, just under the iron staircase, which he had never noticed before. It was a classroom too, but a certain amount of fitting up had been done, and some varnished furniture and quantities of medical gear had been installed.

Was the man who attended to him a doctor? Anyway he had looked at the wound with contempt, like the old gentleman in spectacles. Not contempt for the wound, but for the man who had inflicted it. He seemed to be thinking:

'He's done it again.'

And 'he' was not Frank, but the officer.

He was tended. A third tooth, already loose, was fetched out. Now he had three teeth missing, two right in front of the mouth, and one fairly far back. Now and then, in his sleep, he still felt rather agreeable twinges.

He had not been taken back there. Was that because of the

way the officer had gone about the business? Surely not. Frank remembered the blows he had heard in this very place the morning he arrived.

These were matters of tactics. On many points, on the whole, Timo was right. Timo didn't know everything, but he bad a general idea which was near enough.

Here, Frank had been looked after. He had been taken down to the sick-bay several times. That was the most trying feature, for it nearly always happened at the time when the window was open.

Perhaps that was why he had got better so quickly?

He had pondered over things. The day after he came back from town, he deliberately refrained from marking the day with a line scratched on the plaster of the wall. And again for five or six days running. Then he tried to rub out all the marks he had made earlier.

From now on those marks troubled him. They were the witnesses of a period that was over and done with. He had known nothing yet at that time. He had thought then that life was outside, thought of the moment when he would return to it.

How odd it was just when he was painstakingly scratching a mark on the plaster each day that he was filled with despair.

Now, no longer. He had learnt to sleep. He had learnt to flatten himself on his stomach against the planks of his bed and to inhale his own smell from the sleeves of his jacket.

He had learnt too, and above all, that one must hold on as long as possible, and that that depended entirely on himself. He was holding on. He was holding on so well, he was so proud of it, that, if he could communicate with the outside world, he would write a treatise on the way to hold on.

First of all, one had to fashion one's own private corner, and bury oneself deep in it. Did that mean anything to the people going about the streets?

His worst fear, for ten days at least, was of being summoned downstairs to be confronted with Lotte. She had told him of further visits she hoped to pay him. Evidently they had refused her a permit, so as to prevent her from seeing Frank in his present state. Were they waiting till his face had returned more or less to normal.

He preferred it that way. Lotte had come, or at any rate she had been to one of their offices. She was being very active, as witness the two parcels he had received from her containing, as on the first occasion, sausage, bacon, chocolate, soap and clean linen.

What else did he hope to find in the parcels, that he had searched them as he had done? Every evening in the room above the gymnasium roof a blind was lowered and a light went on, leaving only a golden rectangle.

Was the man there when that happened? Was there really a man? Probably, because of the child, but he too might very well be a prisoner, or somewhere beyond the frontier.

If he came home, what did he do, as he came in from outside, so as to take in simultaneously the flat, the room, the peaceful warmth, the baby in its cradle? And the smell of cooking, and his waiting slippers?

Despite everything, Lotte must come. He would do what was necessary to bring it about. He would be well-behaved for a time. He would appear to be giving them some slack.

By now he knew them well. They ended up by finding out everything they wanted to know. Not the men from the big building, where officers smoked cigars and offered you cigarettes before hitting you with a brass ruler like hysterical women. Frank was quite ready to rate *them* minus nothing.

The real ones were those like the old gentleman in spectacles.

With him it was a different kind of struggle. At the finish, whatever happened, whatever the ups and downs of the game, it would be all up with Frank. The old gentleman would win. That could not be prevented. All that Frank could do was to prevent him from winning too quickly. It was possible, with great effort and much self-mastery, to gain time.

The old gentleman struck no blows. Nor did he have Frank struck by others. After two weeks of personal experience, Frank was ready to conclude that, if someone was being struck the day he arrived, it was because that someone had deserved what he got.

The old gentleman struck no blows, and he was not niggardly with his time. He just didn't know what impatience was. He appeared to know nothing of the general or the notes, and never made the slightest reference to them.

Was it really another sector? Were there watertight bulkheads between the sectors? Rivalry perhaps, or more? In any case, the old gentleman had looked at the gash on his face, still looked at it every day, with dismay.

His contempt was directed, not at Frank, but at the cigar-smoking officer. He did not mention him, acted as though unaware of his existence. He never uttered a word irrelevant to his course of interrogation, which, disconnected though it might appear, and devious though it might be, was following a terribly direct route.

Here Frank was not offered cigarettes. He was not called Friedmaier and he was not patted on the shoulder. No one bothered to put on an air of cordiality.

It was another world. At school Frank had never understood anything of mathematics. The very word had always seemed to him charged with mystery.

Well, here they did mathematics. It was a world without boundaries, bathed in a cold light, in which the things that moved were not men, but entities, names, numbers, signs, changing places and value each day.

The word mathematics was not quite right. What was the name of the space where the stars revolved? He could not find the word. There were times when he was so tired. And then, such precision did not matter anyway. What did matter was that they should understand, that he should understand himself.

For quite a time Kromer had played the role of a star of the first magnitude. What Frank called 'quite a time' was, say, the time taken up by two interrogations. And these were not in the least like the one with the officer, either in rhythm or in duration.

However, Kromer was now practically forgotten. He was

wandering up among the nameless stars, when now and again he would be drawn – fished – back with a careless gesture for a question or two before being thrown back.

The one lot and the other each had their separate logic. There was the officer's logic – he was thinking only about the notes, and probably about the general; and there was the old gentleman's – who, you would swear, didn't give a damn about them, if indeed he knew anything about it.

But the end-result would inevitably be the same. A man who knew what Frank knew could not be set free.

So far as the officer was concerned, indeed, Frank was already dead.

He had hit him in the face, and Frank had not talked.

Dead!

Only, along came the old gentleman, who sniffed and decided: 'Not so dead as all that.'

Because even a dead man, or one three parts dead, could still be turned to account. And the old gentleman's job was turning people to account.

The banknotes and the general mattered little, provided there was *something*.

And there must inevitably be something, since Frank was there.

It need not be Frank, it might be anyone, but there would always be something.

What mattered, if he was to cope with the old gentleman, was to sleep. The old gentleman did not sleep. He had no need of sleep. If he dozed, he must be able to set himself like an alarm clock, and find himself, at the predetermined hour, as active, as cold, as lucid as ever.

He was a fish, a man with a fish's blood. Fishes were cold-blooded. Certainly *he* did not inhale the sweaty smell of his armpits, or watch for a doll-sized silhouette at a far-off window.

The old man would win. The game was already played. He had all the trumps in his hand, and he could allow himself to cheat into the bargain. For Frank it had long since ceased to be a question of winning.

Would he still want to win if that were possible?

It was not certain. It was improbable. It was holding on that mattered, holding on for a long time, seeing the window each morning, the woman leaning out, the napkins drying in the sun on a line stretched over empty air.

What really mattered was, each day, to gain another day.

That was the reason why it would be ridiculous to scratch strokes on the plaster of the walls – strokes which had lost all meaning.

The point was not to give in – not on principle, nor to save anyone, nor on a question of honour – but simply because one day, before he had known why, he had determined not to surrender.

Did the old gentleman sleep with one eye open, like himself?

A fish's eye, then, perfectly round, lidless, unwinking – whereas it was deliberately, voluptuously, that Frank let his belly sink into the earth as into a woman.

2

He bore them no grudge. It was their job to try by every possible means to wear down his resistance. They thought they had him in the matter of sleep. They never let him sleep several hours at a stretch, and they had not guessed – they must never be allowed to guess – that it was they, yes, they, who had really taught him how to sleep.

Since the window opposite was shut, he knew it would not be long before he was sent for. It never happened at the same time two days running. Another of their little tricks. Otherwise, things would become too easy. For the afternoon sessions, and especially those at night, there were often wide differences of timing. When the interview was in the morning, their choice was more limited. The prisoners next door had come in from their exercise. They must loathe him, regard him as a traitor. Not only did he refuse to listen to their messages or answer them: he refused to be a link in the chain. There was another thing that he had understood. Even if the messages were not understood, they were transmitted from one classroom to another, from wall to wall, for there was still a chance that they might reach someone to whom they would be precious.

It was not his fault. He hadn't the time. Nor had he the wish. All that sort of thing seemed childish to him. These folk were preoccupied with outside, with their lives, with trifling things. They were wrong to blame him. He felt sure that he was playing for much higher stakes than they were, and the game was one he simply must win. It would be terrible to go without having won it to the last point.

He was asleep. He had gone to sleep as soon as the window had been closed. He sank as deep as he could into sleep, in order to recuperate. He heard footsteps in the neighbouring classroom, lamentations in the room to his left, where someone – an old man no doubt, or else a very young one – was spending his time groaning.

As always, or nearly always, they would come for him before the soup was brought round. Frank still had a bit of bacon left and the end of a sausage. He wondered why the two parcels had been delivered to him, seeing that without them he would have been much weaker by now.

Frank was not far from crediting the old gentleman with a certain honesty in the methods he adopted, a kind of sportsman-ship. Or was it only the challenge of difficulty Perhaps because of Frank's age – he must think of him as no more than a kid – and in order not to blush for his victory, he was anxious to give him an extra chance.

In the matter of the soup, anyway, they played their little trick again today. What day it was didn't matter, since he no longer reckoned in days or weeks. He had other things to go by. He reckoned according to the main subject of the interrogations, so far as you could call anything the main subject when you were dealing with a man who enjoyed mixing every-thing up.

It was the day after Bertha, four days after the spring-cleaning in the room with the open window. That was enough.

Besides, he was expecting it. He had perceived a kind of rhythm, like the rise and fall of the tides. One day he would be called very early; another quite late; sometimes barely a few seconds before the soup was brought round, when the clash of the dixies could already be heard on the stairs.

He should not, in the beginning, have eaten it down to the last drop. It was poor stuff. It was nothing but hot water with swedes and occasionally one or two beans. However, there were sometimes bubbles on the surface, as on dish water, and then he might have the luck to find a tiny scrap of greyish meat right at the bottom.

That ought not to interest him, when he was favoured with sausage and bacon. But he liked sitting on the edge of his bed, with his tin can between his knees, feeling the warmth go down his throat and into his stomach.

The old gentleman, who was never to be seen in the courtyard, still less on the landings, must have guessed, for he always had Frank fetched down before his soup.

Frank recognized their steps through his sleep – the man in town shoes and the soldier in boots. They were coming for him. Those two were invariably for *him*. It was as though he were the only prisoner to be questioned. He did not lose a single morsel of sleep. Even now he pretended to snore, in order to gain a few seconds. They had to shake him. It had become a game, but they must never guess.

He had practically given up washing, simply to save time. The whole of the time at his command was devoted to sleep. And what he meant now by sleep was something infinitely more important than the sleep of ordinary people. Otherwise it would not have been worth his while scraping up, as he did, the smallest crumbs of time.

He did not give them a smile. They did not wish each other good morning. Everything went forward without a word, in dull indifference. He took off his overcoat to put on his jacket. Down below it was very warm. The first few days he had been most uncomfortable, having brought his overcoat. It was better to risk catching a chill in the gangway or the staircase. His own warmth did not have time to evaporate in so short a journey.

He had no mirror, but he felt his eyelids were red like those of people who sleep too little. They were hot and prickly. His skin was too taut, too sensitive.

He walked behind the civilian and in front of the soldier and, as he walked, went on sleeping. He was still sleeping as he entered the little building, where he was often kept waiting on the bench in the outer room for a long time – as much as an hour – although there was no one with the old gentleman.

He went on recuperating. It was a matter of habit. There were noises, sometimes voices, and at regular intervals the clatter of the tram outside in the street. Children's shouts filtered through to him, doubtless when they were let out of a near-by school.

The children had a teacher. At school you had masters, and there was always at least one who stood to you in relation of the old gentleman. For most grown-ups there was the boss, the chief at the office or the foreman in the workshop, or the owner.

Everyone had his own old gentleman. Frank, having understood this, bore his no grudge. Next door pages were being turned and papers rustled. Then a civilian would appear in the frame of the doorway and beckon him, just as at the doctor's or the dentist's, and Frank would get up.

Why did two civilians remain in the room? He had pondered this question, and found several plausible solutions, but they did not satisfy him. Sometimes they were the ones who had escorted him into town on the day of the brass ruler; sometimes he recognized the man who had come to arrest him in Grünestrasse, and sometimes there were others, but they were not many: seven or eight in all, who alternated. They did nothing. They did not sit at a desk.

They never took any part, however small, in the interrogation: doubtless they would never have dared. They would just stand, looking indifferent.

Was it to prevent him from running away, or from strangling the old gentleman? Possibly. That was the answer which immediately came to mind. However, there were armed soldiers in the courtyard. One of them could have been put on guard at each door.

Possibly, too, they did not trust one another. Off hand, he did not dismiss the idea, incongruous though it might appear, that these men were there to observe the old gentleman's behaviour and note his words. Who knows? Maybe one of them was more powerful than the old gentleman? Perhaps even *he* did not know which one, in reality did he perhaps tremble at the thought of the reports about him which were transmitted to higher authority?

To look at, they were more like acolytes. They recalled the choirboys who went on each side of the priest during a celebration. They did not sit down. They did not smoke.

But the old gentleman smoked, he smoked incessantly. It was practically the only human thing about him. He smoked cigarette after cigarette. There was an ash-tray on his desk. It was far too small, and Frank was irritated because no one thought to change it for a bigger one. It was a green ash-tray, shaped like a vine leaf. Even when the questioning took place in the morning, it was so full that cigarette ends and ash spilt over on to the desk.

There was a stove in the room, and a coal bucket. It would have helped a lot had they occasionally emptied that ashtray into the coal bucket, if no more than once or twice a day.

Nothing of the sort was done. Perhaps the old gentleman did not want it done? The cigarette butts piled up, and they were dirty. The old gentleman was a dirty smoker, and he never took his cigarette out of his mouth. He dribbled, let his cigarette out several times, lit it again, moistened the paper, chewed the loose strands of tobacco.

His finger-tips were brown. His teeth too. And two little stains, one above and one below his lips, marked the place where he always held his cigarette.

What was most unexpected in a man like him was that he rolled his own. He looked as though he attached no importance to material things. You wondered when he ate, slept, or shaved. Frank could not remember having once seen him freshly shaved. Yet he took the trouble, even in the middle of an interrogation, to fetch a pig's bladder containing tobacco out of his pocket. From a pocket in his waistcoat he would produce the packet of cigarette papers.

He was most particular about it. The ritual took time, and it exasperated Frank because meanwhile all life was as it were suspended. Was it a trick?

The previous night – it was almost morning – the old gentleman had mentioned Bertha to him towards the end of the interrogation. As always when he introduced a fresh name into the circuit, he had done it in the most unexpected fashion. He hadn't used her surname. You might have thought the old gentleman was a regular at the flat, or a man like Hamling for whom Lotte's little doings held no secrets.

'Why did Bertha leave you?'

Frank had learnt how to gain time. Was that not the sole purpose of his being here?

'She didn't leave me. She left my mother.'

'It comes to the same thing.'

'No. I never concerned myself with my mother's affairs.'

'But you used to go to bed with Bertha.'

They knew everything. God knew how many people they must have questioned to get to know as much as they did! God knew what that knowledge represented in hours, in comings and goings!

'Because you did sleep with Bertha, didn't you?'

'Sometimes.'

'Often?'

'I don't know what you would call often.'

'Once, twice, three times a week?'

'It's difficult to say. It all depended.'

'Were you in love with her?'

'No.'

'But you used to go to bed with her?'

'When it suited me.'

'And you used to talk to her?'

'No.'

'You went to bed with her, but you didn't talk to her!'

Sometimes, when he was pressed on a subject like this, Frank was tempted to answer with an obscenity. As one was at school. But you could not talk obscenely to your schoolmaster. Nor to the old gentleman either. *He* did not play at getting roused.

'Let's say that I used the fewest possible words.'

'Such as?'

'I don't know.'

'You never talked to her about what you had been doing during the day?'

'No.'

'Or asked *her* what she had been doing?'

'Even less.'

'You didn't talk to her about the men who went to bed with her?'

'I wasn't jealous.'

That was the tone of the conversation. Only, it had to be remembered that the old gentleman chose his words with care, weighing them before he spoke, which took time. His desk was a monumental American one, with numerous pigeon-holes and drawers. It was full of meaningless-looking scraps of paper, which he fished out from here and there, at a given moment, as he required, glancing over them briefly.

Frank knew those scraps of paper. Here there was no clerk. There was no one to record his answers. The two men, who always stood close to the doors, had neither fountain pen nor pencil. That they didn't know how to write would not have surprised Frank much.

It was the old gentleman who wrote, invariably on scraps of paper, on bits of old envelopes, at the foot of letters or circulars, which he then carefully cut off. His handwriting was tiny, incredibly fine, and must surely be illegible to everyone except himself.

If there was a scrap of paper referring to Bertha in the pigeon-holes, that meant that the big girl had been questioned. Was that the right conclusion to draw? Sometimes, when he came in, Frank would sniff, searching for smells, for traces of someone who had been brought there while he was about.

'Your mother used to receive officers, officials?'

'Possibly.'

'You would often be in the flat while these visits were taking place.'

'I must have been sometimes.'

'You are young – full of curiosity.'

'I'm young, but I'm not specially curious, and in any case I'm not a pervert.'

'You had friends, acquaintances. It is very interesting to know what officers say and do.'

'Not to me.'

'Your friend Bertha . . .'

'She was not my friend.'

'She isn't now, seeing she has left you, you and your mother. I wonder why. I also wonder why on that particular day voices were heard in your flat so loud that some of the tenants were alarmed.'

Which tenants? Who had been questioned? Frank thought of old Herr Wimmer, but did not suspect him.

'It's odd that Bertha, who was almost one of the family according to your mother, should have left you just then.'

Had he purposely let it be understood that Lotte had been questioned? Frank was no longer upset by the hint. He had heard so many others.

'Bertha was a treasure to your Mama.' (He didn't know that Frank had never called his mother that, that a Lotte was not the sort of person to be called 'Mama'.) 'Someone said, I forget who' – he pretended to rummage among his scraps of paper – 'that she was as strong as a horse.'

'As strong as a mule.'

'All right, as a mule. We must talk about her again.'

At the beginning, Frank had thought it was just a matter of random discussion, a form of intimidation. He did not imagine that his conduct could be so important in the old gentleman's eyes as to justify setting in motion a machine as complicated as the one which was evidently now at work.

The extraordinary thing was that from his point of view the old gentleman was right. He knew where he was going. He knew it better than Frank, who was only beginning to discover depths which he had never before suspected.

In this place words were not spoken at random. There was no bluffing. If the old gentleman said: 'We must talk about her again . . .', that meant he would do more than talk about her. Poor fat stupid Bertha!

However, Frank felt no real pity for her, or for anyone. He had rounded that cape. He bore her no malice. He did not despise her. He was without hate. In the end he looked on certain people with the fish eyes of the old gentleman, as through the glass walls of an aquarium.

The subject of Kromer gave Frank the proof that the old gentleman did not use words at random. It was right at the beginning, when Frank had not yet understood. He imagined that, as with the officer with the brass ruler, denial was enough.

'Do you know a certain Fred Kromer?'

'No.'

'You have never met anyone of that name?'

'I don't remember having done so.'

'Yet he was a regular at the same places as you, the same restaurants, the same bars.'

'That's possible.'

'You're sure you've never drunk champagne with him at Timo's?'

A nudge in the ribs.

'There are so many people I sometimes happened to drink with at Timo's – even champagne.'

That was unwise. He realized it at once, but too late. The old man was accumulating his spidery scrawls on the little bits of paper. It did not look dignified in a man of his age and position. Yet not one of these scraps was wasted: there was not one that failed to come in at its appointed hour.

'You don't know him either under his first name of Fred? Certain people, in certain places, go only under their first names. For example, numbers of people who used to meet you almost daily don't know your name is Friedmaier.'

'That's quite a different case.'

'A different case from Kromer's?'

Everything counted. Everything had its bearing. Everything was noted down. He spent two exhausting hours in denying his connexion with Kromer, simply because that was in line with the course of conduct he had set himself. The next day, and on the following days, his friend was no longer touched on. Frank thought Kromer had been forgotten. Then, right in the middle of a night interview, when he was literally swaying on his feet, when his eyes were burning, and he was being deliberately kept standing, he was handed a snapshot in which Frank appeared with Kromer and two women on the bank of a river in high summer. They had taken off their jackets. It looked the typical summer excursion. Kromer, naturally, had his huge hand on the breast of the blonde who was with him.

'You didn't know him?'

'I don't remember his name.'

'Nor the girls' names?'

'As if I could remember the names of all the girls I've gone boating with!'

'One of them – this one, with the brown hair – is called Lilli.'

'I expect you're right.'

'Her father works at the town hall.'

'That's possible.'

'And the man with you is Kromer.'

'So?'

He could not recall the photograph, and had never had a print of it in his hands. What he could remember was that there had been five of them that day – three men and two women – an arrangement which never worked. Fortunately the odd man out had been fully occupied with his photography. It was he too who had done the rowing. Even if Frank wanted to tell the old gentleman the fellow's name, he could not have done so.

This proved how much in earnest their investigations were. God knew where they had dug up this snapshot from! Had they searched Kromer's flat? If the picture had been there, it was odd that Frank should never have seen it. The other chap's house? The photographer's where the film had been developed?

This was precisely the good point about the old gentleman – what encouraged Frank and gave him hope. The officer would doubtless have had him shot at once, just to be rid of him, to avoid further bother. With the old gentleman, he still had time in front of him.

To tell the absolute truth he was convinced – no, it was a matter of faith rather than conviction – that the whole thing depended solely on himself. Like all those who slept little, but had learnt to sleep, he thought mainly in terms of images and sensations.

He would have to cast back to his dream of flying, in which he had only to lay his hands flat, to press on nothing with all his strength and *with all his will*, to rise, slowly at first and then quite easily, until his head touched the ceiling.

He could not talk about it. Were Holst here in person, Frank would not confess his secret hope to him. Not yet. It was exactly as in the dream, and it was wonderful that he had dreamt it several times, for it was a help to him now. Perhaps what he was living through now was a dream too. There were moments when he was so sleepy he could not tell any more. This time again, it depended on himself, on his will power.

If he had the energy, if he did not lose his faith, it would last as long as need be.

There was no question of returning outside. For him there was no question of the hopes that the men in the neighbouring classroom must be cherishing. Such hopes did not interest him, they offended him rather.

They were doing what they could. It was not their fault.

For himself, there was a certain lapse of time to be gained. If he had been asked why it was so important, or indeed to specify it in terms of days, weeks, or months, he could have given no answer. And what if he were asked what must be at the end of it?

Come, it was better to argue with the old gentleman. Everything in its proper time. This was a standing interrogation. He distinguished between sitting interrogations and standing ones. A rather childish ruse, really. The object was always to put him in the state of least resistance. He did not let them see he would rather stand. When they made him sit, it was on a backless stool, and in the long run this posture was even more tiring.

As for the old gentleman, he never got up, never seemed to feel the need to take a few paces round the room to stretch his legs. Never once, even during a questioning that had gone on for five hours, had he gone off to go to the lavatory, or to drink a glass of water. He drank nothing. There was nothing to drink on his desk. He was content to go on smoking his cigarettes, but even so he regularly let each one go out two or three times.

He employed a number of tricks. There was the revolver trick, for instance. He would always leave Frank's gun lying on the desk like something overlooked, as though it were an object without context or importance. He used it as a paper-weight. Since the first day, when Frank had been searched, he had never referred to it. Yet there the weapon was none the less, like a threat.

It was necessary to reason coolly. Frank was not the only one in the old gentleman's sector. Despite the time he devoted to Frank, and that was a great deal, it must be supposed that a man of his importance had other problems to solve, other prisoners to interrogate. Did the revolver remain there while he questioned the others? Wasn't it a matter of stage-setting, different for each one? At certain times was not the revolver replaced by some other object – a knife, a cheque. a letter, or some other piece of evidence?

How could Frank explain that this man was a blessing from Heaven? Others would not understand and would take to hating the old gentleman. Without him Frank would not have, ever-present, the notion of the time still left to him. Without him, without these exhausting interrogations, Frank might never have known the lucidity he now experienced, which held so little resemblance to what he used to call by that name.

But he must keep on his guard, and avoid letting the old gentleman gain too much ground all at once. Otherwise, it might go too fast, and then the end would be reached straight away.

It must not finish yet. Frank had still some things to bring into focus. It was a slow business. It was at one and the same time rapid and slow.

All this prevented him from thinking about the men in the classroom next door who were taken away at dawn to be shot. The most sinister thing, indeed, was the time of day chosen for this. The prisoners, half awake, were haggard, unwashed, unshaven; not so much as a cup of coffee had warmed their bellies, and the cold drove every single one of them to turn up his jacket collar. Why weren't they allowed to put on their overcoats? It was a mystery. It could not be on account of the value of the garments. And the cloth, however thick, would not stop the bullets. Was it perhaps precisely so that it should be sinister?

Would Frank turn up the collar of his jacket? Possibly. He did not think about it. He seldom thought about it. Besides, he was convinced that he would not be shot in the courtyard, near the playground with its heap of desks.

Those others were men who had been tried, who had committed a crime which could be judged and entered in the great ledgers of justice. With a little cheating, if need be.

If Frank had had to be tried, it was more than likely that he would have been sent back to the office of the officer who had wielded the brass ruler.

When everything was over, when the old gentleman was satisfied in his soul and conscience, that he had squeezed everything possible out of him, Frank would be made to disappear without ceremony, though, not knowing the building well enough, he could not yet say where. A bullet would be put into him from behind, on a staircase or in a corridor. There was probably a cellar used for the purpose.

When the moment came, he would not care. He was not afraid. His only fear, his obsession, was that it might hapen too quickly, before the time he would have decided on, before he had finished.

He would be the first, if they liked, to say:

'Go ahead.'

If he had a last wish to frame, a final request, it would be to ask them to get on with their little operation while he was lying flat on his stomach on his bed.

Did not all this prove that the old gentleman was providential? He would surely uncover something new. Every day he made fresh discoveries. It was a matter of being on the alert on all fronts at once – of thinking of Timo as well as the people Frank had met at Taste's, besides the nameless tenants in the block. He mixed up everything on purpose, that old devil in spectacles.

What was his latest discovery? He had taken the time to wipe his glasses with a vast coloured handkerchief which was always hanging out of his trouser pocket. He had played about as usual with his scraps of paper. Anyone looking through the window and not knowing what it was all about would almost have thought he was drawing raffle tickets or playing a game of lotto. He really looked as if he were fishing among them aimlessly. Then he rolled a cigarette with infuriating deliberation. He put out his tongue to lick the gummed paper, hunted for his box of matches.

He could never find his matches, buried as they were under heaps of papers. He did not look at Frank. He rarely did look him in the face, and when he did, it was with utter indifference. Who knows? Perhaps the two others – the choirboys – were there to spy on Frank's reactions, and made their report on them afterwards?

'Do you know Anna Loeb?'

Frank did not move a muscle. He had long given up doing that. He tried to think. It was a name he did not know, but in itself, this signified nothing. More exactly, he knew the name of Loeb, as everybody did – Loeb's brewery, whose beer he had been drinking ever since he had been old enough to drink beer. The name displayed in huge letters on the gable-ends of houses, on the glass panels of cafés and grocery-shops, on calendars, and even on the windows of the trams.

'I know the beer.'

'I'm asking if you know Anna Loeb.'

'No.'

'Yet she was one of the women living at your mother's.'

So it was a matter of someone bearing that name.

'You may be right. I don't know.'

'No doubt this will help you to remember?'

He handed Frank a photograph which he took out of a

drawer. He was a man who always had photographs in reserve. Frank had to restrain himself from exclaiming:

'Anny!'

For it was she, though a rather different Anny from the one he had known – perhaps because she was in town clothes, wearing a summer frock and a large straw hat and with her arm linked in that of someone whom the old gentleman covered with his thumb.

'Do you recognize her?'

'I'm not sure.'

'She lived in the same flat as yourself lately.'

'That's possible.'

'She has stated that she slept with you.'

'That's possible too.'

'How many times?'

'I don't know.'

Had Anny been arrested? With *them*, you never knew. It was to their interest to tell a false story in order to get at the truth. That was part of their job. Frank was never entirely taken in by the bits of paper.

'Why did you bring her to your mother's?'

'Me?'

'Yes, you.'

'But I didn't bring her to my mother's.'

'Then who did?'

'I don't know.'

'Are you trying to imply that she turned up of her own accord?'

'That wouldn't be at all unlikely.'

'In that case, we should have to presume that somebody gave her your address.'

Frank did not yet understand where this was leading, but, scenting a trap, made no answer. There were thus long silences, which made these interrogations last an eternity.

'Your mother's activity was an illicit one on which there is no need to dwell.'

That might also mean that Lotte had been arrested too.

'So it was in your mother's interest that as few people as possible should know what was going on. If Anna Loeb turned up at your mother's, it was because she knew she could find refuge there.'

The word 'refuge' acted as a warning to Frank, who had to struggle simultaneously against sleep and against hazy thoughts which, at the least inattention, took possession of him, and which he put aside with reluctance, for in reality they were now his whole life. He repeated, like a sleepwalker:

'Refuge?'

'Are you claiming that you don't know Anna Loeb's past?'

'I didn't even know her name?'

'What name did she go by?'

It was what he called paying out line. He had to do it.

'Anny.'

'Who sent her to you?'

'Nobody.'

'Your mother took her on without any references?'

'She was a good-looking girl, and she was prepared to make love. My mother asks nothing more.'

'How many times did you go to bed with her?'

'I don't remember.'

'Were you in love?'

'No.'

'Was she?'

'I don't think so.'

'But you slept together?'

Could there be in the old gentleman a touch of the puritan, or the pervert, that made him attach so much importance to such questions? Or again, was he impotent? It had been the same when they were discussing Bertha.

'What did she say to you?'

'She never said anything.'

'How did she spend her time?'

'Reading magazines.'

'Magazines which you used to go and fetch for her?'

'No.'

'How did she get hold of them? Did she go out?'

'No. I don't think she ever went out.'

'Why?'

'I don't know. She only stayed a few days.'

'Was she hiding?'

'It didn't look like it to me.'

'Where did her magazines come from?'

'She must have brought them with her.'

'Who posted her letters?'

'No one, I imagine.'

'She never asked you to post letters for her?'

'No.'

'Or to take a message for her?'

'No.'

This was easy, since it was true.

'She went to bed with the customers?'

'Naturally.'

'Who with?'

'I don't know. I wasn't always there.'

'But when you were there?'

'I wasn't interested.'

'You weren't jealous?'

'Not in the least.'

'All the same, she's very pretty.'

'I'm used to that.'

'Were there any clients who came only for her?'

'That's a question you must ask my mother.'

'She has been asked.'

'And what did she answer?'

Thus almost every day he was forced to live over again some small part of the life of the flat. He spoke of it with a detachment which obviously surprised the old gentleman, the more so because he felt Frank was being quite sincere. 'No one ever rang her up on the telephone?'

'There's only one instrument in the block that works, and that's the janitor's.'

'I know.'

Well, then – what was he trying to find out?

'Have you ever seen this man?'

'No.'

'Or this one?'

'No.'

'This one?'

'No.'

People he didn't know. Why did the old gentleman go to such pains to conceal part of the photographs, to leave only the face visible, and to prevent Frank from seeing the clothes?

Because these were officers, of course! Very senior officers, perhaps?

'Did you know Anna Loeb was wanted?'

'I never heard it spoken of.'

'You didn't know either that her father had been shot?'

It was at least a year since Loeb the brewer had been shot because a whole arsenal had been found concealed in the vats at his brewery.

'I didn't know he was her father. I have never known her family name.'

'Yet it was your place she chose as a hide-out.'

It was really extraordinary. Frank had slept two or three times with the daughter of Loeb the brewer, one of the richest and best known men in the town, and he had never known. Each day, thanks to the old gentleman, he plumbed new depths.

'She left you?'

'I don't recall now. I believe she was still at the flat when I was arrested.'

'You're not sure?'

What should he reply? How much did they know? He had never felt any sympathy with Anny, who seemed so contemptuous – no, not even that, so absent, which was worse – when he made love to her. Now, none of that mattered. Had she been arrested? Had they really deployed a drag-net since he had been in prison?

'I think so. I had been drinking the night before.'

'At Timo's?'

'Maybe. And elsewhere.'

'With Kromer?'

He never forgot anything, the old crocodile!

'With heaps of people.'

'Before taking refuge with you, Anna Loeb had been the mistress of several officers, one after another, and she used to pick them carefully.'

'So!'

'More for the post they held than for their physique or their money.'

Frank did not answer. He was not being asked anything.

'She was in the pay of a foreign power, and she had gone to find shelter at your place.'

'It's not difficult for a tolerable-looking woman to be taken into a brothel.'

'You admit it was a brothel?'

'Call it what you like. There were women who made love with the customers.'

'Including officers?'

'Possibly. I was not on sentry duty at the door.'

'Nor at the fanlight?'

He knew everything! He guessed everything! He must have visited the flat and gone over it with special care.

'Did you know their names?'

'No.'

Could the old gentleman's sector by any chance be working against the other sector, the one where Frank had been struck with the brass ruler? The word 'officer' was recurring with a frequency that fascinated him.

'Would you know them again?'

'No.'

'Sometimes they stayed a long while, didn't they?'

'Long enough to do what they had come there for.'

'Did they talk?'

'I wasn't in the bedroom.'

'They talked,' said the old gentleman emphatically. '*Men always talk.*'

You would have thought he had Lotte's experience. He knew where he was going, with his patience and his attention to detail. He had all the time he wanted. He took, a piece of thread, delicately, and unravelled the skein.

The time for soup had passed. The fluid would be ice-cold in its mess-tin, as Frank found it almost every day.

'When women make men talk, it's in order to tell somebody else what the men have said.'

Frank shrugged his shoulders.

'Anna Loeb made love with you, but you maintain she said nothing to you. She did not go out, and yet she sent messages.'

His head was reeling. He must hold on to the end, until he could reach his bed, reach the planks where he would sprawl at last, eyes shut, ears drumming, listening to the blood flowing in his arteries, feeling his body live, thinking at last of something other than all these idiocies which made him endure, thinking of a window, of four walls, of a room with a bed, a stove – he dared not add the cradle – thinking of a man who left in the morning knowing he would come back, of a woman who stayed behind and who knew that she was not alone, that she never would be, thinking of the sun rising and setting in the same places every day, of a tin box carried under the arm like a treasure, of grey felt boots, of a geranium in bloom, of things so simple that they were unknown, or despised, or even complained about by those who possessed them.

His time was so terribly short!

3

That night, he had been through one of the most gruelling sessions of all. It must have been the middle of the night when he was awakened and he was still in the office when a volley was heard in the courtyard, followed, as usual, by a single fainter shot. He had looked at the windows and seen that it was dawn.

It was one of the few occasions when he almost lost his temper. He really felt that the interview was being dragged out for the sake of dragging it out, that he was being asked just any questions, at random. There had been talk, among others, of Ressl, the editor. Frank had answered that he did not know Ressl, that he had spoken to him only once.

'Who introduced you?'

Kromer again. It would have been much simpler and less wearing to land him in the cart once and for all, the more so because, as far as Frank could judge, Kromer had taken care to go to earth somewhere out of their reach.

There had been talk of people Frank did not know. He had been shown photographs. Either this was done to tire him out, to break his resistance, or else they imagined that he knew much more than he really did.

The air, when he came out of the office, had the smell of dawn, with the tang of the chimneys of the neighbourhood. Had he seen the open window? He couldn't tell. He had seen it, but, faced with the old gentleman, for instance, and in answer to close questioning, he could not have sworn whether or not it had been in a dream. But he must have opened his eyes, he was sure of that.

He couldn't tell, now, really. And here he was being dragged out of bed already. With the civilian in front of him and the soldier behind, he walked, framed in the noise of two pairs of boots. He was still sleeping. There was time. Usually he was kept waiting on the grey-painted bench. This time he was not kept waiting, he was led across the outer room without stopping and straight into the office.

And in the office were Lotte and Minna.

Had he looked at them with annoyance? He didn't realize it. He saw his mother start, open her mouth as if to utter a cry, restrain herself, and then stammer, her voice full of a pity he no longer understood:

'Frank!'

She found she had to blow her nose on one of those lace handkerchiefs which she invariably doused with scent. As for Minna, she had not moved, or said a word. She stood very upright, very pale, with tears running down her cheeks . . .

He had forgotten: it was his missing teeth, his beard, probably too his reddened eyelids, and his now quite shapeless jacket. He had not troubled to change his shirt.

Obviously they were deeply moved. But not Frank. He was almost as icy as the old gentleman. At the very first glance he had noted that his mother was dressed in grey and white. It was an old craze which seized her whenever she wanted to appear distinguished. She had dressed pretty well like that when she came to visit him at school – the real school – and even then she used to wear light-coloured eye-veils, although they had not yet come back into fashion.

She smelt nice and clean. She smelt of scented powder. So she had come from home. If she had been in prison, she could not have turned herself out with such care.

Why had she brought Minna? To look at them, you would have said they were mother and little cousin come to visit the young man. Minna looked very much the cousin in her navy-blue tailor-made and white blouse, and she had scarcely any make-up on. She was thinner.

He looked round for the suitcase, the parcels they had brought. There was none in the room, and he thought he understood: Lotte's embarrassment proved he was right. She did not know how to begin. It was the old gentleman she was looking at, rather than her son; perhaps she meant thus to convey to Frank that she had not come entirely of her own accord.

'They have been good enough to let us see you, Frank. So I asked if I could bring Minna too – she's always talking about you – and this gentleman kindly gave permission.'

It was not true. Frank was ready to swear it was an idea of the old gentleman's. A fortnight ago he had been interested in Bertha. A week ago he had been talking about Anny. Now, with his air of leisurely progress, he had reached Minna. He had not needed to hurry, because he had her ready to hand. Minna was embarrassed, and turned away her head.

All the same, it was mighty clever. For Frank did not believe in chance. The old gentleman had at length realized that, if there was one girl among the many who had passed through the flat – if there was one Frank could feel a little differently about, it was Minna.

In reality Frank did not love her. He had been harsh to her, on purpose. He couldn't exactly remember now what he had done to her. There were plenty of things he had done outside and had erased from his conscious memory. Notwithstanding, he still felt a certain humility towards Minna. He was uncomfortably aware of having behaved shabbily towards her.

All three were standing. It was rather ridiculous. The old gentleman was the first to realize it, and had chairs drawn forward for Lotte and her companion. With a wave of his hand he gave Frank permission to use the stool which featured in seated interrogations.

Then he resumed his air of being engrossed in something else. To look at him, you would have sworn that what was going on had nothing to do with him whatever. He ruffled through some files, found scraps of paper and docketed them.

'I must speak to you, Frank. Don't be frightened.'

Why did she add these last three words? What should he be frightened of?

'I've thought such a lot about things, these last six weeks.'

Six weeks already? Or was it *only* six weeks? The phrase was like a blow. He would have liked to look at her less sternly, but he couldn't. For her part, she did not dare to raise her eyes to his face for fear of bursting into sobs. Was he so dreadful to look at? Because two of his front teeth were missing and he had given up looking after himself?

'You see, Frank, I'm sure that, if you've done something wrong, even something serious, it's because you've let yourself be led astray. You're too young. I know you. I was wrong to let you go about with friends older than yourself.'

She was lying clumsily. Usually, she was a practised liar. When talking about her customers, or about men in general, she would boast of fooling them at will. Was she lying clumsily on purpose, to let him know that she was here under duress?

There was no car in the courtyard. They must have come by tram.

'I've had some advice from responsible people, Frank.'

'Who?'

'Herr Hamling, for one.'

If she mentioned that name, it was because she was permitted to do so.

'I know you don't like him much, but you're wrong there. Later, you'll understand. He's an old friend, perhaps my only friend. He knew me when I was a girl and if I hadn't been such a fool . . .'

Frank's eyes narrowed. An idea he had never had before had flashed into his mind. If, despite Lotte's more than dubious position, the chief inspector visited them so often and on such familiar terms, if he seemed to take her more or less under his protection, and if he seemed to assume the right to speak to

Frank as he had sometimes done, might there not be a very good reason?

Frank was almost as tense as before. For a moment his face again wore the expression of the worst days in Grünestrasse, and Lotte, who had perhaps been on the point of confiding something to him, retreated hastily.

He preferred it so. If by any chance Kurt Hamling were his father, he would give anything not to know.

'He has always taken an interest in us, in you . . .'

Frank cut her short:

'All right.'

'He knows you better than you think. He too is sure you've been led astray but that you won't admit it. As he rightly says, it's a false sense of honour, Frank.'

'I have no honour.'

'These gentlemen are being very patient with you, I know.'

So! What did that mean?

'They've let you receive parcels. Today they allowed me to come with Minna, who is worrying herself sick over you.'

'Is she ill?'

'Who?'

'Minna.'

Why had he interrupted Lotte's train of thought? There she was, not knowing what answer to give and trying to question the old gentleman with her eyes.

'No, no: she's not ill. Where did you get that idea? I had her thoroughly examined last week. A young doctor, who doesn't know anything about these things, wanted to operate, but it isn't necessary, the other doctor said. She's better already.'

He sensed something mysterious, something oppressive. Quite at random, he said:

'Well, now she's got time to rest.'

His mother hesitated. Why? Then, as the old gentleman did not seem inclined to protest, she ventured:

'We've opened the flat again.'

'With women?'

'There are two – new ones – apart from Minna.'

'I thought your friend Hamling had advised you to shut up shop.'

'At the time, yes. He didn't yet know how much harm Anny might have done.'

Now he understood. All of a sudden he understood why they were there. He understood everything. The old gentleman never let any opportunity slip.

'You've been asked to keep the business going?'

'It was explained to me that it would be better from all points of view.'

In other words, the flat in Grünestrasse had become a sort of rat-trap. Who, on behalf of these gentlemen, was peeping through the fanlight and trying to hear what was said?

That was why Lotte was so embarrassed . . .

'In short,' he said carelessly and without even a touch of irony, 'all goes well at the flat.'

'Very well indeed.'

'Is Sissy better?'

'I think so.'

'Haven't you seen her?'

'Well, you know, there's so much to do. I don't know whether it's the weather . . .'

What more could they say to one another? They were worlds apart, on either side of an infinite gulf. Even to that scented handkerchief which, in this room, became so prominent that Lotte, noticing, stuffed it into her bag.

'Listen, Frank.'

'Yes.'

'You're young.'

'You've said that already.'

'I know better than you do that you're not bad. Don't look at me like that. Remember that I've never thought of anything but you, that everything I've done since you were born I did for your sake, and that now I would give the rest of my life to see you happy.'

It was not his fault if, in spite of himself, he was inattentive.

He barely took in the meaning of the words. He was looking at Minna's red handbag. But for its colour, it was exactly like the black one Sissy had had, the famous bag with the key in it which he had waved at arm's length on the waste ground, and which he had finally placed on a hummock of snow. He had never known whether she had come to get it.

'I told them you knew Kromer, because it's true. He was your friend, and I don't want you to deny it any longer. I shall never get it out of my head that he was your evil genius and now he's been clever enough to get out himself and leave you in the lurch.'

Was that, when all was said and done, what she had come to tell him – that Kromer was in safety? Frank was too close to the stove. He was hot. Through the window – it was the first time he had been put in that particular place – he could see the iron gate, the sentry-box, the sentry and a bit of the street. It did not affect him in the least to see the street again, the passing trams.

'It is essential that you tell them the whole truth, everything you know, and they'll take it into consideration. I'm sure – I'm confident of that.'

Never had the old gentleman appeared so remote.

'Tomorrow perhaps I shall be allowed to come and leave a parcel for you. What would you like me to put in it?'

Frank was ashamed for her, for himself, for them all. He was tired. He felt like replying:

'Muck!'

He would have done so, before. Since then, he had learnt patience. He muttered:

'Whatever you like.'

'It's not fair that you should pay for the others, do you understand? I too have done a lot of harm, without wanting to. I realize that now.'

And she was paying by letting her brothel be used as a lechers' trap! The most astonishing thing was that four or five months ago it would have seemed perfectly natural to Frank. But even now he did not become indignant. He was thinking of something else. He had been thinking of something else throughout the visit, never realizing that his eyes were glued to Minna's handbag.

'Tell them frankly what you know. Don't try to be clever with them. You'll get out of here, you'll see. I'll take good care of you, and . . .'

He did not hear any more. It was all very far away. Of course, he was always sleepy, and at certain times of day, especially in the morning, he had dizzy spells. He was so tired.

She rose. She smelt nice. She was a pastel of rustling clothes, with a bit of fur round her neck.

'Promise me, Frank. Promise your mother. Minna, you ask him, too . . .'

Minna, who dared not look at him, articulated with an effort: 'I'm very unhappy, Frank.'

And Lotte:

'You still haven't told me what you'd like me to bring you.'

Then, he said it. He was the first to be astonished. He had thought that it would happen much later, at the very end. Suddenly, he felt too weary. He spoke without thinking, without realizing that he had taken a decision.

He said, almost inaudibly, conscious of what the words meant for him, but for him alone:

'Could I see Holst?'

There was something stupefying in what happened then. It was not his mother who replied. Besides, she couldn't have understood, she must be quite out of her depth. As for Minna, she choked back a kind of sob which might have passed for a hiccup. Minna knew far more than Lotte about this.

It was the old gentleman who raised his head, who looked at him, who asked:

'Do you mean Gerhard Holst?'

'Yes.'

'That's odd.'

He rummaged among his scraps of paper, finally fished out one which he scrutinized carefully, and all this time Frank scarcely breathed.

'He has just submitted an application for a visit.'

'A visit to me?'

'Yes.'

Surely he was not going to jump for joy, or dance round the room in front of them all! But his face was none the less transfigured. Now he was the one who, like Minna, had tears in his eyes. Yet he still dared not believe it. It would be too much. It would mean he was not mistaken. It would mean . . .

'He has asked to see me?'

'Wait . . . No . . .'

His blood froze. The old gentleman must certainly be a sadist.

'It's not exactly that. A certain Gerhard Holst has applied to the higher authorities for a visit. He applied very high indeed. But not for himself.'

Quick! My God! And Lotte who was listening as she would to the radio!

'It is for his daughter.'

No! No! No! He must not weep. He must do anything, but he must not weep. Otherwise, he might bungle everything. It was not true! It was impossible! The old gentleman would pick up another bit of paper and discover that there was a mistake.

'You see, Frank,' said Lotte, in a blissfully tremulous voice, as though she had just heard a sentimental record played over the radio, 'you see that everybody believes in you. I told you that you must get out of here and, for that, must listen to these gentlemen.'

Fool! Idiot! He couldn't even feel vexed at her, and it was better she should never know how wide was the gulf between them.

It was Lotte again who asked, with the pious look of a devout old lady addressing a bishop:

'Have you given permission, sir?'

'Not yet. The application has only just been referred to me by another office. I have not had time to examine it.'

'You would be making her so very happy, I think! She lives just across the landing from us. They've known each other for years.'

That was not true. If she would only be quiet. Or rather, what did it matter what she said? Even if it were to miscarry now, even if Sissy were not to come, there would still remain the fact that Holst had put in the application.

They had understood each other. Frank was right. Let Holst come and it would be the same, not quite, but it would have the same meaning.

Oh God, let them finish! Let them do him the favour of not questioning him any more that morning, of allowing him to go back home upstairs. Funny! He had thought simply: 'home'. To throw himself down on his bed, with this truth to hug to him while it was still warm, this truth which must not be allowed to evaporate.

'She's a well brought up girl, a real young lady, believe me.'

How could one be vexed with someone so stupid, even if it was one's mother? And the other, with her bogus cousinly air, who took advantage of their having stood up to get close to him and touch him furtively!

'I thought,' interrupted the old gentleman, 'that you were asking just now to see Gerhard Holst?'

'Him or her.'

'You have no preference?'

Frank could only hope he wasn't making a blunder.

'No.'

A glance through the spectacles was enough to tell the choirboys that it was time to take him away. He didn't know how he got out of the office. His mother and Minna stayed on. What more would Lotte have to say about Sissy?

He reached his room almost at the same time as his soup-tin. It was still warm, and he was content to hold it between his knees, without eating, just to let its warmth penetrate his body. The window was shut up there, beyond the gymnasium. It did not matter. From now on he could manage without it if he had to. His throat was tight. He wanted to talk. He wanted to talk to Holst as though Holst were present.

First of all, there was a vital question to ask him.

'How did you come to understand?'

It seemed impossible. It was miraculous that such a thing should be possible. Frank had done everything so that no one should understand. Besides, he had not understood himself. He had simply prowled round Holst and, at times, he had forced himself to believe that he loathed him, or despised him; he had laughed at the tin box and the ill-fitting boots.

When had it happened?

Was it that night when Holst, on his way home from the depot, had found him hugging the tannery wall with an open knife in his hand?

He must stop. It was too much for him. He must remain calm, remain seated quietly on the edge of his bed. He would not even lie down, because then it would be worse. He couldn't really begin to howl, could he, looking at the window?

He would not go mad. This wasn't the proper time. Little by little he would recover his self-control. If it had happened, it meant that the end had almost come.

He had always understood that. That was one of those certainties you didn't try to explain. In any case he would not have the strength to hold on much longer.

Holst had understood!

And Sissy?

Had she too always known that this was how it would turn out? Frank had known. Holst had known. It was a terrible thing to say. It sounded like blasphemy. But it was the truth.

Holst ought to have come and killed him that Sunday night, or next morning, and he had not done so.

And thus it had to come to pass. Frank could not do anything else. He didn't yet know why, but he felt it.

If he had not been frightened of torture, of the officer with his ruler, or of the old gentleman and his acolytes, it was because no one could ever cause him such suffering as he had caused himself when he had pushed Kromer into the bedroom.

Would the old gentleman say 'yes'?

Most certainly he must be given an inducement, to make him think that allowing the visit would serve some purpose. Frank was impatient to be fetched. He would make no promise – that would be too clumsy – but he would hint at being much more talkative *afterwards*. If only they would come for him quickly!

He would pay out some line. This very day he was going to pay out line – a good stretch. On any subject they chose. About Kromer, for instance, since that didn't matter now that he was safe.

In reality he had reached the point of wondering which he would rather do – talk to Holst or to Sissy. To Sissy he had nothing to say. He needed simply to look at her. And to have her look at him.

'Tell me, Herr Holst . . .'

'*How did you find out, Herr Holst, that man, whatever he may be . . .*'

Words failed. There was none to express what he would like to say.

'*You can drive a tram, can't you, or do whatever it may be. You can wear boots that draw a stare from the street urchins and a shrug from the spivs. You can . . . you can . . . I understand what you're going to say . . . It isn't that which counts . . . It is enough to accomplish what one has to accomplish, because everything matters equally . . . But I, Herr Holst, how could I have?*'

It was not possible that Holst should have asked for a visitor's permit for Sissy. Frank began to weaken, to question his own belief, to doubt. Perhaps it was some machination on the part of the old gentleman. Then, then, if such was the case, how bitter the hatred with which Frank would hound him to the pit of hell!

And that Holst, who avoided all contact with the occupiers, who had no doubt suffered at their hands, should have applied, in the old gentleman's words, to very high authority indeed! To do that, he had been forced to go through intermediaries, to compromise himself, to humiliate himself in front of others.

Still Frank was not fetched. It took so long. He could not sleep. He did not want to sleep. He would like to get done with this, at once.

Yet he had lain down, without realizing it. He couldn't

remember whether he had put the tin of soup on the floor. If he knocked it over, it would smell foul all night. That had happened once. He wanted to cry. He would not tell Holst that he had cried. Or anybody. No one saw him. He stretched out an arm, as though there was somebody beside him, as though it were still possible that one day somebody would be beside him.

That might have been, but everything would have had to be different.

He refused to accept that Kurt Hamling was his father.

Why did he think of that?

He thought of nothing. He cried, like a baby. He was sleepy. At such times his foster-mother used to put a feeding-bottle between his lips, and he would snuffle two or three times, start sucking and settle down quietly.

It would not be so much longer. And it wasn't time that mattered. How old was the woman at the window? Twenty-two? Twenty-five? Where would she be in ten years, in five? Perhaps her companion would be dead. Perhaps he was dead already. Perhaps she herself carried in her body the seed of some disease which was destined to carry her off.

What would Holst say to him? How would he behave?

Sissy would be silent, he was sure. Or else she would simply say:

'Frank!'

The old gentleman would be there. That didn't matter. Frank was hot. Was he feverish? If only he didn't fall ill, just at this moment. The old gentleman wore spectacles, was dressed in black from head to foot. Why, when he usually wore grey? Frank was a Catholic. He had had Protestant friends and he had sometimes attended their services. He had seen their pastors.

He must be careful: the American desk was changing its shape and turning into a kind of altar. It was ridiculous of Lotte to dress as she did. She got herself up like that whenever she thought it necessary to appear distinguished. And then she overdid the grey and white. He remembered vaguely the photograph of a queen who used to dress like that, in an even softer, more ethereal style. But she was a queen. Lotte kept a brothel, and she was ethereal too. As for poor Minna, she looked as if she had stepped straight out of a convent. She was Cousin Minna.

Why was she crying? Lotte dropped the handkerchief she had crumpled into a ball, and it was Holst who stooped to pick it up and hand it to her at arm's length. He said nothing, because it was not the moment to speak. The old gentleman was reading from his scraps of paper and in danger of getting into a muddle. It was a very complicated prayer and of the utmost importance.

Sissy was looking into Frank's eyes, with such intensity that his own eyes ached.

There was no revolver now, but a key. A key was to be given them instead of a ring. The idea was not so stupid. Frank had never heard of that being done, but it was very apt. Who was to be given the key? It was clearly the key to a room with a window and a blind. It was dark already. The blind would have to be pulled down, and the lamp lit.

He looked. His eyes were open. The naked bulb in his classroom had just been switched on. The civilian was standing by his bed and the soldier was waiting at the door.

'I'm coming . . .' Frank stammered. 'I assure you, I'm coming . . .'

He did not move. He had to make a violent effort. His legs were stiff and his back hurt. The man was waiting. The courtyard was dark. The searchlight swept it like a lighthouse on the sea-shore. Frank had never seen the sea. He would never see it. He knew it only from the cinema, and there there were always lighthouses.

He had been to the cinema with Sissy, twice. Twice!

He put on his jacket. He had the feeling of having forgotten something. Oh yes – he must behave very nicely to the old gentleman, so as to put him in good heart.

The little office. The purring stove. It was much too warm. On purpose too, perhaps. He was left standing, it was a standing interview, whereas today, he didn't know why, it would have been a comfort to sit down.

'Suppose you started talking about Kromer?'

He never missed a trick, did he? He well knew that this was the right moment!

'I'm willing.'

He would sooner have talked about the revolver, which he saw lying on the desk. He would then have done with its threat, which was doubtless being reserved for the very end.

'Why did he give you the money?'

'Because I procured some goods for him.'

'What kind of goods?'

'Watches.'

'He was in the watch business?'

Frank wanted to implore:

'Won't you give the authorization?'

All through the interrogation he kept choking back that question.

'Someone had asked him for some watches.'

'Who?'

'I believe it was an officer.'

'You believe?'

'He told me it was.'

'What officer?'

'I don't know his name. A senior officer, who collects watches.'

'Where did you meet him?'

'I never saw him.'

'How did he pay you?'

'He paid Kromer, and Kromer handed over my share.'

'How much was that?'

'Half.'

'Where did you buy the watches?'

'I didn't buy them.'

'You stole them?'

'I took them.'

'Where?'

'From a watchmaker's I used to know. He's dead now.'

'Was it you who killed him?'

'No. He died a year ago.'

This was going too fast, much too fast. Normally there would

have been matter enough for three or four interviews, but Frank
was seized with giddiness. It was as though he were now the one
who forced the pace, so as to reach the end faster.

'Who had possession of the watches?'

The old gentleman referred to one of his scraps of paper. They
knew. Frank could have sworn they had known the whole story
from the very beginning. Then why this farce? What more did
they want to learn? What were they hoping for? Because, after
all, it was their own time they were wasting far more than his.

'They were hidden at his sister's. I went there. I took the
watches and I left.'

'Is that all?'

Sullenly, like a kid caught in the act, Frank blurted out:

'I went back to kill her.'

'Why?'

'Because she had recognized me.'

'Who were you with?'

'I was alone.'

'Where did this take place?

'In the country.'

'Far out of town?'

'Seven or eight miles.'

'You went there on foot?'

'Yes.'

'No!'

'You're right; no.'

'How did you go there?'

'By bicycle.'

'You haven't got a bicycle.'

'I borrowed one.'

'Who from?'

'I hired it.'

'Where?'

'I don't remember. At an upper town garage.'

'Would you recognize the garage if you were taken to the
upper town?'

'I don't know.'

'And if you were shown the truck you used, would you recognize it?'

So they knew that too. It was depressing.

'You will see it tomorrow morning in the courtyard.'

He did not answer. He was thirsty. His shirt was soaked under his arms, and his temples were beginning to throb.

'How did you get to know Karl Adler?'

'I don't know him.'

'Yet he was driving the truck.'

'It was dark.'

'What do you know about him?'

'Nothing.'

'You must surely know that he was in radio?'

'I didn't know.'

'There was a transmitting set in the truck.'

'I didn't see it. It was dark. I didn't look in the back.'

'Who was in the back?'

'I don't know.'

'There was somebody?'

'Yes.'

'Then you must have been introduced. Who by?'

'Kromer.'

'Where?'

'In a bar opposite the cinema.'

'Who was he with?'

'He was alone.'

'By what name did he introduce his associates?'

'No name.'

'Would you recognize the man who was in the back?'

'I think not.'

'Describe him.'

'He was fairly stout with a moustache.'

That was a lie. But it was time gained.

'Go on.'

'He was wearing a mechanic's overalls.'

'In the bar?'

'Yes.'

They didn't know the chap. Frank could feel that. So there was no risk.

'Wait. I think he had a scar.'

'Where?'

Frank thought of the brass ruler. He improvised.

'Across one cheek. . . . The left . . . Yes, that was it . . .'

'You're lying, aren't you?'

'No.'

'I should be very sorry if you were lying, because that would prevent me without further consideration from issuing the permit I've been asked for.'

'I swear I don't know him.'

'What about the scar?'

'I don't know.'

'The description?'

'I don't know either. No doubt I should recognize him if I saw him, but I can't describe him.'

'The bar?'

'That's true.'

'Karl Adler?'

'I only wonder why his name has stuck in my mind. I saw him again twice in the street. He didn't recognize me. Or else he pretended not to.'

'The transmitting set?'

'They didn't mention it to me.'

Would he get his permit? In agony he scanned the face of the old gentleman, who was doubtless finding a quiet pleasure in appearing more inscrutable than ever. He rolled a cigarette. Then he spoke, slowly and softly:

'Karl Adler was shot yesterday by another service. He did not talk. It is necessary that we find his accomplices.'

Then, suddenly, Frank flushed crimson. Was he going to be offered a deal like the one Lotte had accepted?

He knew nothing at all, that was true. They must have begun to convince themselves of that. But he might find out. They could use him to find out.

He could hardly breathe. He did not know where to look. He

was ashamed yet once more. What would he do if the question were put bluntly to him, take it or leave it? What would Holst do?

He shut his eyes, steeled himself. It would have been too much. He mustn't count on it any more. It never would happen. He was not crying. This was not a time when he would start crying.

He waited. No doubt the old gentleman was fiddling with his scraps of paper. Why was he silent? There was nothing to be heard except the purring of the stove. Time passed. Then Frank ventured to open his eyes and saw the acolyte standing beside him, ready to take him back. The soldier was already at the door.

It was over. Perhaps for a little while, perhaps until tomorrow?

Nothing was said as he left. Here there were no greetings, no good-byes. It was probably one of the customs of the building, and it left a feeling of emptiness.

It was very cold outside, much colder than the past few days. The sky was clear and bright as a blade of steel, and the roof-ridges stood out more sharply than usual.

Tomorrow morning there would be frost flowers on the window panes.

4

It was odd. Frank had spent the greater part of his life – so much the greater part – in hating fate with an almost personal hatred, to the point of seeking it out in order to challenge it and come to grips with it.

And now, suddenly, when he had stopped thinking of it, fate was making him a present.

There was no other possible way of putting it. One could, of course, suppose that the old gentleman, for all his fish's blood, had had a moment of weakness, of compassion. He might also have committed a tactical error, but that was scarcely plausible, seeing that so far he had never made a mistake. More likely it had been brought about elsewhere, in another sector, that very high sector to which Holst had applied, where someone who knew nothing about the case had scribbled on the application an initial which meant 'yes'.

Holst was downstairs! Holst was in the little office, close to the stove, and at his side, standing back a little, was Sissy.

They were there, both of them!

Frank had had no warning. He had been fetched as though for an interrogation. It was about five days since his mother and Minna had come, there had been twelve or fifteen questionings, he had almost no more line to pay out, and he felt so weak that he had occasional fits of absence.

Holst was there, and Frank stopped short upon looking at him. He had seen Sissy too, but he continued to look at Holst, and his feet would not move, his body did not stir. The marvellous thing was that Holst did not think of opening his mouth.

To say what?

As if in understanding the question in Frank's eyes, as if in answer to it, Holst gently pushed Sissy forward.

The old gentleman was certainly there, behind his desk. The acolytes were at their stations too, beyond a doubt. There was the stove, the window, the courtyard, the sentry close to his box.

But actually, there was nothing at all. There was Sissy, in a black coat which made her look very thin, with her fair hair escaping from under a black beret. She looked at Frank. She did not want to cry, like Lotte. She was not moved to pity, like Minna. Perhaps she did not even notice his two missing teeth, or his beard or his crumpled clothes.

She did not come to Frank. They did not dare, either of them. Would they, if they had dared? It was by no means certain.

Her lips parted. She was going to speak. She said first of all, as he had so surely foreseen:

'Frank . . .'

She wanted to say more, and he was afraid.

'I've come to tell you . . .'

Embarrassed, he whispered:

'I know.'

He had thought she was going to say, he had been afraid she would say:

'. . . that I hold nothing against you.'

Or again:

'. . . that I forgive you.'

But those were not the words which she slowly uttered. She kept on looking at him. Surely never had two beings looked at each other with such intensity. She spoke simply:

'I've come to tell you I love you.'

She had her bag, her little black bag, in her hand. Everything was happening almost as in Frank's dream, except that the old gentleman, who had just rolled a cigarette with the utmost care, stuck out his tongue to wet the gummed paper.

Frank made no answer. He had no answer to make. He had

no right to make any answer. He must hurry to look at her. He must look at Holst too. Holst was not wearing the felt boots he used to put on to drive his tram. He was wearing shoes like anybody else. He was dressed in grey. He was holding his hat in his hand.

Frank did not stir, dared not stir. He could feel his lips moving, but not to speak. Perhaps it was nerves: he didn't know. It was then that Holst stepped forward, taking no notice of the old gentleman and the choirboys, and laid a hand on Frank's shoulder, exactly as Frank had always thought a father would do.

Did Holst think he owed Frank an explanation? Was he afraid that Frank had not altogether understood? Was he still harbouring some doubt?

His hand pressed lightly on Frank's shoulder, and he recited, he really seemed to be reciting, in a voice at once grave and toneless which recalled certain ceremonies of Holy Week:

'I had a son, a boy a little older than you are. His ambition was to become a great doctor. He had a passion for medicine, and nothing else mattered to him. When I ran out of money, he decided to go on with his studies at all costs.

'One day some expensive materials – mercury and platinum – disappeared from the physics laboratory. Then complaints started about petty thefts at the university. Finally, a student coming unexpectedly into the cloakroom found my son in the act of stealing a wallet.

'He was twenty-one. While they were taking him to the rector's study, he jumped out of a third-floor window . . .'

The pressure of the fingers had increased.

Frank would have liked to say something to him. There was one thing in particular he would have liked to tell him, but which meant nothing, which might be taken amiss: he would have liked to be Holst's son, he would like to be Holst's son. It would make him so happy – and ease him of such a burden – if he could say the one word:

'Father!'

Sissy had the right to do that – Sissy, whose eyes never left him. He could not tell, as he had with Minna, whether she was thinner or paler. That didn't count. She had come. It was she who had wished to come, and Holst had agreed. Holst took her by the hand and brought her to Frank.

'There,' he concluded. 'It's a tough job to be a human being.'

He seemed to smile feebly as he said the words, as if to excuse himself.

'Sissy talks to Herr Wimmer about you all day. I have found work in an office, but I finish early.'

He turned towards the window, so that they might look at each other, just the two of them.

There were no rings. There was no key. Neither were there any prayers, but Holst's words took their place.

Sissy was there. Holst was there.

They must not stay too long, for Frank might not be strong enough to stand it. He had just this. He would have nothing but this, ever. It was the whole of his share. There had been nothing before, and there existed no afterwards.

This was his own marriage! It was his honeymoon, it was his life, which he must live in one close-packed instant, near the old gentleman fumbling among his scraps of paper.

There would be no window that opened, no washing hung out to dry, no cradle.

If there had been all that, there would perhaps have been nothing at all, nothing but a Frank raging desperately against fate. It did not matter how long a thing lasted. What did matter was that it should exist.

'Sissy . . .'

He did not know whether he had murmured her name, or whether he had only thought it. His lips moved, but he could not stop them. His hands moved too, constantly working forward with a motion which he always halted in time. Sissy's hands were doing the same. Sissy had found a way of keeping herself in check by clenching her fingers round her bag.

For her sake too, and Holst's, it must not go on too long.

'We will try to come again,' said Holst.

Frank smiled, still gazing at Sissy, nodded in agreement, though he well knew it was not true, as Holst, and doubtless Sissy, knew too.

'Yes, you'll come again.'

That was all. Frank's eyes could hold out no longer. He was afraid he would faint. He had eaten nothing since the day before. He had spent the last week almost without sleep.

Holst went up to his daughter and took her arm. It was he who said:

'Courage, Frank.'

Sissy did not speak. She let herself be led away, her head still turned towards Frank, her eyes clinging to him with an expression he had never seen in human eyes.

They had not touched one another, not even their finger-tips. There had been no need.

They were gone. Frank could still see them through the window, against the whiteness of the courtyard, and Sissy's face was still turned to him.

Quick! He was going to scream! It was unbearable! Quick!

He could no longer keep still, he walked up to the old gentleman, opened his mouth. He was going to gesticulate, speak vehemently, but no sound issued from his throat and he stood motionless, as though transfixed.

She had come. She was there. She was in him. She was his. Holst had blessed them.

Through what aberration, or unheard-of generosity, did fate, after a gift such as so few men are allowed, now grant Frank another? Instead of questioning him, as in all likelihood should have happened, the old gentleman got up, put on his hat and coat – a thing that had never occurred before – and Frank was taken back to his room.

He owed it to himself not to sleep on his wedding night, and it was not interrupted.

It was better that he should no longer feel his fatigue, that he should be so calm on getting up, so entirely master of himself.

He waited for them. He looked at the window over yonder, but it hardly mattered that they came for him before it was opened.

Sissy was in him.

He walked behind the civilian, in front of the soldier. He was kept waiting, but that did not worry him. It was the last time. It must be, it had to be the last time. Evidently there was a new light in his face, for the old gentleman, looking up, paused for a moment in amazement and then examined him with anxious curiosity.

'Sit down.'

'No.'

It was not going to be a sitting interrogation, that he had decided.

'First of all, I ask your permission to make an important statement.'

He was going to speak calmly and deliberately. That would lend more weight to his words.

'I stole the watches and I killed Fräulein Vilmos, the sister of the watchmaker in my village. I had already killed one of your officers, at the corner of the alley by the tannery. I did it to get his revolver, because I wanted a revolver. I have committed other much more shameful deeds; I have committed the worst crime in the world, but it has nothing to do with you. I am not a fanatic, nor an agitator, nor a patriot. I am a rotter. Ever since you started questioning me, I have used every trick I knew to gain time, because it was indispensable that I should do so. Now it's all over.'

He spoke almost without drawing breath. It might have been thought that he was trying to assume the icy voice of the old gentleman, but at times his voice sounded more like Holst's.

'Of all that you would like to learn, I know nothing. That I solemnly declare. If I knew anything, I wouldn't tell you. From now on you can question me for as long as you like, I shan't answer one word. You have the power to torture me. I'm not afraid of torture. You have the power to promise me my life. I don't want it. I want to die, as soon as possible, in whatever fashion you choose.

'Don't think ill of me for speaking in this way. I have nothing against you personally. You have been doing your job. For my part, I have decided not to talk any more, and these are the last words I shall speak to you.'

He had been beaten. He had been brought downstairs three or four times for beating. The last time he had been stripped naked in the office. The men with moustaches set about their work without heat and without malice. Doubtless under orders, they struck him hard with their knees in the genitals, and he blushed, because for an instant he had thought of Kromer and Sissy.

He had nothing but the soup to live on now. The rest had been taken away from him.

It would not be long now. If they did not hurry, it might come of itself.

He still hoped that he would be taken down to the cellar. Still his old bent for demanding to be treated differently from others.

There was always the window above the gymnasium, the window that might have been his window, the woman who might have been Sissy.

They finally made up their minds, one morning when it had started to snow again. They seemed to be early, because the sky was dark and low. They had gone into the other classroom first. He had not thought that it would be like this. Then, leaving the three men they had picked out to wait on the gangway, they pushed his door open abruptly.

He was ready. No use putting on his overcoat. He knew all about it. He hurried. The three others were cold, and he did not want to keep them waiting. In the gloom he tried to make out their features, and it was the first time he had shown any curiosity about the men of the other classroom.

They were made to walk in single file along the gallery.

Funny! He had turned up his jacket collar, like the others!

And he had forgotten to look at the window, he forgot to think. Of course he would have plenty of time afterwards.